MASHKIKI
RAPIDS

MASHKIKI RAPIDS

Author: Anne Rud Miller
Book and cover design: Roslyn Nelson
Printed in the United States of America

ISBN 978-0-9892822-0-8
Library of Congress Control Number: 2013937527

Publisher: Little Big Bay LLC
littlebigbay.com

A Novel by

ANNE RUD MILLER

MASHKIKI
RAPIDS

Mashkiki is the Ojibwe word for medicine

Little Big Bay LLC
LITTLE PLACE ~ BIG IDEAS ~ ON THE BAY
www.littlebigbay.com

DEDICATED

TO THE MEMORY

OF MY PARENTS

Eileen Edson Rud
and
Harlan Carl Rud

AND TO THE "MILLER GIRLS"

Hallie Robyn
Jo Ellen
and
Jenna Leigh

ACKNOWLEDGEMENTS

Spring 2013

There are several people I must thank for the success of this book finally reaching the printed page.

Thank you for early, intermediary and final readings and suggestions: Karla Kroeplin, Harold Rud, Terri Wagner, Jeff Orthmann, Laurie Otis, Heidi and Don Knoke, and above all, Roy Lindquist, who never let me stop revising and never let me down.

Thank you for background information: Russell Horton (reference archivist, Wisconsin Veterans Museum), Don Kassien, Mavis Kingbird, and Dr. Howard N. Sandin.

Thank you for encouragement and suggestions: Dr. Laurel Yourke, UW-Madison and all the disciples in her writing workshops

Thank you for the best editing expertise anywhere: Ros Nelson, and by proxy to Liz Woodworth who steered me to Ros.

Thank you Kim Miller Welty for supplying me with the perfect cover photo of her parents, Laverne and Richard "Mouse" Miller.

Thank you to my former Ashland High School students who told me for thirty-four years to write a book and promised to purchase it.

I've done my part.

TABLE OF CONTENTS

CHAPTER ONE

late August 1953

Her father banged the tabletop, jostling the salt and pepper shakers perilously close to the edge. Elaine hoped she wasn't cringing as she struggled to meet his eyes. He hated blubbering and brooked no sentimentality from her. Even as a small girl she was forbidden to cry. When she dared look up she saw anger was in them, yes, but what else? Surely betrayal, but was that loathing as well?

"How could you, Elaine? How did this happen? Do you have any idea how much of a disappointment you are?" Though quiet, her father's voice had power, each syllable ricocheting off the counters and appliances lining the kitchen. "After all I've given to you? A first class college education, spending money, my trust! Your first day back from summer school and this is how you reward me? With loose behavior and now a bastard child in your belly? And you don't even know the fellow's name? Good God, Elaine! I'm glad your mother isn't alive to see this! It would kill her! As much as if–"

He broke off suddenly but Elaine could hear the rest of the accusation hanging in the air like a frigid and deadly icicle threatening to impale her on his shiny, newly installed linoleum.

Just like you killed your mother when you were a child. His words pounded in her head. It made her feel as sick as when she heard them the first time as a little girl after Dad had too many cocktails. It was your fault your mother died, Elaine. It was your fault she left us. An elderly aunt told her that she wasn't really to blame for her mommy's death. She'd just turned four when her mother ran from the kitchen to the basement stairs and caught the back of her high heel on an uneven step. That misstep catapulted her down until her newly permed head struck a thick lead pipe lining the wall and halted her descent. Did Elaine clearly recall standing at the top of the stairs and seeing her mother sprawled on the bottom step, her shoe off, the heel broken? Going to the neighbor's house in tears because Mommy wouldn't wake up? She thought she could remember hearing the thump of her mother's head meeting the pipe. Had that recollection too been supplemented by her aunt's account?

It didn't matter now. Elaine struggled to pick up what her father was saying. Something about a home for unwed mothers in Duluth or Minneapolis, it was up to her. Wait, wait! She'd just told him she was expecting a baby. And she knew exactly when it would be born. Though she refused to give details, name names, she knew exactly when it was conceived. It wasn't hard to remember your one and only time with a man. What was he saying? It was hard to concentrate. Up to her? Had they talked through other possibilities? Were there other choices? Duluth sounded best; her father was saying, further away from this part of Illinois, more secluded and run by the same order of nuns from their local parish. He would give her a few hundred dollars to get there. The Mother Superior could contact him for more when she was settled. Pack tonight. He'd take her to the train station tomorrow.

Would he ever forgive her? Ever love her again? Had he ever loved her? Would he someday allow her back in this Chicago suburb home, the place where she had grown up, the only place she had ever called home? Probably not. He always warned her that some transgressions could never be forgotten, let alone forgiven. She knew what the consequences were.

"The Adventures of Ozzie and Harriet" played on the kitchen Philco as her father poured himself another martini. Elaine left the kitchen feeling even less sure of herself now than she had in all her twenty years.

—Ↄ

The late morning August sun was barely visible when Elaine's father purchased her ticket, handed her an envelope containing cash and turned to the parking area. He offered no farewell hug, not even a pat on the shoulder. His only remark was, "When you get to Duluth, take a cab to St. Mary's Maternity Home." He wore his disappointment visibly, like coffee splashed on a white shirt. His brow was furrowed and he didn't look back as he straightened his shoulders and departed in his shiny new DeSoto. Elaine's disappointment was replaced with chagrin when she realized that a soldier standing nearby had witnessed her humiliation before moving on to the ticket booth.

Names, slang and symbols long forgotten were etched under the much varnished surface of the train depot bench. A winter coat, too bulky to pack, was slung over her arm. Elaine hefted the old leather satchel and directed herself to an empty spot near the end of the varnished plank. Spotting an equally determined traveler heading in the same direction, she hastened her step and parked herself before he reached the destination. She tried not to feel guilty for depriving the mature gentleman of his seat, but there were other spots available and most likely his ankles were less swollen than hers. This pregnancy thing would take some getting used to.

From somewhere in the bowels of the building came snippets of Frank Sinatra. Twin toddlers, girls dressed identically in Betsy McCall outfits, stomped their feet and marched around a bench as their mother conversed with the ticket agent in front of them. Their mother delivered what she probably hoped was a stern "Girls, sit down there, now!" The little girls just laughed and stomped their feet even louder. They tapped their own cadence much to Elaine's delight. Stomp, stomp, giggle, stomp, giggle. The older gentleman leaned back against the wall, huffing and sucking on a White Owl too stubborn to stay lit. Elaine checked her watch and opened her purse.

Counting out her money, she calculated that it might last three or four days if she was careful. Three or four days to consider if she wanted to go to Duluth. After all, the notion of that northern city as her destination was her father's idea, not hers. Not yet. She would give herself a few days. After that she wasn't sure what she would do for cash if she dismissed her father's plan. But what choice did she really have? It wasn't as though there was a sweetheart anywhere. Or any close family to take her in. If she were honest, there wasn't even a friend she could confide in.

The call came to board her train. A porter helped her up the step and into the club car. Pockets of fellow travelers dotted the area. She draped her winter coat over her arm and held it in front of her. No need to advertise her condition. At three months, she could see a difference in her waistline but she wasn't sure about the detection of others. Here and there she could see groups of servicemen, returning from overseas duty now that the war in Korea had ended. Seeing so many together reminded her of the nights earlier in the summer when she and her roommates frequented the USO and ... best get my mind off that, she told herself.

A jostling at her shoulder made her drop her coat and prevented any further daydreaming. Elaine bent to retrieve her wrap.

"Ahh jeez," A loud, irritated bark came from the young soldier trying to pass her. Laden with two stuffed and heavy duffel bags, he scowled when his progress was stopped. His ill temper abated a bit when he saw he wasn't expected to pick her coat up.

"Sorry," she said automatically as she turned to face him. Too late she realized he was the soldier who had overheard her father's remark. He was very handsome but his eyes were as cold and penetrating as her father's. Was she imagining contempt as his gaze swept over her body? It was as though she had traded in one judgmental stare for another. His glance slowed at her breasts, then at her thickening waistline, and finally stopped at her left hand. No ring there. Was he evaluating her as her father had done only hours before? She straightened but before she could cover her belly, his voice softened.

"Yeah, okay, no harm done," he grumbled and bumped past her to a seat in the rear. More soldiers filed by her, heading toward those seats as well. Some called out to one another in familiar fashion. A few nodded at her but kept moving toward what sounded like a card game.

Making herself comfortable in these seats was a chore. Amazing how every contour of her body had changed in just a few months time. Sitting next to the window seemed like a good idea; she put her purse on the seat next to her. Maybe she'd be lucky and have both seats to herself. She tuned out the conversation of the couple behind her and the quiet whoops of the card players. Maybe a little nap was what she needed. Do what Scarlett O'Hara advised—think about things tomorrow.

Stretching a few hours later, she noticed the denser green of the north's vast pinery. Denser, and speckled with lakes and rushing rivers. Here and there, boulders of impressive size pushed out of the Wisconsin pastures. She tried to calculate how far they might be from Minocqua, the last stop on this line today. Her thoughts turned to her present conundrum.

It was times like these that she missed her mother or the notion of a mother. For what had to be the hundredth time in the last few days, tears sprang to Elaine's eyes. If only her mother was here to stave off this loneliness and reassure her that this wasn't the worst thing in the world. That the one careless, fanciful night at the Chicago USO with her college roommates, the beer, the dancing, all the handsome young men returning from Korea, the kissing and the clinging wouldn't really ruin her life forever. Things might be bad for a while but surely these circumstances could be altered.

She hadn't thought about the baby as being permanent. She needed to consider those places her father mentioned: places where girls in her predicament could go for help. Isn't that just what her father wanted? She'd heard whispers about these places when they were discussed among her high school classmates. There were girls who went for the summer to their "aunt" and came back overly cheerful but never seemed to rise above the rumors. Girls, who if they did return to school, endured the stares and snickers from sophomore boys at their lockers. Ahh, but the tears right now … they must be addressed before they spilled down her cheeks onto her pale blue sweater.

Fumbling for a Kleenex and trying not to sniffle, she rummaged through her purse, found the tissue and looked up to see another soldier stopped next to her seat. He was one she noticed when he boarded this morning, grin at the ready, his gait slightly off stride, telling all who might care to hear that he was heading home after 14 months of active duty, part of it in Korea. He was not overly handsome–not nearly as handsome as the rude GI who reminded her of her father–but his strong and distinctive nose caught her eye. That and the way his eyes sparkled when he said "home."

Now here he was again; in his khakis, looking down at her. She pretended to be absorbed in her book. She could feel his eyes on her and peered into her purse for a comb, her new Coty lipstick, anything. When she dared peek in his direction; he was looking at her with a hint of a smile. She smiled back. As they made eye contact, the train lurched and he plopped down in the empty seat beside her. Oh Lord, did he interpret her returning glance as an invitation to join her?

"Hello there. Guess the train thought we needed to visit a spell." His voice was pleasant enough, indeed very pleasant. Were pregnant girls–fallen girls, her aunt would say–supposed to smile at strange young serviceman, be grateful for the kindness in their eyes? Those blue gray eyes seemed full of backwoods sincerity and boyish solemnity. Perhaps he was playing an innocent boy-meets-girl thing with her. Using her as a way to pass an hour or two before he departed. The possibility of some mild flirtation brought another gush of tears to her eyes.

Before Elaine could steel herself for his "line," his Army come-on, the soldier spoke. "Are you alright, Miss? You seem a bit …" He faltered, looked for the right word, "… distressed." He offered a clean, white handkerchief. "Here. Please feel free to use mine. Looks like you need it more than me."

The linen that resembled an altar cloth found its way into her hand as the soldier leaned toward her. Not too close but perhaps close enough.

"You're not sick, are you?" His voice was soft.

Elaine thought about her vomiting before re-boarding the train in Madison and smiled weakly. He didn't mean morning sickness; that queasiness that had rendered her as wilted as week-old lettuce. He was asking how she felt now.

"Hey girl, it's nice to see that smile." He sounded more sure of himself now.

She started at his familiarity, as sweet and welcome as the remark sounded. He stammered and hurriedly continued. "I'm sorry ... I hope you don't ... sorry. I don't usually strike up conversations with just any pretty girl I spy on a train and nearly squash. Honest." He showed the wide grin he'd shared with the others in the depot. The grin looked, well, friendly. How long had it been since she felt friendliness? Although it might all be a line, an army line designed to make girls swoon at the feet of a returning soldier, maybe it was okay. They were in a public place and conductors roamed by with regularity. Perhaps she might trust him for a few minutes. What could it hurt?

"Are you getting picked up in Minocqua or are you going on to Ironwood tonight? I think we should be there in less than an hour," he told her.

Elaine was puzzled until he pointed to the temporary timetables posted at the front of the car. The wallboards were scarred and needed a scrubbing to remove the months of tobacco residue left by travelers. She focused on the list of departures. A train for Ironwood, Michigan left Minocqua yet this evening. One for Minneapolis and Duluth was due out in the morning. She hesitated. Was she going on? Or was there an inexpensive hotel where she could again count her money and weigh her options?

"Ellen?"

Elaine looked back at the GI. He expected a response, but who was Ellen?

"I have an aunt named Estelle, though we call her Lovey. A little on the odd side, but we like her fine. Plus she makes a dang tasty gravy." Another grin punctuated this disclosure. "She and my Uncle Roland are picking me up tonight. The conductor said we'll be a few minutes early so I may have to wait ... Eleanor? Estelle? " He smiled and pointed at her chest.

What on earth was he talking about? Elaine rose, planning her escape from this amiable lunatic when she realized he was gesturing at the *E* monogram pin on her sweater. A chuckle escaped. The soldier joined in with a pleasant and throaty murmur.

"Elaine," she told him. She drew a breath, sat, and then blurted, "My name is Elaine Reilly and I'm alone, and yes, I'm pregnant, and I don't know if I'm going on to Ironwood tonight." What was she thinking? Her first words in this casual conversation were about being knocked up? Was she truly losing her mind? Horrified, she turned her gaze to her companion.

His eyes widened, but the soldier's voice betrayed no surprise at her revelation. "Well, hello, Elaine," he drew out the hello to almost three syllables, calm at the announcement that had startled her, shaken her to her knees. He extended his hand and shook hers. Before she had time to react, he continued. "Maybe I can help. At least I can listen. My name is Harlan Tilden, but everyone calls me Bud."

CHAPTER TWO

Elaine realized that unlike the tall soldier who jostled her earlier, Bud hadn't seen her standing in the aisle, or noticed her baby bump. Well now, in for a penny, in for a pound; she dried her tears and answered his questions. She admitted her father's lack of support, her withdrawal from college, and her finances. Bud didn't require much explanation. He nodded once or twice and waited until she was all talked out. Then he described his birthplace and family. He laughed often. To her, the flow of his words was like moving a boulder from damming up a small creek. He told her about home in a small town called Mashkiki Rapids. "Mashkiki is the Ojibwe word for medicine," he explained. This was where his family owned and operated a lodge claiming to be "the northernmost quality resort in the county."

"My grandfather built it and named it Tilden's Last Resort; my grand-dad had quite a sense of humor. We cater to tourists and hunters and have a restaurant that also serves the locals." Pride was evident in his voice. The family lived near the restaurant in a house his father built when his parents were first married. He and his brother and sister grew up in that house, a place Bud could hardly wait to see.

"Elaine, Rapids is just the prettiest place under the sun. Loads of small little lakes surrounded by these majestic pines and hard-woods. There's nothing more beautiful than all that natural glory right outside your doorstep! I know I probably sound like a cheesy travelogue magazine but it's true."

Elaine learned more. His father and Bud's younger brother, Perry, maintained the grounds, the cabins and upkeep of the main lodge while his mother managed the kitchen and the books. An older married sister, Madlyn, no longer worked at the family's business unless there was a shortage of help.

Two or three seasonal workers lived on the premises and received room and board in addition to a modest salary between spring and early winter. Generally, the business closed after hunting season, usually right after Thanksgiving. In the winter months, his father and brother did some logging, and cut and delivered firewood. Bud was also hoping to do some logging and use some of his GI earnings to purchase a truck and start his own small-scale trucking business. Elaine could tell he was thrilled to soon be back with people he loved dearly.

Bud had called his father to let him know he was being discharged. "But that process involved more time than I first thought. If I'd known about all that other folderol, I'd've refused to be part of all that jazz, but—" Bud shrugged and hurried on. Was she missing something?

When Bud learned a worker had recently left and made everyone's responsibilities a little more of a burden, he changed his travel plans. Instead of being picked up at the base, Bud told his father that he'd come home by train. "Shoot, I was at the largest training base in Illinois. Now my dad is no hick but I figured it was easier for me to come home by train as soon as I finished mustering out ... and all that other stuff ... ." Another blush and he again hurried on. "Otherwise, he'd leave work for a day or two to fetch me in the middle of all that chaos, being short handed. So I said just have my aunt and uncle fetch me from Minocqua."

He thought a few seconds. "Plus if my mother came with Dad, Perry'd have to run the place alone. I'm not sure anyone would feel comfortable about that. My brother would be apt to have his own party and forget the paying guests!" He laughed comfortably. Elaine sensed his assessment of his brother was not necessarily realistic, maybe just a possibility. Somewhere in his epic about the extended Tilden family, Bud offered the idea that perhaps Elaine might want to come with him tonight.

"I doubt you'll find a room any place in Minocqua with Labor Day so close and who knows? Maybe you could get a job cleaning cabins and do some work in the kitchen. Not the kind of work a fancy college girl might aspire to but you might just like it. The pay isn't too shabby and it could give you some time to think about– " He stopped abruptly and tried to reclaim the thread of conversation without intruding on her privacy. As if she had a sense of privacy after her outburst!

"... yourself," he continued. "And where you want to land. What do you say? If you don't like it, I'll borrow Perry's truck and bring you back to Minocqua tomorrow to catch another train." He sounded as if solving someone else's problem was the easiest thing in the world.

It didn't sound too crazy. She could give herself a few days grace to mull things over and decide on her own where she might end up. She nodded. Bud picked up her satchel and steered her to a vacant bench outside. Bud acknowledged the soldier who bumped her in the aisle. "Hey Lloyd." Instead of answering, his counterpart scowled and stared at Elaine before shaking his head and moving out into the dusk.

Bud shrugged. "One of my high school classmates. Still kind of a jerk, I guess. Well, I can't see my aunt and uncle but they should be along shortly. I've timed that route from Mashkiki Rapids to this station when I was picking up or delivering lodge patrons. I've got it to the minute." As if on cue, a rather dusty but comfortable looking Studebaker pulled into the parking area. A horn honked and the dark gray vehicle stopped. Elaine saw a plump female arm emerge from the passenger window waving a white handkerchief.

"There they are!" Bud took off at a run, leaving his duffle bag and her satchel behind as he sprinted to the car. He looked back over his shoulder at Elaine. "Don't move! Be back in a sec!"

Gentle amusement filled Elaine; an amusement mixed with mild envy. She would never elicit this kind of homecoming from her father. A short, heavyset woman wearing a billowing dress emerged from the car. She was followed by the driver, an even shorter, balding man who grinned at Bud.

"Buddy boy!" the woman exclaimed, "Oh Bud! It is so good to see you!" Further conversation was quelled when Bud stooped to hug her. Chin resting on her head, Bud reached a hand around his aunt to his uncle who pumped it vigorously. Then the man threw both arms around Bud and his aunt. Again tears welled in Elaine's eyes. How many times had she cried today? No matter, this was different. It was almost a privilege to be privy to this tableau.

Bud pointed toward Elaine, then came back to retrieve the bags. The woman waddled behind him, one eye trained on Elaine, insisting she could help. His uncle opened the Studebaker's trunk. Elaine could hear conversational snippets as Bud stood before his aunt. "No, I didn't wear the medals, you can see them later ... brought a friend ... she's coming to the lodge with us ... treat her nice." Bud's aunt craned her head around his torso and focused on Elaine.

The lady nodded and turned back to the car. "Well, help her Bud, don't leave her standing there to get a chill. Let's get going. We can complete the introductions on the way home."

Bud walked to Elaine and crooked his head, double checking. Was she still coming? She gave the smallest of nods. He grinned, and took her valise. "Well, all right then. I guess we're off."

After the cursory introductions, she settled into the backseat with Bud. Lovey did the lion's share of the talking. Uncle Roland occasionally looked into the rearview mirror and gave Elaine a sweet, gentle smile. She contented herself with the patter between Lovey and Bud.

"I know," Bud was saying, "I wasn't sure how long they were going to parade me around before they turned me loose."

"Well, goodness sakes, Bud! How many war heroes did they have there anyway? Of course they wanted to let people see you! It was probably like those war effort rallies from the last war. Remember those, Roland? Didn't we have a few rip-roaring assemblies here in '43 or so? You can bet that if we had an honest-to-God hero ... ."

Bud cut his aunt's narrative by blowing her a kiss. "Okay, now Aunt Lovey, we don't want to bore Elaine."

Elaine was confused but before she could pursue it, Bud's voice rose. "Can you see those lights over to the right there through the trees? There it is! That's my home town!"

Aunt Lovey definitely wanted to continue the narrative about her nephew but Uncle Roland lifted his hand from the steering wheel, patted his wife and communicated something to his wife with his quick glance. Then Elaine saw a few lights and a sign announcing "Mashkiki Rapids." No turning back now.

Lovey gestured to the town marker and turned once more to her nephew, "We're thinking of attaching a small sign to the bottom of that big one, 'Birthplace of Harlan Tilden, Korean War Hero'."

Bud burst in again, overlapping her speech. "Hey, not now Aunt Lovey!"

"Well, I don't think it's such a bad idea, Mister Smarty Pants. Even so, your mother made us promise not to tell anybody else you were coming home tonight or there'd be everybody in the county at the lodge. Maybe even a marching band." Her enthusiasm expanded. "A parade! With you in a big vehicle leading the way ... and a sign! Oh Bud, just think!"

Again, her husband interrupted. "Leave the boy be, Lovey. Maybe he don't want to talk about all that ceremonial stuff just now. Probably had enough these past few weeks, right, Bud?" Roland glanced once more in the rearview at Elaine. Definitely some kind of secret here. Just who was this soldier who had befriended her?

The car turned at a crude sign directing traffic to the Langholz Fish Camp. After another mile a weathered wooden sign, "Tilden's Last Resort" directed them down a gravel driveway into a small parking area. Light shone from the dining room of a restaurant. Each window was rimmed in dark green matching the roof shingles. A long porch set with painted Adirondack chairs, small wooden tables, and a generous sized porch swing completed the welcome. The gallery led to wide, high double oak doors at the lodge's main entrance. The structure was regal without being pompous.

"Here we are," Lovey announced. "I 'spect Richard and Perry've been keeping an eye on the road." Sure enough, before Roland could shut off the motor, the doors of the lodge opened and two men of near identical height and build emerged. One called to someone inside the lodge before turning back to the parking area. Elaine immediately noticed their resemblance to Bud, despite the age differences. Their profiles with prominent noses and strong jaw line were carbon copies of Bud. They bounded down the steps and reached Bud simultaneously.

The older one placed his hands on Bud's shoulders and spoke quietly to him. A tiny sob escaped as he embraced the soldier son before him. When his father released Bud and turned away to wipe his eyes, the younger man hesitated, then flung himself at Bud with a loud whoop. Arms pinned, it was now Bud's turn to be lifted from the ground and spun about by this fellow.

Everyone, including Elaine, laughed at Bud's inability to disengage himself from the young man who looked like his twin. Bud mock struggled but gave up when he realized his laughter sapped his strength. Bud was righted, and flanked by both men, their arms around his back and shoulders as they propelled him toward the porch. Lovey turned to Elaine. "Come on, honey, we don't want to miss Dorothy seeing her boy come home. This will beat all my radio soap operas six ways to Sunday!"

Elaine followed Roland and Lovey through the main doors and saw the folks gathered in the entryway. She took in the details of the massive, timbered doors. Over seven feet tall, they were impressive; the swirls and patterns in the grain of the wood were made more distinctive by the high sheen on them. She would have to look at them more carefully in daylight. She walked out of the chill and was enveloped by warmth in the lobby and restaurant area.

A handsome, dark-haired woman came out from what might be the kitchen area. She stood still for a long moment, wiping her hands on her green and yellow flowered apron before she dropped her hands and walked toward them. Elaine could see tears spilling from her eyes. As Elaine glanced at Bud, she saw he had his mother's amazingly beautiful eyes. They were an undeniably startling shade of blue and his own tears now threatened to cascade down his cheeks.

"Oh, Ma," he murmured simply as he wrapped his arms around her and raised her to her tiptoes. Her head on his chest, they stood that way for a moment or two while the others in the room looked on. Finally, the woman pushed away from Bud and looked up into his face. He kissed her forehead and turned to the others.

A younger woman with glossy auburn hair gave Bud a tight hug and was also twirled around before Bud set her down to look her full in the face. "Hello, Livvie," he sighed as he brushed her hair from her forehead.

"Oh, Bud!" the woman exclaimed. "You have no idea how I prayed for this day! I am so glad to see you in one piece! You're home now for good, right? I don't have to think about you going off again, do I?" She kissed his cheek, linked her arm in his and turned to face the rest of the room. Her eyes rested on Elaine standing near the door, her battered suitcase at her feet. This young woman gave Elaine a genuine and welcoming smile.

Bud turned to his mother. "Ma, this is a friend, Elaine Reilly. Elaine, this is my mother, Dorothy. And my dad, Richard and brother Perry." Richard smiled and dipped his head at the visitor. Perry scrutinized Elaine from the top of head to her scuffed toes before settling back on her face. His grin widened and he winked.

Bud tightened his arm around the young woman he'd addressed as Livvie. "This pretty woman right here is my sister-in-law, Per's wife, Olivia. I guess Madlyn's home with the babies?"

A nod from her mother confirmed this. "She had to get home to the girls. She'll be here early since she's filling in for us. She's anxious to see you." She smiled at Elaine. "Then she can meet your friend, too."

Elaine thought she should explain that she and Bud weren't truly friends; they had met only a few hours before but Bud brought the attention back to his mother.

"Ah, just look at my sweet Ma. She may look old and tired but I'll bet she's still one feisty creature, eh, Dad?" Bud dodged a playful slap from his mother while the others laughed. He gestured again in Elaine's direction. "I brought her because she's looking for a job. I told her she could probably find one here easy. At least until after hunting season, am I right?" There was no mention from Bud about meeting her on the train, no reference that a few scant hours earlier they were pure strangers. His introduction suggested that he'd known Elaine for a good bit and Elaine felt no compulsion to correct that now.

The group took measure of the new friend, but Dorothy was first to speak. "Any friend of Bud's is welcome here. And yes, you are most assuredly hired if you want a job. We can talk about particulars tomorrow." Bud smiled at Elaine and she could hear his "told you so" as clearly as if he'd spoken aloud.

What he did say was directed to his mother. "I know the kitchen's officially closed but what are the chances of Elaine and me getting a bite to eat? I can smell the remnants of your famous backwoods stew. Enough left for us, do you think? Maybe some pie, too? Or did Dad finally figure out where you hide the dessert leftovers?"

Laughter again erupted and the broad grin on Richard's face indicated that Elaine was made privy to a family joke. How good it felt to be included in family references kinfolks took for granted.

"Oh hush, you!" Dorothy swatted her son once again, this time gently connecting with his shoulder. "Of course we have enough. I'll warm some up. And there is pie, if Richard didn't eat it all while we were cleaning up. Lovey? You and Roland'll be staying for pie and coffee? Good, we've got plenty."

"Is there a room around back that Elaine can have, Dad? Maybe the middle one?" Bud received a nod, picked up Elaine's bag and started down a narrow hallway. "Come on with me. I'll show you where you can put your things and freshen up. There's three separate rooms and a private bathroom in this back hall where the workers stay." He seemed like he wanted to say more.

His brother's voice interrupted him. "Okay, war he-ro! How about you help with these chairs? You thinking you can mingle a little with us commoners or are you too busy dangling your medals for that pretty girly girl there?" Laughter came from the other men when Bud again appeared flustered.

Elaine reached for her travel bag. "Okay, let me unpack a few things and maybe use the bathroom. Then I'll take you up on that stew and pie. But Bud? What do I say about ... ." she gestured to her belly.

"Don't worry about it. Nobody's gonna judge you. Not here, Elaine. I'll handle all the explanation that's necessary. You don't have to say a thing." Bud turned toward the dining area.

"Wait," Elaine said. Bud stopped and faced her. His smile turned questioning.

Elaine's voice was quiet. "Thank you. I'm a little overwhelmed but thank you." Bud's smile returned full force as he nodded and headed back to his brother.

CHAPTER THREE

After a delicious sleep, Elaine woke to the smell of coffee, muffled female voices and a musical giggle from the hallway. Slipping into her robe, she peeked out. Two young women in green and yellow printed aprons were moving toward the kitchen entry until they heard her door creak. An older, darker blonde identified herself as Rachel. She offered a smile and handshake before gesturing over her shoulder that she needed to get to the kitchen.

The younger of the two was a shorter, sturdier woman who didn't look much older than 17. She was also blonde, her hair almost white. "Hey, hi ya. I'm Charlotte Mickelson–Lotty–and you must be Elaine. Dorothy and Richard were still in the kitchen when I came in late last night and told me about you. Rachel and I are glad to have the help and I know Madlyn'll be glad. She's busy at home with Tommy and the girls and doesn't like coming in if she doesn't have to. Well, I'm off to the kitchen now. Dorothy says if we saw ya to tell ya to come in for a breakfast and then afterwards, she'll tell ya what's what. OK, now?" Before Elaine could respond, the girl strode off.

Getting dressed took some thought. Finally Elaine chose a white blouse and a plain, gathered gray skirt that wasn't too tight across her stomach. Maybe it didn't completely hide her pregnancy but it still managed a bit of camouflage. She stepped from the hallway into the kitchen. There she saw Dorothy moving assuredly from an over-sized stove top to a griddle now sizzling with sausages and pancakes. A brunette was at the sink, washing dishes and stacking clean glassware in the drainer and also wearing what must be the lodge's trademark green and yellow apron. Though a busy place, the area was spotless. Through another doorway she saw Rachel moving among a half dozen occupied tables in the dining room, coffee pot in hand. The customers sat in plaid shirts and jackets, caps hung on the knobs of their chair backs.

"Morning." Elaine ventured, raising her voice just a little to be heard above the radio.

Dorothy and the woman washing dishes turned. "Morning, Elaine. How did you sleep?" Dorothy gestured to the woman at the sink. "My daughter, Madlyn. Madlyn, this is Elaine Reilly. We didn't get everything squared last night but I think Elaine is your replacement."

Obvious that she was Bud and Perry's sister, Madlyn possessed the build, dark hair and startling blue eyes of her mother as well as her father's characteristic nose. All three siblings apparently shared the same family traits. .

"Hello, Elaine, nice to meet you. Thank God Bud brought us a friend to work here because this means I'm probably excused from kitchen duty." A glance at her mother made her add, "After today, I mean. Of course, I'll finish out today."

"Sit down over there, Elaine. You get breakfast served to you today because you're still company." Dorothy smiled. "Tomorrow, if you decide you want to work here, you'll help yourself, eat when you aren't busy here in the kitchen. Have you had any waitressing experience?" Elaine shook her head as Dorothy continued. "Thought not. Maybe helping me in the kitchen with prep and dishes would suit you initially. You'll switch off with Lotty when it comes to supper detail and days off. We'll work those particulars out later. Shouldn't think that was overworking you too much."

Elaine nodded as she moved to the table. Was the "overworked" comment directed at her pregnancy? "Thanks. You don't need to serve me, I can get my own."

"Nonsense. Besides, today it'll be easier for me to get it for you instead of having to tell you where everything is."

"Relax while you can, Elaine!" laughed Madlyn, with a wink at her mother. "She'll run your legs off tomorrow!"

Elaine sat at the kitchen's broad oilcloth-covered table. Dorothy placed a heaping plate of scrambled eggs, a pancake and two sausages before her. Dorothy patted Elaine's shoulder.

"Coffee's over there. And you can surely have more than one pancake but they're pretty generous as you can see and the girls generally only want one. Diets, they say. But don't let them make you feel self-conscious." She lowered her voice. "Eating for two can stimulate an appetite." Elaine could feel her cheeks begin to color as Dorothy returned to the griddle. Had Dorothy just acknowledged Elaine's pregnancy with an invitation for more food and that's all there was to it? No interrogation? No pitying looks? No hidden judgments? That was it?

Overwhelmed by the abundance of food before her, Elaine hoped her stomach would cooperate in staying settled. When she took her first bite, she sighed. How could eggs taste this good? She buttered her pancake and poured a dab of syrup from a Mason jar. It too was uncommonly delectable. Madlyn caught her pouring a bit more over the flapjack and smiled. "That's from Daddy's last batch of maple syrup. I think it's extra yummy this year."

"Hmm," rejoined her mother. "You say that every year, Madlyn. I don't think your dad's ever had a bad batch."

Both women turned to their chores as Rachel and Lotty moved smoothly in and out the door to the dining room. Busy, no one expected small talk. Instead Elaine enjoyed every morsel and chased a stray bit of egg around her plate. She lingered over her milk and considered having one more pancake, a smaller one.

At that moment, Richard, Perry and Bud breezed through the side door. The cool air chilled Elaine's legs and made Dorothy hunch up her shoulders. Each man found and filled a mug with coffee and sat to join Elaine.

Bud grinned. " Well, city girl, I see you decided to make an appearance." His label for her made Elaine feel she'd known Bud for longer than 15 hours. Maybe it appeared so to his family, too. How else to explain their kindness and hospitality to her? Perry chuckled and faked a yawn.

Richard smiled before he spoke. "Don't let either one of them get to you, Elaine. If I hadn't told them last night I was getting started early today, they'd both be straggling in, too. In fact, I told Bud to take it easy today; no reveille anymore, eh, son? But he must've taken one to the head there in Korea ... he was up 'n at'em instead of sleeping in today." Everyone looked at Bud. Elaine was glad the focus moved from her.

"What is it you do so early in the morning?" Elaine asked. "I'm enjoying your fine maple syrup here. Is that one of your businesses, Mr. Tilden? Where you've been today? Gathering the syrup?"

A mild burst of laughter emerged from the Tildens as a flush appeared on Elaine's cheeks. Bud jumped in. "No, wrong season. Spring's when he gathers sap for the syruping but that's just a side interest of Dad's." He was interrupted by Madlyn and Perry.

"Yeah right, a side interest like the wood delivery and the strawberries." This from Perry who looked directly at Elaine and widened his grin.

"Or the woodcarving and the snow removal." Madlyn was laughing now at her father's mild discomfort.

Elaine felt a flutter in her stomach that had nothing to do with the baby. The Tilden siblings were teasing their father. She wouldn't dare have this kind of gentle interplay, this teasing with her own father. Could that ripple be a minute flash of jealousy?

"Okay, okay," Richard waved his brood quiet and looked at Elaine. "First off, it's Richard, not Mr. Tilden. We don't stand much on ceremony here, but I am pleased you seem interested in what I do for a living. I probably seem different than your father? But no doubt much more handsome, eh, Elaine?" The entire kitchen erupted once more at that.

Elaine saw Richard smiling at her with encouragement. What to say about her father? About his attitude? Maybe just stick to the basics. "My dad's an insurance adjustor," she managed. "He lives just outside Chicago. He's been with the same company for almost thirty years." She bit her lip and tried to think of another tidbit to offer about her father.

"Ah," said Perry, turning the coffee mug around in his hand, "A shirt and tie man."

"Alright now, Per, no more teasing this early. Well, I don't have an office job like your dad unless you count this," Richard's hand swept the expanse of the room. "And of course, Ma there is my boss!" Again laughter from the three grown children.

Richard pretended to ignore his progeny. "As to what I do for a living, this is pretty much it. For almost six months, the lodge, and the cabins, and restaurant keep us pretty busy. Tourists make up most the business but Ma here has gained a pretty fair reputation for serving a good meal at a fair price. We're closed most of the winter and then we usually open the restaurant up in April and get ready for the visitors who'll start showing up in May for the fishing opener and such. In between I do a little of this, a little of that. We don't starve and I don't get much down time, right, sweetheart?" His last remark was directed at his wife who beamed at her husband. He blew her a kiss before turning back to Elaine.

"So what about the rest of your family, Elaine? Your ma, any brothers or sisters?" Richard asked. At a look from Dorothy, he added, "Not trying to be snoopy, just curious. There is a difference, Dorothy." Another chuckle from the brothers and Madlyn before they turned, as one, to Elaine.

Oh, my. What to say but the truth and hope they left it at that. "My mother died when I was a little girl, so there's just me." She paused. "I have an aunt in California I see once in a while. She's alright ... ." Elaine's voice trailed off. Her summary of familial ties sounded pitiful to the ear.

Sympathetic sounds accompanied the announcement of her mother's early death and blended into Bud taking command of the conversation. "And then she went to college in Chicago and that's where I met her when she was doing some volunteer work at the USO club there."

Elaine tried not to choke at that comment. Had she told him about going to the USO club while waiting for his aunt and uncle last night? She must have. How else could he manage to weave that detail into the falsehood he was offering to his family? Her volunteering had been total fabrication. She tuned in to what Bud was saying.

"Yes, I did spend some time at the USO," Bud held up his hands, palms out. "Well, I had to find some way to spend the time whilst those generals decided on where to exhibit me next."

"Now Bud," Madlyn piped in, "You can't blame 'em. How many times could they get their hands on a real life hero? I would guess they'd want to make the most of it. And we're all so proud of you. When we heard-"

"Maddie" Bud cut his sister off. "How about we wait a bit for all the guts and glory details, okay? Elaine doesn't want to hear this."

"What do you mean, Bud? Didn't you and your city girl have time to share your cham-peen stories there at the USO? Or were you too busy ... you know ... ." Per waggled his eyebrows like Groucho Marx and jiggled the fork in his hand like a cigar.

Elaine blushed. Was he implying she and Bud were a couple? Could he somehow have missed the fact that she was pregnant? Or did he— no, the Tildens couldn't possibly think the baby was Bud's. They had to figure he was nowhere near Chicago when she became pregnant. After all, she was beginning to show and ... .

Bud chuckled and then swatted at his brother's hand. The fork clattered to the floor just as the Tilden clan began talking at once. Elaine felt she was present at a tennis match as she swiveled to keep track of the conversation. It ended when Lotty emerged from the dining room and proclaimed, "Hey! The customers want to know if they're missing some of the good stuff in here."

That stopped all words. Elaine expected them to look irritated, but they just grinned at one another and the men returned to their coffee. It was Dorothy who walked to Bud's chair and gave him another quick hug. She seemed to be the only Tilden who noticed the puzzled look on Elaine's face. She took a seat across the table from Elaine.

"Well, I can tell Bud didn't say much to you about his service record while he was in that USO club, now did he?" She glanced at her oldest son and waved away his protest. "I'll let Bud tell you the details in his own sweet time, just like someday he will tell us all he cares to tell." She threw a pointed look at her son. "But the truth of the matter is that my boy is a war hero. Shush now, Bud. Yes, you are!" Her glance returned to Elaine. "And he's got some medals to prove it, too."

Dorothy cleared her throat and continued. "That's why he couldn't come back to his mama as fast as he should have. Those higher-ups needed him for some recognition stuff, some morale boosting things. Pictures and interviews and such. Giving little speeches here and there to some politicians, and auxiliary volunteer groups, and Gold Star Mothers. Take some time to make those other mothers, the ones whose boys didn't come home, feel a little better."

Dorothy turned to her son, held him with her eyes and then looked in turn at the rest of her brood. "And I am proud to death of him! I want to go out in that parking lot and whoop like a crazy person and tell all of Vilas County how proud I am of my boy, but I won't. I won't because I know what Bud's thinking about now. About those boys who didn't come back. Wouldn't be right of me to be too showy while there are other mothers still grieving." She gave her eyes a quick swipe and deposited another kiss on Bud's cheek as she returned to her chores.

Richard pursed his lips. "Dorothy and Bud are right, it's Bud's story to tell, but that doesn't stop any of us from being impressed with my boy's bravery. It isn't everyone who is awarded the Distinguished Service Cross."

Simultaneously Bud and Elaine spoke.

"Dad!" from Bud.

"The Distinguished Service Cross?" Elaine overrode Bud's protests. "The Distinguished Service Cross? Holy smokes! The Distinguished Service Cross! The only thing awarded that's higher is the Congressional Medal of Honor! Bud! No wonder your folks are thrilled!" She lost all reserve and her voice grow in volume and intensity. Last night she'd been leery of this hero, this man who must have undergone terrible adversity! And he was worried that she didn't have a place to stay. Maybe her father was right. She was too caught up in herself and gave no thought to anyone else. The Distinguished Service Cross!

"Bud!" She reached across the table and took his hand, held it until he looked at her. "Oh Bud, I am so ... " What words would suffice here? She stumbled on. "... honored. Really, I had no idea." She needed more detail; this wasn't about her anymore. She swallowed and smiled at him. "Thank you for your service. And I'm glad too that you made it home to your parents."

Bud held her gaze, then blinked. A hint of a smile played upon his lips. Richard raised his cup in Elaine's direction, a mock salute, and proclaimed, "Yep Bud, she might be okay. Might be a keeper!" When they laughed this time, she was pulled into the warmth of their shared joy, a part of it.

It was mid-afternoon as she steeled herself to write a note to her father. Writing the letter lifted a cinder block from her chest, but she didn't expect an answer. She told him that she was not in Duluth, that she had no intention of going to Duluth–or anywhere else that boasted a home for unwed mothers. At least not yet. She told him she had a job and supplied the phone number of the Last Resort in case he needed to reach her. In her own mind she was convinced she would give the baby up for adoption. But it would be on her terms, not her father's, so she did not discuss her long-range plans. How could she include that information when she had no clue herself?

Chapter Four

early September 1953

It was the end of Elaine's first day off from her job. She spent it in a blissfully mundane fashion. She slept in and later in the morning rode to the village with Richard. She walked the Main Street and found the tiny public library where she registered for a card and checked out a book. She noted the feed-store, a gas station and a hardware store. Next to the post office was a tiny pharmacy and gift shop. Her last stop was Marge's Dry Goods and General Store where a few late-season tourists still lingered, fingering picture postcards and asking for directions.

Marge's Dry Goods appeared to be Mashkiki's answer to a department store. Here she could find books, rudimentary clothing, cosmetics, cookware and household items. Counting out her change for a new compact and a candy bar, Elaine was surprised by the cashier. "Don't let Richard Tilden work you too hard, now. Tell him Marge said so. Hope to see you again," the woman said as she handed Elaine her change. Apparently in a village of 600, a recent addition to the population was big news.

An hour after leaving him, she met Richard near the general store for her ride back. Her plan was to eat lunch in the resort kitchen and then let the book and a nap round out her day. Two weeks down and money in her pocket. Most of her duties at the Last Resort were not terribly taxing and were comforting of a sort; folding clean laundry, straightening rooms and delivering towels and linens to the cabins gave her the satisfaction of a job completed.

She liked kitchen duty best of all. Part of it was the warmth of the big room, its temperature and charm. No matter how chilly the dining room got with the huge, burnished oak doors opening and closing against the wind, the laughter and brightness of the kitchen cheered her each time she entered. She loved the shiny pots hanging from the rack over the huge stove and griddle. The mingled aroma of coffee and the day's special were the perfect greeting to each morning. She delighted hearing the chorus of laughter: giggles from Lotty accompanied by the lower register chuckles of the teasing Tilden men. Above all, she liked the way no one had asked her any questions about her pregnancy. She wasn't sure what Bud told his family but his explanations and admonitions must have filtered down to her co-workers. No one broached a discussion of her condition. So far.

In the lodge kitchen she was part of all transpiring with the Tildens. Sometimes she felt like an interloper, an eavesdropper on a closed society. But little by little she was drawn into the social side of her work-place. Dorothy kept up a lively conversation, commenting on the news and music from the radio, sometimes encouraging Lotty to sing along, gently drawing Elaine out on her Chicago background. She learned Doro-thy's formal education ended with high school but her intelligence was obvious and entertaining. It wasn't everyone who could converse readily about Sweden's Dag Hammarskjold as the new U.N. chief and intersperse it with a 30-item grocery list. Bud's mother was a wealth of information, a talented businesswoman, and was more than willing to talk Elaine through one of her recipes, giving Elaine tips and the mothering she had never received.

"Hold your hand like this," Dorothy said, demonstrating how she made up a batch of her trademark backwoods stew and the accompanying biscuits. "See how it makes a little cup? That's what you use to measure flour when there's not a measuring cup handy. This is how much I add at first. See? And then you stir it occasionally. If it seems to run a little thin, add a dollop more." In short time Elaine learned what a dollop was, figured what comprised a smidgen, and ascertained how much extra coffee Richard wanted when he requested just a swallow.

With her current kitchen and cabin duties she avoided restaurant customer stares at her burgeoning belly and sidestepped any conversation with a well-meaning guest. Her luck was bound to run out soon. When Elaine entered the kitchen, intending to take a glass of milk and sandwich back to her room, she discovered Lotty having trouble keeping up with lunchtime orders. Rachel, Elaine was told, had twisted her ankle and was ordered to prop it up with an ice pack for the rest of the day.

"Here Lotty, why don't I give you a hand until the worst of the lunch rush is over?" Elaine looked at Dorothy, got a broad smile of approval, and grabbed a green and yellow lodge apron. Lotty pointed her toward the far corner of the dining room. "If you can handle those four tables, I can get caught up."

It looked easy, delivering water glasses, pouring coffee and writing down an order for two house specials. She approached the last table of lingering diners with a full coffee pot, ready to pour refills when one head turned and she heard a familiar voice.

"Ah, so this is where you ended up. Shoulda known ole Bud couldn't resist shepherding a stray." It was the rude soldier from the train, the one who'd bumped her in the aisle. The unbelievably gorgeous one Bud called Lloyd. Elaine saw his eyes sweeping down her torso yet again. What did that remark mean? A stray? As in a strayed woman? Was that how pregnant girls were labeled here?

Cheeks flaming, she turned to the other men. "Need a refill?" She filled all the proffered cups but Lloyd's. Then she turned on her heel and started back to the kitchen.

"Hey miss! Missy? I think you forgot me!" Lloyd's voice followed her. "Don't I get any more coffee?" Laughter erupted from the table from his companions.

"Guess not, Lloyd," one of the men ventured. "Looks like you might need to turn on the charm if you expect an extra cup from that one."

Lotty stopped her at the kitchen door. "Don't pay any attention to that creepy Lloyd Defoe," she whispered. "I hear from all the local girls that he's always been a real jerk. Now I hear he got hired back at his old job. He's a welder full time at Mashkiki Mechanical. Good pay but– he sure does seem like a pain in the you-know-what." Lotty sighed. "If only he wasn't so good looking. Not just handsome but movie star handsome. Looks a little like Rock Hudson, don't you think? Maybe a little younger but Rock Hudson seems like he'd be nicer! What a waste."

Elaine glanced again at the corner table. All the men were focused on their conversation but Lloyd peeked over his shoulder, saw her and narrowed his eyes before turning back to his cronies. He murmured something and all eyes turned her way once more as a few of them threw a smirk her direction. Damn him! She pushed the swinging door and re-entered the kitchen.

Twenty minutes later things calmed down. After acknowledging Lotty's gratitude, Elaine passed into the dining room heading for her room in the staff hallway. She rounded the corner and collided with another body. A flat hard chest, and spicy aftershave accompanied the strong grip on her arms, stopping her stumble. Lloyd.

"What– what are you doing back here?" Elaine sputtered. "This area is employees only. The men's room is down the hallway on the other side of the kitchen."

"Yeah, I know," he answered. "I was waiting for you." He didn't elaborate, but seemed to take some pleasure in her mild discomfort.

Rather than asking "Why?" she lifted her gaze and cocked her head. Two could play this game. Whatever this game was.

Lloyd's smile broadened. "Hey, I just wanted to apologize for getting you flustered in there." He jerked his head toward the dining area. "I didn't mean to rattle you. I remember you from the train. I guess I was surprised to see you here at the lodge. After I saw you with Bud, I shoulda known you knew the Tildens and were heading for Mashkiki."

"I didn't know them then." The words flew from her before she gave a response any thought.

Lloyd's eyes widened at her comment. Why did she tell him that? Why did he deserve any kind of explanation at all? And why did his face register some pleasant reaction to her pronouncement? She tried to move past him but a slight shift from Lloyd blocked her again. She looked up at him once more. "Are you going to let me by or is this little dance going to continue?"

Lloyd's smile gained intensity. "Dance? Now that is a splendid idea! Here I was just going to apologize and be on my way and you go putting other notions in my head! Well, Miss Elaine, I think that a dance could be arranged. There's a little tavern here in town—a respectable place—where people gather on a Saturday night and socialize. Charlie has a pretty good jukebox there and people have been known to dance a little. What say I pick you up around eight?"

What? Now he was asking her for a date? Didn't he realize she was pregnant? But of course he did. It seemed obvious from the way he stared at her on the train and again in the dining room. And what about his remark to his pals? Wasn't that a reference to her? She studied his face. His way of looking at her through his eyelashes recalled her father. Ugh. But this guy was undeniably handsome. Definitely a resemblance to Rock Hudson. With an even better smile. Maybe the "stray" remark was a reference to Bud. Or to the Tildens. She could sort it out later.

"Well?" he asked. "Whadda you say? Let me make up for my poor manners. Maybe I could buy you a drink and lead you in a polite waltz around Charlie's dance floor. Come on, pretty Missy. Eight o'clock?"

Could the wattage on that smile get any brighter? Maybe she misjudged him. Just because she was pregnant didn't mean she had to stay cooped up in her room, did it? There was no father to grant permission, none to disappoint; none to give judgmental looks or offer any remarks that made her feel so worthless. It was Saturday night, and she was responsible for herself now. And Lloyd did seem sincere. And he was so gorgeous.

" All right," she answered quickly before she could change her mind.

"Eight o'clock it is. I'll be in one of those chairs on the lodge porch, waiting."

He nodded and moved around her. "Good. I'll be there. Don't you be keeping me waiting."

Did she have anything in her wardrobe that might be suitable to wear out on a Saturday night? That looked sort of dressy and made her feel pretty? That might camouflage her condition a little? Maybe she should settle for one that still fit.

—☙

There wasn't much time for chit chat. It was only a two to three minute ride from the resort to the center of Mashkiki. Elaine considered telling Lotty about her date but didn't want to defend her decision to the younger girl. When Lloyd showed up at eight on the dot; he had even gotten out of his vehicle to open her door. She felt that perhaps this evening would turn out better than she hoped. Then she could tell Lotty about it!

On the way, Lloyd made a few comments about the lack of night life here in Rapids compared to big cities like Wausau. Before she had much of a chance to respond, they arrived at the Dew Drop Inn. At first glance, it looked like any backwoods roadhouse, built like an overgrown toy Lincoln Log structure. They approached the door and Elaine noticed fresh paint around the windows. The frames were a bright and shiny scarlet, and several coffee cans filled with red geraniums lined one side of the building. The geraniums were probably on their last weeks outside, frost would be coming soon but they added a homier touch than most country bars might offer. Strains of a pleasant ballad greeted them as Lloyd opened the door and ushered her inside.

A few couples gathered near the bar. Most of the women were seated, talking with one another as the men stood behind them. A pool table was in the center of the main room. To one side was an alcove with four tables and a small area where two couples were dancing and singing along to "Don't Let the Stars Get in Your Eyes." She noticed Perry and Olivia seated at a small table, and what appeared to be a look of surprise on Perry's face. She managed a small wave at them before Lloyd steered her to a table and helped her with her coat. He draped it over the back of one chair and motioned her to a chair where she could see the dancers and still get a view of the bar.

"What can I get ya? You want a beer or something stronger?"

"Maybe just a wine spritzer? Would that be okay?"

Lloyd looked puzzled. "A wine what?"

"A spritzer. Just a little red wine with a splash of 7UP."

"Ooohhh. So that's what you call a spritzer, huh? Is that fancy or are you living dangerously tonight?"

Before Elaine could answer, Lloyd was swaggering to the bar, calling out to the bartender. "Hey Charlie, could I have a cold beer? Hamm's is fine. And the little lady over yonder wants a red wine spritzer. She tells me that's a little red wine with some 7UP mixed in."

"Yeah, yeah, I know. I've actually made one or two before, Lloyd. Not everyone was brought up in a barn. I'll start a tab and bring the drinks over to your table so I can meet your friend." Charlie sent a friendly smile over Elaine's way and turned to fetch some glasses.

Lloyd clapped the shoulder of one of the men Elaine had seen him with this morning, as he returned to the table. She noticed when Lloyd passed the man, the fellow rolled his eyes and rubbed his shoulder. As he neared his chair, Lloyd declined pulling it out and swung his leg over the back before settling in. He reached in his shirt pocket and withdrew a pack of cigarettes. He extended the pack to Elaine and when she shook her head, he lit his smoke and blew a stream upward from the corner of his mouth.

A whiff of Aqua Velva signaled the bartender's appearance. He set their drinks before them and wiped his hands on the apron before extending a hand to Elaine. "Hello there, Miss. I'm Charlie Lowell, owner and proprietor of this little establishment. You must be Elaine Reilly." He noticed the puzzled look on her face and added, "I'm pretty good friends with Richard Tilden and he mentioned that he hired a friend of Bud's to finish out the season. Hope you're enjoying all that Mashkiki has to offer. Lloyd doesn't treat you right, you just let me know. It looks like you have Hank's approval." He motioned to a dog at his side. Elaine gave the dog a pat before it turned and followed Charlie back to the bar.

Lloyd gave a little snort as he watched the bartender leave. "Can't believe he allows that mutt in here. Someone abandoned it in the parking lot and ol' Charlie seems to have adopted it. So Miss Elaine, what should we talk about?"

Elaine blinked. Now that they were settled in and alone maybe her lack of dating experience would be showcased. Didn't most guys like to talk about themselves?

"Well, I don't know. Have you read any good books lately?" She thought this was a safe topic.

" Books! Not hardly! I think the last book I read all the way through was one I had to read for a high school English class. Dull as dirt. Pret' near killed me."

Books were out, as were most music compositions. Her interests in college had been art and literature but neither of those was one of Lloyd's long suits. Somehow they managed to struggle through fifteen minutes. They were saved from too much awkward silence when a couple stopped by their table on the way to the dance floor.

"Hey now, Lloyd," the man exclaimed. He was tall and skinny and appeared a bit older than Lloyd. "I heard you got back on the same train as Bud. How ya doing?"

A brief smile flickered over Lloyd's face. "Hello Ed. Yep, I got back a few weeks ago and just got settled in at the old Fulton place. Got my old job back, too."

"Good for you. And who's the pretty lady here?" Ed turned to Elaine.

Before she could answer, he threw his arm across the shoulders of the woman standing next to him and pulled her closer to the table. "We're the Gundersons. I'm Ed and this is my Scottish lassie, Morag. Heard the Last Resort had some new help but didn't catch a name." He extended one hand toward Elaine.

Lloyd was sipping his beer so that appeared to be Elaine's cue to complete her own introduction.

"Verra nice to meet you, Elaine." Morag Gunderson's eyes crinkled as it registered with Elaine that the woman's surname didn't match her brogue. "P'raps we'll have a chance to talk more later. Come along Ed, you promised me a dance." The couple tossed Elaine and Lloyd another smile and headed to finish a two step.

Lloyd went to the bar for another beer. Elaine searched for a topic she could approach when he returned. She recalled her giggling roommates making oblique and whispered conversation with their dates about sex. That certainly wasn't something she'd introduce in tonight's conversation.

In addition to being embarrassing, truthfully it wasn't something she understood well. Surely there was more to it than the fumbling and discomfort she'd experienced. Attraction was all well and good, but didn't decency and kindness and compatibility figure in there somewhere? She could imagine her roommates laughing if she'd asked that.

Lloyd returned and for several minutes they just listened to the music. Lloyd made small talk with some of the other patrons who passed their table. As Elaine tried to tune in on what Lloyd was saying, she noticed his second bottle was empty.

"... so in another couple of months I should get a decent pay bump and with a union job o'course the benefits are good. Yep, I think I should make out just fine, despite what them who thought I'd amount to nothing might think. Maybe I should flash my pay stub at them. Maybe they'd change their tune then." He glanced to his right and tipped his beer bottle to direct her eyes. She saw only Perry and Olivia seated in that vicinity and realized he was referring to the young Tilden couple. Maybe all the Tildens.

"You don't seem to like Perry much, do you? Why's that?" She was curious and wondered if there was something she'd misread about her employers and their extended family.

"No, I don't care for Perry! Nor his folks or his snooty sister and for sure not Bud! Stuck up ass! Always was the kind that thought he was better'n anybody else and now there's this he-ro stuff. Like the rest of us who wore the uniform didn't matter a bit. Damn do-gooder. It's enough to make you puke." Lloyd's voice was low but there was no mistaking the contempt in his remarks or the sneer on his face. "Yeah, that whole Tilden bunch! You don't have to think they're God's gift, they think it plenty for themselves. A-holes!"

Elaine was surprised by Lloyd's vehemence. "Maybe, but I have to say they've been good employers to me. So far anyway." She didn't want to create a scene and what did she know? Maybe there was something about the Tildens that she didn't know. They had taken a chance on hiring her with no questions asked, just Bud's say so, but maybe she was giving them too much credit. Oh, oh. She was starting to be a little suspicious, and think like her father would. Hard to believe she'd adopt his attitude about anything.

"You don't know 'em. Give them time. Then you'll see I was right." Lloyd found a topic he could expand upon and his words were steeped in conviction. He looked at her half empty glass. "You want another or are you ready to dance a little?"

Maybe a dance was better than trying to steer any conversation into safer territory. And it might slow Lloyd down in the drinks department. Elaine rose and took Lloyd's hand as he led her a few steps onto the dance floor. On the jukebox Jo Stafford was singing "You Belong to Me" and Lloyd surprised her by pulling her close to him and moving effortlessly into a professionally executed waltz. No doubt, he was a good dancer. Probably one of the best she'd ever partnered with. She could see others glancing their way, the men giving their companions a gentle nudge in the ribs and friendly smiles on the lips of the women.

She wished he would not hold her quite so closely. Her stomach pressed up against him in a way that felt familiar and unsettling. Maybe she should just let herself enjoy it. From what she read in her old college biology book, in a few weeks this baby would be kicking. Old Lloyd could be getting a swift poke from the little bun in her oven. A bubble of a laugh escaped before she could squelch it.

Lloyd squinted down at her with irritated eyes. "What's the matter with you? You laughing at me? Something wrong with the way I dance?"

"No, no, it isn't that," she was quick to assure him. "Of course not, you're a great dancer, Lloyd. It's just that I'm not used to being the center of attention." She nodded toward the barroom spectators and then tilted her head back to focus on her partner. With some relief she noticed the song was ending and turned back to the table. "Maybe I should sit and finish my wine and you can get yourself another beer."

"That's a good idea. Ready for another? No? Well, I'll be right back."

Lloyd returned, and set two more bottles before his place. "Thought I'd save myself a trip. These are going down really easy tonight." He grinned at her. "Nothing like a little lubricant to oil up the process."

Now what did that mean? She felt like she was missing something in his remarks. Was he more of a master at double entendre than she gave him credit? Maybe this outing wasn't such a good idea. As though reading her mind, Lloyd drained an entire bottle in a long pull and then reached for the other. "Here, just let me finish these and we can leave. That okay with you, pretty Missy?"

He tapped his foot while he drank the remaining bottle, and soon was helping her with her coat. A few goodnights to his friends and they were out the door. Once settled in the vehicle, Elaine smelled the boozy exhalations coming from Lloyd. Was he drunk? This date hadn't gone too badly, it probably could have been worse, but she was in no hurry to repeat it. Right now, she'd be just as happy back in the lodge, snuggled in to the sweet smelling quilt Dorothy had provided.

A few moments later she noticed Lloyd wasn't following the familiar road back to The Last Resort. If she had her bearings right, they were headed west, not north. "Where are we going?"

"The evening's still young, Missy. Thought you might like to see the splendors of Trout Lake." He hooked an arm around her and drew her closer to him across the bench seat while glancing speculatively at her. He gave her upper arm a firm squeeze and then began to rub her shoulder.

"Umm, Lloyd? Maybe I should just go back to ... ." Her words were cut off by a sloppy kiss from the man next to her. The truck veered across the center line before he righted his course. "Lloyd! Watch your driving!" What was he doing? She wiped her mouth with the back of her hand and scooted toward the passenger door as he returned both hands to the steering wheel. Then he slowed the vehicle and pulled onto a side road.

"Mmm, baby, you sure smell good. Taste pretty good, too. Come on back over here and I'll double check that opinion. Although I'm generally pretty accurate when it comes to the fairer sex." He gripped her now with both hands and pulled her toward him. "Ahh, sex. Now maybe that's a topic you'd care to pursue. Cuz it appears as though you've already pursued that a little with someone else. Yessir, maybe that's something we've got in common here. Whadda think?" His big hand reached inside her open coat and groped her breast.

"Stop it! What are you doing!" Elaine screeched. She slapped at his arm but he shook her off as though she were a mild irritation, like he was shooing a fly from his face. His hand again gained purchase on the front of her blouse, fumbling at buttons, grasping the material. She pulled his hand from her chest and heard the rip of fabric. She put her hand on his chest hoping to establish some distance and push him from her but he caught it firmly in his and placed it on his groin.

"Whadda think, missy? Think you can handle this? At least we don't have to pretend that you don't know your way around this! Or that you'll say no because you're afraid of getting knocked up. There's something to be said for pregnant girls and sloppy seconds." He leaned toward her again, mouth open, intent on another kiss.

"No! Stop it!" Her voice was a shout though no one would hear her. Squirming didn't help; Lloyd was holding her hand too tightly. Reflexively,

Elaine raised her left elbow and connected with his face. A tiny yelp came from him as his head jerked back. With the aid of scant moonlight, Elaine saw that his lip was split. Eyes locked on hers, Lloyd touched his fingers to his mouth and looked at the smear of blood on them. Before she knew it, he'd exited the truck and in a few quick strides was at her door. He opened the door and pushed his face into hers, blood seeping from his lower lip and down his chin. "You see what you did? Good thing it was my mouth. If you'd hit any harder and caught my nose, ya might've broke it!" He jerked her arm and pulled her from the seat of the truck.

Lloyd held her closely before him by both shoulders. Only a few inches separated them and she could smell sour beer on his breath. His voice grew louder and he gave her a shake. "You snooty little bitch! Who do you think you are? Ain't too many guys who'd even be willing to take out a hussy like you! You think you're the Virgin Mary or something instead of a big city slut!"

Her head snapped with one final shake before Lloyd pushed her back a few feet and with a parting shove released her. "You can get yourself back to the lodge. A little hike won't kill you. Might improve your disposition." He slammed her door and marched himself back to the driver's side. She heard a wad of spit land somewhere on the pavement before he heaved himself behind the wheel and pulled away.

Elaine was shaking and could hear the huffing of her own breath as she looked around her. She stood for a few seconds watching his taillights vanish as she got her bearings. A good thing the moonlight was so bright. Ahead she could discern the wooden sign pointing to Langholz's Fish Camp, one she noted on her first ride into Mashkiki Rapids. That meant she was only a mile or so from The Last Resort.

If she let the moon guide her feet and stuck to the middle of the road, if she sang loudly, clapped her hands and scuffed her feet to ward off any stray bears, she could probably be home in twenty minutes.

Home? Right now it sounded right.

Chapter Five

early October 1953

"I know I think Mashkiki's heaven but you normal mortals might like a cruise into another civilization." Bud jerked his head in the direction of the county road which led to Minocqua. "I'm heading into Minocqua so if you want a change of scenery from the pinery, now that your shift's over, here's your opportunity."

The day was blustery and Elaine was grateful she had remembered to grab the plaid, woolen scarf from the peg behind her bedroom door. Never mind her hair, a day like this called for comfort and protection, not worrying about style. She wasn't sure why Bud was going into Minocqua. She hadn't asked. After that miserable night with Lloyd, she hadn't strayed much from lodge property. She knew Bud had worked only four hours this morning and she was just "along for the ride." She thought about stores where she could window shop and a larger public library where she could browse.

"Are you in any hurry to get back? Have you got other plans. Maybe meeting Lloyd or somebody later?" Bud's voice interrupted her thoughts.

"What? No, no, I don't think I'll be seeing any more of Lloyd unless he comes in the lodge for a meal." She hoped Bud wasn't going to ask her any more about the fiasco with Lloyd. To head him off she asked, "What is the deal with Lloyd anyway? Were you two ever friends? And why is he so ... so contrary?"

A chuckle escaped from Bud. "Contrary? Yeah, I suppose that's as good a word as any to describe Lloyd. I don't know that you can say we're friends but we did play on the same sports teams and such. We've had our share of differences over the years, and I know he can be pretty rough and a blockhead sometimes, but I guess what it all comes down to is he's our blockhead, you know? One summer he came crying to my mother. He had found a kitten and his mother said he couldn't keep it. Said if he tried, she'd get on of her boyfriends to drown it. So he brought it to Ma and begged her to keep it."

"Did she?"

"Sure. She's a sucker for stray critters and Lloyd counted on that. He's had a rough upbringing and I guess my take on Lloyd is that doesn't excuse his behavior but it explains it. Don't know if that makes any sense to you."

"Hmm." She wasn't sure if that information made things any clearer but Elaine knew she didn't want to waste any more time discussing Lloyd. "So what are you going in to Minocqua for today?" She was more than a little shocked when Bud told her he had taken the liberty of scheduling a doctor's appointment for her.

"You what!?" She wasn't sure if she heard him correctly. Anger started to build in her. "What makes you think you could make an appointment for me?"

Bud heard the vexation in her voice. "Sorry. I know you can take care of yourself, but I thought just this once you might accept a shortcut. Doc Bremman's son was one of my best friends in school and I knew I could get you in without too much fuss. From now on I'll stay out of your business. I promise."

Elaine took a few breaths and let her irritation subside before she answered. She could detect no judgment or accusation in his voice. She was grateful for a friend, and realized she had put this on the back burner for too long. "Okay. I guess I should've thought of that myself. Thanks."

"Good enough. Maybe afterward you'd like to do some shopping? I'd be happy to show you some of the stores. Maybe you'd like to buy some material and thread or something."

Fabric? She looked at him quizzically. "For maternity outfits," he went on. "My sister calls them hatching jackets and there sure isn't anywhere around here that you can buy some. Well, I don't know. Maybe a Sears catalog? But then you might have to guess about the fit. Most women I know sew their own." His voice trailed off.

Elaine was horrified. She hadn't given much thought to the notion that in a very short time none of her clothes would fit. A few skirts were already too tight around the waist. Was this Bud's way of telling her she looked lumpy? Was she now expected to craft her own wardrobe? With her supposed intelligence was she really this ignorant in the ways of the world? "Sewing, no, I don't … ." Her voice was choked.

It was Bud's turn to be flustered. "Well, I know you probably won't need them right this week but won't you need them sometime? I mean, at some point don't you expectant ladies need to change your wardrobe? I just thought … maybe you have an idea of when … ."

He let his voice again drift away and Elaine realized he was attempting to broach the subject of her due date. From years of eavesdropping on neighbor ladies and what she had read in her college biology books, she knew what the normal gestation period was. And since she had engaged in intercourse only that one time, she had a very clear idea that this baby would be born near the end of February. How much information did she want to tell Bud? How much did he deserve to know? Maybe she could consider these questions while she waited at the doctor's office.

For now she contented herself with studying the symmetry of the oaks and pines and birches along the side of the roadway. That little nature game she played always calmed her before. She liked making patterns of the russets, the peeling whites and deep rich green before that vision was replaced by one of the many small lakes that seemed to be tucked around every curve. What word described the color of the water today? She could see why Bud loved this area; everything here spoke of peace. Maybe some of that natural mashkiki, that medicine, could be a soothing tonic for her, too.

In no time Bud was dropping her off at the clinic door. He showed her where the coffee shop was, only a short four blocks from the medical offices. He'd wait there for her and promised to treat her to coffee and a cinnamon roll "though they're not as good as Ma's."

The appointment went well. Oh yes, there were some tears shed and a few moments where Elaine relived some shame and anxiety at her predicament, but the physician was kind and asked only a few questions regarding her baby's paternity. He seemed more businesslike than judgmental when Elaine had few details to supply. Overall, he was far more understanding than her father was. Even the nurse patted her hand and gave her some pamphlets to tuck in her purse. She encouraged Elaine to come with a list of questions next time.

The walk to the diner was refreshing. Twenty minutes after sliding into the booth across from Bud, Elaine drained her cup and licked her fingers which had become coated with a delicious sticky cinnamon and sugar combination.

Elaine took a breath. With her appointment behind her, Elaine's thoughts were more organized. She looked for a good way to begin. "Okay Bud, I want to talk about my pregnancy." She stammered. "About how I wound up like this." She paused and took another breath. Maybe this recitation wouldn't be as easy as she hoped, but she owed Bud the truth. After all, he had rescued her, at least for the short term. "You see, there was this sailor and ... ."

"No, no," he protested, "You don't have to go into any of that, Elaine. I mean, it's not really my business and I have no right to know what happened between you and your sweetheart so ... ." He averted his eyes from hers and seemed to take a sudden interest in the menu. "I shouldn't be bringing up those bad memories for you. For all I know, maybe he could have died or gotten hurt somehow. For sure he couldn't have deserted you. I mean, I suppose he could have but what guy would."

"Bud!" She spoke a little sharper than necessary to quiet him. "There was no sweetheart! That's what I want to explain to you. Maybe I need to. I know that I want to because nobody knows the real circumstance. Surely not my father. Not even my friends, if I even had a friend who might understand this." She smiled at him ruefully. "Right now you're about the only friend I have and I only want to tell this once. Is that okay with you?"

He looked at her in a shocked silence and she registered once more the intensity of those glacial blue eyes. There was a barely perceptible head bob from him.

"Okay. Sorry, Lainie. Haven't been around many girls lately. I'm running off at the mouth here. This is your story. Go ahead, shoot." Bud gave her a lopsided smile and cocked one eyebrow.

"Okay. Thanks. I think." A nervous little laugh escaped from her and her eyes began to water. She reached for a napkin to dab her eyes and was amazed to see that Bud's eyes looked misty as well. He cleared his throat and his voice held a measure of concern.

"It's alright, Lainie. You can talk about it ... or not. It's up to you. Just know that we can take as much time as you want and you can stop whenever. You're not obligated to me."

He sounded so serious, Elaine almost laughed again but knew she needed to begin her saga now or she would never speak of it. She took yet another deep breath, and looked at Bud before focusing on the faded and oft-washed red, Formica table top.

"At my college I attended what we called short term. The spring term is over in late April but the profs and record keepers have until the end of May to get all the exams and term papers graded for the graduates. Some students go home or travel but you can take one class that month if you want. Four hours a day and get a semester's credit. Anyway, I was getting a C in one of my spring classes and my father told me I had to retake it or drop out of school. He said if he was paying for a college education that I needed to be more serious about it. C's don't make it. He's pretty strict that way and I don't remember ever crossing him. I was planning on summer school anyway so ... ." She saw an odd look pass over Bud's face when she spoke of her father's edict.

She took another breath and continued. "The dormitory where I had lived was being repainted so I shared a flat with two girls I knew from my freshmen dorm. We weren't real close friends but I knew them and it was a better arrangement than living with complete strangers through the summer. We didn't do much together as far as socializing. They weren't as serious about the classes they were taking as I was." She sighed and forged ahead.

"Then the last week in May came and I knew I was going to do well in my class, for sure getting an A or even an A plus." There was a slight note of pride in her voice before she stopped and shook her head. "And I suppose I was kind of mad at my dad for forcing me to retake it and maybe I was tired of staying in every night doing all that studying when Maribeth and Suze went out. Anyway, I told them that I would go to the USO Club near Chicago with them that last Friday before Memorial Day." She glanced at Bud and fiddled with a salt shaker before she continued.

"I'd never been to one before and I was a little overwhelmed when I walked in. The lights were so bright and the dance floor was crowded. The music was real loud and it sounded good! Wonderful, just like in the movies. And before we could even find a table, all these sailors and soldiers were walking by us and asking for a dance or wanting to get us a drink. Everyone was laughing and smiling. So many of those boys were saying things like 'Hey, pretty lady! You spoken for?' It took a few seconds before I realized they were talking to me!"

Her eyes brightened. "No one had ever told me I was pretty before! And there were all these handsome, eligible men in those spanking, newly-pressed uniforms! I just knew I was going to have fun. I felt I deserved it, and I was kicking myself for not coming before." Elaine paused a minute. She knew she sounded feisty and that her face was flushed. In her mind she was back in Illinois at that club.

"I wore new shoes and they were a little tight but I was determined to dance as much as I could and it was great! Of course, there was the matter of all those drinks that kept coming to the table. I'd been to a couple of beer parties while I was going to college but never had that much alcohol before. I'm not trying to make excuses and I suppose that sounds a little Miss Goodie Two-Shoes to you but that's the way it was. I was never very popular, I guess. Anyway … ." Her voice trailed off as she felt herself choke up.

"Elaine?" Bud looked anxious. "Elaine, you can stop if you want to. I'm sorry if I pushed. You can quit telling me this if you want to. I didn't mean for you to get upset." He sensed that he was making her relive her humiliation.

"No, no, it's alright." Elaine toyed with the salt shaker, the sugar dispenser and the napkin holder. Her eyes again studied the table top. "I danced a lot. Drank too much. It was great! Toward the end of the night, I couldn't find Maribeth and Suze. I knew they probably connected with the same servicemen they'd run into the last couple of Fridays. They'd talked about them on the way to the club–how cute Maribeth thought they were and what good kissers they were."

Elaine laughed here. "It was just so much fun for me! All that anticipation. Me feeling like I was a real part of their group. I know that sounds silly but that's the way it was." She cleared her throat and picked up the story. "We agreed that if we got separated we'd meet in the parking lot at midnight and I had almost an hour before they'd be showing up. By that time, most of the other guys had figured out I wasn't a real ball of fire so they had kind've drifted off .

"I'd been talking with this young sailor, some shy, skinny, blond kid from northern Illinois. He was just out of the hospital. I think he had been burned because he kept referring to some kind of burn medication and there was a scar … ." Elaine paused here and her hand moved up to the side of her neck to indicate the location of the wound. She dabbed her eyes before continuing.

"He was only 18 and he was more of a duck out of water than I was. From the teasing that his buddies were throwing at him, I don't think he'd ever had a date before. They kept asking him if his hometown even had any girls in it, it was so small. We were all laughing when they said that. He offered to walk me outside since I was feeling pretty woozy. I remember his arm was around my shoulder ... ." Her voice drifted off and her eyes closed for a few seconds. "And then we were kissing. I was hiccuping and trying not to get sick. He kept patting my shoulder and stuff. The next thing you know I was in his buddy's car, my skirt was all twisted up and ... and he was crying and holding my hand."

She paused to look at Bud and felt a single, lonely tear trickle down her cheek. "Yeah, he was crying. Crying hard. Maybe we both were. Somehow he thought I was, I don't know, more experienced, I suppose. It was his first time, too and maybe he was upset about hurting me." She stopped and wiped her face, embarrassed that she had given more details than she intended. Bud looked uncomfortable.

"So that's it. No sweetheart involved, Bud. Just a poor homesick kid and a silly college girl who couldn't hold her liquor. Certainly not very romantic. More like a story in one of those cheap magazines they sell at a big city bus depot."

Bud opened his mouth, but Elaine shushed him as a waitress walked by. "Miss? Could we have another cup of coffee here, please?" She turned to her companion. Bud studied her face. It probably was good for her to get this out but she didn't intend to continue blabbing all the details of her private life at the drop of a nickel. She was done.

"I am sorry," Bud told her. "That couldn't have been easy for you and I didn't mean to make you go through that again. I shouldn't have ... ."

Elaine stopped him, wanting the conversation to return to normal, whatever normal was after baring your soul about the why's and therefore's of an unplanned pregnancy. "That's okay, it's natural, I guess, to be curious. You and your family have been so good to me, I guess you deserved to know."

"No Lainie, it's not that." Again his eyes lowered and his voice dropped. Elaine realized then that sometime during her narrative he'd taken her hand, was holding it yet. His smile was odd, even a little shy. "Now it's my turn to confess." He stopped and then all his words came in a rush.

"Can't you see that I care about you? When I heard about you and Lloyd—Perry gave me a report about seeing you together at Charlie's— I was sick. I was thrilled when that didn't seem to go anywhere!"

If you only knew! Elaine kept quiet as Bud continued. "I feel so selfish now. I wanted to know about your baby because I ..." Bud stopped and swallowed before he picked up the conversation. "I wanted to jar myself out of how I feel about you. I thought if I knew about a sweetheart who was going to swoop in here one day and carry you away, I'd be able to just get on with whatever life has in store for me here in Mashkiki and forget about all the thoughts I've been entertaining about this beautiful and smart city girl."

Elaine was flabbergasted. It took effort to align her reaction to his words as Bud continued. "Never had anyone tell you you were pretty before? Ha! Don't you know how sweet and gorgeous you are, Lainie? What was wrong with all those big city boys you grew up with? They all blind or something?"

Elaine felt her mouth opening and shutting like one of those gasping fish Richard described in his ice fishing stories. Her? Sweet? And pretty? Bud thought she was pretty? Even when she felt so dumpy and unattractive? Him? This appealing and handsome soldier?

Bud squeezed her hand. "Come on Lainie, that's enough intense talk for today. I think we better get back home before we feel like we're acting out one of Ma's radio stories." His smile was radiant as he pulled her to her feet and helped with her coat.

—❧

They didn't speak much on the ride home but something in their relationship shifted. More and more Bud showed up when her shift ended in the kitchen. He helped her close the dining room and then sat with her for hours at the big table while she ate her supper. He poured her extra glasses of milk. Sometimes, when the late evening air was mild and the stars were visible, they went for a stroll around the resort property before he walked her back to her room. Now and again their goodnights included a kiss or two at parting. Sweet, comforting, enough to make her feel that she wasn't a troll.

November neared and Elaine knew her employment was ending. Not only did she need to make more concrete plans about the baby but she knew she might have to deal with the absence of Bud, probably the closest friend she'd had since junior high. She decided she'd adopt the attitude of her movie heroine, Scarlett O'Hara, and think of her options later because "tomorrow is another day." True enough she told herself, but I'm not Vivian Leigh and I don't expect my life to have a Hollywood ending. And my days alone, without a baby, are running out.

CHAPTER SIX

November 1953

Thanksgiving dawned cold and clear and with it came the traditional close of the resort for the season. Dorothy and her kitchen crew fed the few last hunters a hearty breakfast and the Tilden men helped them load the deer carcasses on their vehicles as they aimed their cars southward. Elaine overheard one of the hunters ask Bud if he'd be back at guiding next year. "I don't think so," Bud had responded. "I've had enough of guns for a while. Kind of swore off hunting this year." Later she had heard him tell his mother that while he respected the sport involved in hunting, he didn't think he could ever point a gun at a living thing again. Evidently his war experiences had a greater effect on him than originally noted.

As soon as the last hunter rolled out, Dorothy and Richard began to prepare in earnest for the Thanksgiving feast. Madalyn, Tommy and their girls were coming in later as well as Perry and Olivia. Some of the extended family planned to show up in the evening for pie and coffee.

From what Lotty and Rachel told her, Elaine knew the crew was welcome to join the family in the lodge that evening. Officially this was her last day of work. She had a tidy little sum saved and she knew from her conversations with Bud that the Tildens would not push her out until she had made some plans. On her last visit to the doctor's office, the nurse had given her some options and names to contact. Adoption for her child might be the best choice. There was no baby's father to help, no family of her own to count on, but she still balked at the idea. "After Thanksgiving," she told herself. "After tonight, I'll make these decisions."

Last night when she finished in the kitchen she bundled up and sat on the porch for a few minutes to watch the northern skies. Bud joined her and told her not to worry. More than that, he promised her he had a plan when her work ceased at The Last Resort. She hadn't given his statement much thought. It was so like the Bud she'd come to know to want to fix things. Nevertheless, it was still a surprise tonight when the pie was served and the coffee and brandies passed round, Bud rose from his seat and clinked his fork against a water goblet. "Thank you for the wonderful meal, Ma. It was as delicious as I dreamed of when I was eating that army chow last Thanksgiving. What I would've given for some of your fantastic pumpkin pie then!" Laughter accompanied that remark since Bud consumed nearly an entire pie by himself this evening.

"We're just glad you're here now, son," Dorothy countered.

"Amen to that!" Richard mouthed before spearing another bite of his own dessert.

Bud smiled. "Now before all the kids get too sleepy and you all start making noise about getting home and out of the clean up, I've got an announcement to make."

Perry, settled back with his arm flung around the back of Olivia's chair, spoke up. "Now, now, big brother. You're not leaving Mashkiki for some high-falutin' job in Wausau, are you? Tommy told me the paper mills are hiring and giving veterans first preference, but I think Ma'd skin you alive if you tried to leave Rapids so soon after getting back."

Everyone saw Dorothy glance at Richard who merely shrugged and fiddled with a toothpick. The question was unspoken but evident in her eyes. Did her husband know if Bud was planning to leave? Where was this leading? Elaine, seated at the end of the long table next to Olivia and the kitchen door, looked down the long line of Tildens at Bud. She started when she realized his eyes were locked on hers.

"No, nothing like that." Bud assured them. "But I think this might be even better than any announcement about a new job. Shouldn't be any secret to any of you that what I've wanted my whole life was to have what Ma and Dad have. Being in a place you love, with someone you love and raising a family. Madlyn, Perry, remember when we were little and begged Dad for a story? No matter how the story started, it always ended with a handsome man named Richard finding his angel and her name was Dorothy?"

The assemblage laughed again as Richard leaned over to kiss Dorothy's cheek and she pretended to wave him away. Bud smiled more broadly as he continued. "Okay, you all know what I mean. Little did I know a few months ago that I'd be bringing my own angel home with me on the train." Elaine could feel a burn starting up her neck. Was she hearing him right?

A murmur came from Aunt Lovey, and Madlyn actually squealed as Bud continued. "Elaine, I know I've never said it but I think you know how I feel about you. So I'm asking you right here, right now, to marry me and I'm hoping that by asking you in front of everyone in the world I love, you'll take pity on me and say yes."

Bud walked down the length of the table toward her. In his hand was a small velvet jeweler's box. "What about it, Lainie? I love you. Will you take this ring? Will you do me the honor of marrying me?"

Elaine wondered later if her hesitation showed or if it really took only a second for so many thoughts to race through her mind. He loved her? Loved her? Really? Did she love him? Would this be the answer for her? What did the Tildens think of all this? Would they accept her? Could she do this? Should she do this? It would certainly solve all her problems and she did feel something special when she was with him. It was gentler and more satisfying than any time she spent with any other boy. It probably was love. If it wasn't, it could become love, couldn't it?

Everyone's eyes were on her. She could feel the love and joy that seeped to every corner of this beautiful rustic room. She didn't remember saying anything but she did remember rising, throwing her arms around Bud's neck, laughing as he lifted her off her feet and twirled her around the dining room as his family cheered and applauded. "Yes," she whispered into his ear. "Yes, I'll be your wife. I love you, too."

Somehow a chair materialized and Bud moved next to Elaine. He gripped her hand tightly and an enormous smile played across his face. Elaine felt her own smile match his.

"Well, congratulations the two of you!" Richard beamed. He stood and raised his glass. "I was wondering if there was something more than met the eye when you showed up with this smart city gal. So, what are we thinking? A June wedding maybe?"

June! Elaine came back to earth. By June her baby would be born. The baby! What about the baby? She'd never discussed the baby with Richard or even specifically with Dorothy. She looked at Bud to see if he would field his father's query. Before Bud responded, Dorothy slid next to her husband and raised her hand to stop her son's reply. Her eyes sought Elaine's as something definite registered in them.

Bud's mother smiled at the two lovebirds but her words seemed to be addressed to Elaine alone. "It's not my wedding so I shouldn't be pushy but I always wished one of my children would get married right here, in this great room, at the lodge fireplace at Christmas. Wouldn't a holiday wedding be perfect? What do you think, Elaine? I know it's soon but do you think we could press you into a small family wedding at Christmas?"

She knows, thought Elaine. Dorothy is no dummy; she knows how pregnant I am. She's trying to help me save face. Elaine looked at Bud who nodded. It was up to her. "Thank you, Dorothy, I think a Christmas wedding would be wonderful."

CHAPTER SEVEN

December 1953

Would she remember all the details of her wedding night when she was an old lady, sentimental and forgetful? When her children asked about it? She looked around her now at all the faces creased with smiles, with all the laughter erupting from the children who were dancing to the radio, stealing extra pickles from the buffet table set up at the side of the dining room and rubbing their eyes when their mothers weren't watching. None of them wanted to be shuttled off to bed, not when they looked so handsome in their Christmas finery.

At Elaine's request, Dorothy designed her a dark green velvet dress. Elaine didn't want traditional white and always dreamed of a pretty Christmas gown just like the one that emerged from Dorothy's sewing machine. Her future mother-in-law understood the dress was not to be too fitted but instead should hang loosely from gathers in a yoke. It had an attached belt sewn into the side seams and could be tied in the back as snugly or limply as one wished. The color set off her eyes and was just, well, perfect.

On Christmas Eve morning, Dorothy knelt at the foot of the chair where Elaine stood. A pincushion strapped around her wrist and pins in her mouth, she adjusted the hem of the dress. "Elaine, this looks lovely, if I do say so myself. You'll make a very pretty bride." Dorothy paused and looked upward. "But Elaine, I've got to say something to you before tomorrow. If I don't, I'll burst. You're not family ..." She smiled up at Elaine. "Not yet, so I hope you'll understand this."

Elaine's fingers pinched the sides of the dress as she tried not to fidget. Surely, Dorothy wouldn't pick this moment to lecture her. She knew things were happening quickly but the fondness she felt for Dorothy and Richard was so genuine, she didn't want to imagine how life would change if Dorothy chose this moment to voice her disapproval. She nodded at Dorothy to continue.

"I might not be the smartest woman in these backwoods and certainly not the most charitable, though I try. But one thing I do pride myself on, Elaine, is that I consider myself a good mother. Hush now, I need to get this out and I need you to just listen, okay?" With a yank on the hem, Dorothy rocked back and sat on her heels, her eyes trained on Elaine's.

"I'm proud I raised my kids to think for themselves. To think carefully and consider the consequences. To trust their hearts and have the courage to follow through. Now I must admit, I was a little flummoxed when Bud asked you to marry him so soon after his return. I won't pretend that I believe the baby you're carrying is his. And my talk with Bud confirmed that. I'm sorry, Elaine, but I had to ask him! He's a grown man but he's still my precious baby and I couldn't stand to see him hurt. I was worried this baby's father might come swooping in here some day to carry you off and leave Bud high and dry. But—no Elaine—no puddling up just yet now! What you need to hear from me is that after talking with Bud, I understand. How this baby came to be, doesn't matter. Not to me, not to Richard. What matters is that we've got our boy home in one piece and that he's happy. We believe he loves you, and we have faith that his future is going to be a happy one. We know that future includes you and this baby, and we're happy for you."

No further words were spoken between them; none seemed necessary as Elaine wrapped her arms around the older woman.

The lodge tables were decorated with white linen, poinsettia plants, and balsam boughs. The center of each table held a lit candle. Pine garlands framed the fireplace. Uncle Roland, upon hearing that Elaine's father would not be present, insisted on giving the bride away. She carried a small bouquet of red roses and white mums. At the last minute, Bud declined his mother's wishes to wear his dress uniform and wore a dark charcoal suit. The circuit judge, a distant cousin of Richard's, met them in front of the fireplace to officiate. Lotty, whose fine voice had been heard for months over the clatter of dishes and pans in the lodge kitchen, agreed to sing for the occasion. Not only did she perform well at the ceremony with her rendition of "O Promise Me" but she also led the gathered group through dozens of Christmas carols after the meal was consumed.

As it neared midnight, Elaine and Bud were surrounded at his car. Perry went out first to start it and get it warmed for the bridal couple. Bud booked a night's stay at a hotel nearby but was wise enough not to divulge the exact location in case Perry and some of the other men decided to conduct a chivaree. It didn't take much time at all to drive the ten miles or so and find their room; Bud had already procured a key yesterday.

And now, they sat together on the bed. Bud reached over and took her hand. He waited until she turned to look at him. "There's no hurry here, Lainie. And in case you're wondering, I don't think you're unappealing, even with your tummy. On the contrary, I think you're gorgeous. Yes, you are. And yes, some of it's the stuff my Aunt Lovey talks about. All that inner beauty stuff. And Lord knows you've got more than enough of that. But you're also very easy on the eyes, girl. You've got the most beautiful hair and I love the way the sun catches on your eyelashes and shows itself in those faint freckles on your face. Yes, I do like them.

"And your eyes—they make me think of summer and freshly mowed lawns and how the air smells after a rain. Now maybe that's not the most romantic speech a fella could deliver to his bride on their wedding night but Lainie, I am nuts about you. And part of the reason I'm nuts is because who'd've thought a beautiful, smart, brave girl like you would even consider starting a life with a lunk like me? I feel so lucky."

Elaine didn't know what to say. She felt something tender for this noble man seated with her but somehow she couldn't bring herself to face him or articulate something meaningful.

"You okay, Lainie?"

She nodded. Bud laughed then and averted his eyes. "So anyway, tummy or no tummy, I think you're damn appealing." He cleared his throat and dipped his head, staring at the floor. "Also, I have something to tell you. I suppose I should have talked to you about this before. It's kind of like how you feel about your stomach but my problem's even worse. Your belly'll be fine in a couple of months but me ... "He nudged his left shoe off and crossed his leg over his right knee. "You know I was in an army hospital for a while. There's a gunshot wound on my leg and I've got a shiny little scar on my ribs, too, but I also had trouble with frostbite. Lots of us did and I ended up having two toes amputated. My little toe and part of the one next to it on my left foot. And even though what I'm going to show you is pretty ugly, I feel pretty lucky, considering."

Elaine heard of frostbitten appendages and seen the devastation in photos of amputees in the newspapers. Now she remembered the occasions when she noticed a slight wobble in Bud's step. She thought it was new, ill fitting shoes. She steeled herself as she watched her husband–her husband!–peel off his sock. Ahh, the skin was smooth and shiny, his foot slightly misshapen but still strong and muscular. Tears filled her eyes as she looked up at Bud. A look of pain crossed his face.

"Oh Lainie, I'm sorry, I know it's ugly and I should have had you look at it earlier but what do you say to a gorgeous girl you want to impress? 'Hi honey, want to go on a date and oh yeah! Maybe you'd like to take a gander at my ugly foot?'" He shook his head "I just couldn't find a way to do this before now. I should have ... ." His words were cut off when her fingers pressed across his lips.

She held his gaze and slowly shook her head. "No need, Bud. No need. I am so proud of you. And I love you so much."

His arms closed round her as he lowered her into the bed.

CHAPTER EIGHT

January 1954

Bud let the storm door shut behind him and readied, steadied himself for the cold. Radio said darn near 30 below and he was inclined to agree. His eyes were already tearing from the impact of the subzero temperature. He let his gaze settle on the battered, old Dodge truck. Thirty minutes earlier he trudged this same path with some embers and ashes from the wood stove in an old cake pan and placed it under the motor, hoping to warm it a bit. Would the Beast start this morning?

Snow squeaked and crunched under his wolverines. He was glad he paid heed to Lainie's admonition to put on an extra pair of socks. His breath hung in the air and he pulled up the scarf hanging about his neck and burrowed his chin down to escape some of the to-the-bone chill. When he reached the truck, its door opened reluctantly, requiring some effort to overcome the frozen hinges. Key in the ignition, he pressed the accelerator, saying a prayer that the motor would turn over. A low moaning sound came from under the hood, like an old man being told to don a tie for a church supper. Have to coax it, maybe wheedle a little. He pumped the gas again, moved the worn silver key 45 degrees and resumed his prayer.

The engine finally caught, sputtered and settled into a muffled whine.

Not strong, but steady enough. Satisfied it would continue running, he turned the heater up, grabbed the scraper and exited the truck. Circling his vehicle, he swiped again at the crusted snow and kicked the rock-like stalactite hanging from the wheel wells of the old Dodge. Implement in hand, he began the task of chipping the stubborn ice and frost from the windshield.

Earlier Bud had tried to get Lainie to call and cancel the doctor's appointment but she was adamant about driving into town for her checkup. She looked healthy enough to him and she seemed fine, no odd cravings or unexplained aches and pains. Was this trip really necessary?

"Are you sure you have to go in today, honey?" he asked her. "It's terrible cold. Maybe you'd be better off staying here near the heater with a nice blanket and a book. I could put some soup on to simmer and maybe come home to have lunch with you. What do you think?"

Lainie bit the inside of her lip as her gaze focused on the frost-covered windows. "Well, if you think the truck won't start, I suppose I can cancel and try to get in next week but... ." Her voice faded off.

Bud hoped that concentrating on the snow and ice before her would make her put her fears into perspective. After all, women have been having babies since the beginning of time, most without benefit of a regular monthly checkup from a physician. Was there something she hadn't told him? What did he know? He was a man.

"What do you think, Lainie?" he asked.

It looked like she was forcing a smile. "Why don't I leave it up to you, Bud? You're more of an expert on the cold and ice here in this neck of the woods than I am. I guess I could reschedule if I need to."

Good, a half hour ride in the bitter cold was not how he envisioned this morning and now Lainie seemed more agreeable than when she had awakened him and reminded him of the appointment. Was that a tremble he now spied on her lips? It looked a tad like the expressions on the faces of the young recruits when first joining his company in Korea and were unsure of what was expected of them. Could she be a little scared?

Back a few weeks, his mother offered advice while he hauled sacks of flour into the lodge storeroom. He was grousing a bit, just a bit, about Lainie's mood swing of the night before. Dorothy was perched on a high stool in the kitchen rather than her corner "office" in the dining room.

"Don't forget she's just a scared young girl, son. A smart, city girl sure, but one without a mother to talk to and without loads of aunts, sisters and cousins to turn to when she has questions. We're all here for her when she's puzzled about having this baby, but my guess is you will be her prime nursemaid, hon. Be patient."

Lainie did ask so little, he hadn't the heart to disappoint her now. "I guess a ride into Minocqua is okay as long as we're bundled up real good and stick to the main roads. No detouring to look at the sparkle of the frozen falls off County D today," Bud told her. A smile appeared on her face before she ducked her head and headed to the back of the house.

He kept scraping, wondering if a person's frigid breath could really freeze in exhalation and just hang there on the air for a minute before falling and shattering like one of his mother's glass Christmas ornaments. He laughed inside the woolen scarf covering the lower part of his face. Maybe Lainie wasn't the only one given to the odd thought these days.

Chapter Nine

late February 1954

Elaine filled her cup with weak coffee, sat at the window seat and gazed out across the yard. Although she'd been out a few minutes earlier, and wanted to finish the laundry tasks, her back was twinging so she thought a short break was warranted. The snow was gone for a couple of days even though she knew it would return. Bud said to expect at least one more good storm in February and another in March. But for today, mild as it was, she could pretend it was spring and hang a few clothes on her new line.

A small flick of movement pulled her eye to the edge of the woods where not one but two does, already heavy with the fawns ready to be born in another two months made their way to the exposed foliage. Maybe she was imagining it, but to her untrained eye they seemed to walk as gingerly and slowly as she did, their bellies drooping, their faces turned downward. She sipped her drink and when the does returned to the woods, her cup was empty. "Time's up; back to the clothesline." Elaine giggled a little and wondered if all pregnant women talked to themselves. Well, what was the harm?

Elaine searched for the beaded, Indian-style moccasins had Dorothy given her. Normally she was a trifle vain about her feet; she liked to admire her rather sensual arch and long, slender toes and how nice they looked in high heels. But now she admitted her mother-in-law was right in the choice of this more practical birthday gift she received a few weeks back.

"Soon hon, your feet will swell even more and look like those tootsies belong to Elroy Hirsch, instead of a sweet, pregnant city girl. You'll be happy to plunk your feet into these," Dorothy told her. "Maybe some of the maskiki, the village medicine, will rub off on your sore feet."

The north wind switched abruptly and the sheets, hung a scant half hour earlier, slapped her arms, and then the metal pole. Thunk ting, thunk, ting as she moved down the line, hanging the rest of the whites. Was she markedly heavier than last week when she waddled to the clothesline to air out an old quilt? The moisture seeping up from this early thaw crept into her moccasins, chilling her toes. She looked to the side of their little house where lilac bushes would soon bloom. She could hardly wait for the fragrance Bud promised would fill the backyard when they sat out here on a warm spring day with the new baby. "Soon," she told herself.

Bud would love it when he crawled into bed tonight. Both of them found they loved the feel of clean sheets with the smell of the outdoors on them. "One of those little pleasures that I appreciate," he told her. She'd tried to tease him and said she would win a Proctor and Gamble sweepstakes. Then they could hire a maid, and buy a mansion, and live in the lap of luxury. Clean fresh sheets everyday! Bud had laughed.

"No, no Lainie. That would be terrible. That once-in-a-while treat would lose its appeal and it wouldn't be special anymore. No, no, I want to keep that one just as it is." He smiled indulgently at her and then added, "And ya don't have to be telling Perry or any of those other yahoos that I like smelling clean sheets. Instead of being impressed with this small town hero crap, they'd think I went off and turned sissy on them."

She laughed delightedly at that notion. Bud so rarely spoke about his service record and when he did, no mention was ever made of the medals he received while recovering from his wounds in the field hospital. It was over coffee a few weeks ago when Olivia finally told her some of the details about Bud's bravery. About his concern for his buddies and how he risked his life when he returned to pull three comrades to safety even though he was wounded himself. She was fortunate; she had a kind sweet man who loved her—and a war hero to boot.

There were days when she thought about last fall and her arrival at Mashkiki Rapids, her involvement with the Tilden clan, even her misguided evening with Lloyd. She heard from the kitchen help that he had taken a week off in January and gone to Missouri near Fort Leonard Wood. She heard he returned with a bride, someone he knew while he was stationed there. A widow with a small son who he reportedly courted with a vengeance. No one knew much about the newly-minted Mrs. Defoe but Elaine hoped that maybe being married would settle Lloyd down. She heard that often happened with some rough men.

The towels and underwear were hung. Lainie spied a couple of those smoothed wooden clothespins that rolled out of the basket and debated trying to pick them up. Bending these days was near impossible. Some days the walk to the mailbox and back was a chore. Now who was the sissy? She nudged the clothespin with her toe and then took a deep breath as she bent to retrieve it.

Halfway in her reach, Elaine felt a tiny stab of pressure. Simultaneously she felt a gush of water coursing down her legs just as Bud and the Beast pulled into the yard. He spied the puddle around her feet as he walked toward her. The concerned look on his face was replaced by a smile unlike any she'd seen on his face before. His appearance was transformed as he rushed to her and was assured by his wife that "Yes, it was time."

CHAPTER TEN

The young, speckled, freckled nurse poked her head in the door. "Alright, Mr. Tilden, you had your ten extra minutes. I know you're a proud grandpa but you've got to leave and let the new mother get some rest. Visiting hours are over." She smiled but her voice was purely no-nonsense.

Richard gave her a grin and bobbed his head. As she disappeared, he turned to Elaine and patted her hand. "You done good, honey; that boy's a keeper for sure. And Dorothy said to tell you she's just as pleased with the name as I am." He looked delighted as he smiled at Bud.

Earlier, Bud asked if she had any preferences for a name. They finally decided on James Richard. James for Bud's best buddy in Korea, a boy who hadn't made it back to his hilly Arkansas farm. And Richard, of course, for his father, a man Elaine was also coming to cherish.

"You are sure that's okay, hon?" Bud asked her again this morning when the nurse double checked for the birth certificate. "You sure you don't want to stick your father's name in there? Or a favorite uncle? Anyone?"

She was sure. There was no hesitation on that. In the last six months, even before she became his daughter-in-law, she formed a close bond with Richard. She knew him to be accepting and principled, not in any way comparable to her father and his rigidity. She hoped someday things might be smoothed out with her father but that didn't seem to be scheduled anytime soon. The terse letter she received in reply to the letter she sent him shortly after her arrival in Maskiki left no doubt of that. "Once you arrange a suitable adoption for the child, you may come back, Elaine. Not until." Somehow she was convinced that Richard would never have pushed Madlyn out into the world on her own because of a surprise pregnancy.

No, Richard was more than fine as the baby's middle name, just as Jimmy seemed to be the right sobriquet for the infant from the first time the nurses had allowed her to hold him.

Richard gathered his jacket now and stepped back to her bedside. He kissed her on her forehead, and took her hand. "We are sure glad to see the roses back in your cheeks too, Elaine. You had us scared there for a while." Then he clapped Bud on the shoulder and left the room. When he reached the threshold, he addressed Bud, "If you won't take the whole day off tomorrow, at least take the morning off, son. You need to spend some time with this new mother here. Maybe catch up on some sleep of your own."

Ahh, the first time she was alone with Bud since yesterday morning when he drove her to the hospital. Elaine wanted to take in all that was around her, now that they were a family. The last two days had been so jumbled. The rush to the hospital, the pains, the excitement, the pains. The baby boy's emergence into the world and then the nurses' anxiety. Doctor Bremman's concerned face. His pronouncement of placenta accreta and the need for an emergency surgery for her. Reassurance that the baby was fine and that soon she would be fine as well. Somehow in her muzzy-headed daze, she understood that there would be no more babies. This little boy was fine, perfect even, but there would be no more. The truth of it seeped in with every drip through the IV in her arm. It happened.

Now she was aware that Bud had taken her hand and she drew her thumb over the knuckle of his index finger downward to his thumb, and back again. Over and over; now familiar territory. She could see a small bouquet of flowers, probably purchased from the gift shop on first floor. There was also no doubt that the card said "Love, Bud," probably in her mother-in-law's handwriting. Bud had been too distracted and worried to remember flowers but Dorothy most likely had stepped in. No matter, they were lovely. She took a deep sniff to commemorate the smell.

"You alright Lainie? Is it too cold in here for you, sweet stuff?" Bud looked frazzled. "I can get another blanket for you." He rose from the chair placed so close to her that it seemed a lopsided extension of the hospital bed.

" No, I'm fine. Really, I'm fine. I expected your mother's reaction to the baby but I can't believe how excited your father is. That is so nice." She started to sniffle in earnest but before she could fumble for a handkerchief, Bud scooted up next to her in the hospital bed, strong arms encircling her as she nestled into his shoulder. "Oh Bud," Lainie wailed softly, "I can't stop this crying. What time is it? I've been crying since last night. I've got a beautiful baby and the doctor said he's so healthy. I know there can be no more babies. Is that okay, Bud? Are you okay with that? And I didn't die! And the baby is perfect! What's wrong with me?" She knew she was babbling but she didn't' seem able to stop. Her eyes and cheeks felt puffy. She wondered what she looked like.

"Shh now, Lainie, it's okay. You've been through a lot. The nurses told me it was to be expected that you might be a trifle weepy after you had the baby. Maybe there will be more after you go home too, so don't feel bad about a little blubbering. Ma says she's available to help you. We all are. Doc said no lifting for a while."

"Oh, your Mom's been great! I don't know what I would have done without her the last few months. But, your dad; I didn't expect you dad's reaction. He seems so happy and so proud. Oh Bud, it's like he thinks Jimmy is his own grandson, his real grandson ... ." Her voice trailed off as she thought about some of Richard's remarks of the last month, of him hoping that the baby was foremost healthy but "if the Lord could see His way to making this babe a boy, well, a grandson to carry on the Tilden name would be a bonus."

Elaine pulled away from the comfort of Bud's shoulder, twisting gingerly in the bed, to look her husband full in the face. His eyes were loving, sure, so deep and fiercely blue they seemed like a hybrid of cornflowers and sapphires. Eyes often commented upon, "They're way too pretty to be wasted on a male!" She could not take her eyes from his. Richard's enthusiastic outbursts made sense to her now. "Your dad, Bud, your dad thinks Jimmy is yours doesn't he? Your mom knows what the deal is but does your father? Does he think we were sweethearts before you brought me home? Did you tell him that? To protect me? Did you tell him Jimmy was your baby?"

Bud continued to gaze into her eyes. She detected a tiny flicker somewhere deep in the blue recesses and a twitch at the corner of his full lips. Was he hiding some irritation, some disappointment? "Are you upset because now you won't ever have a baby of your own?"

"Oh, hon, what are you talking about? I was so scared for you. I am just so thankful you are going to be fine and I am thrilled with this little boy. I didn't have to tell my father anything 'cause Jimmy is mine." Bud shifted himself further onto the side of her bed, and then, as they held one another, they heard the approach of the floor nurse.

They ignored her instructions to Bud to get off the bed. "It needs to be kept as sterile as possible. Mr. Tilden, no visitors permitted on the bed!"

Instead they continued to cling to one another and swipe at their eyes.

Chapter Eleven

May 1954

The jingle of bells on the door of the tiny grocery signaled the arrival of another pedestrian on the walkway. It was Elaine's first solo trip to the village after Jimmy's birth. Elaine looked up to see Morag Gunderson emerging from Tollefson's Grocery, arms laden with two large brown paper bags, her head swiveling from right to left as she looked down the street. It was the first time Elaine had seen her since that ill-fated night at the tavern with Lloyd.

"Hello, Mrs. Gunderson. You need some help? I saw your husband's truck down the street there at the feed store. From what I could hear it didn't sound like he'd be leaving real soon." Elaine shifted her purse under her arm and reached for the shorter woman's bag.

"Thank you, Elaine. I'd be verra grateful for the help. And my name is Morag. Mrs. Gunderson is Ed's mother." She sent a bright smile in Elaine's direction.

Elaine loved it when a bit of Mrs. Gunderson's Scottish burr emerged. She knew Morag was what they called a war bride, from Scotland. She also knew Ed met her when he was stationed on one of the air bases in Britain in the mid 40's, married her there and brought her back when his service ended. Now she, Ed and their daughter lived at the edge of town where Ed had a motor repair business.

Morag nodded toward the group assembled across the street. "Fine bunch, there, eh?" she said in a quiet but derisive tone. "What my Ed would say for certain is there's a wind row of assholes if ever he saw one. Oops." Morag looked quickly at Elaine, poised to apologize. Elaine let a small guffaw emerge.

"Are you headed anywhere in particular now?" Morag asked. She appeared delighted in this impromptu conversation.

"No, I stopped to deliver some fresh aprons to the lodge. I've been doing the laundry for them now. I was just feeling a little restless and my mother-in-law told me to take a walk while she fed my baby so I did." Elaine felt a little embarrassed admitting her lack of purpose here on Mashkiki's main street.

Morag merely smiled, glad for the opportunity to visit. "Ah and it's thank God sometimes for a good mother-in-law. That's just where my little girl is now, too. With her Granny Gunderson. Have you been into Marge's store of late? She's some lively spools of ribbons in. Lovely, lovely colors though I can't help but wish they had a bit of plaid ribbon to choose. I want to get some to tie up my Mary's hair in pigtails when she sings in the children's choir at church. And of course, there's school next fall. Can ye believe it? My babe is almost ready for the classroom. Kindergarten they call it here. Achh!"

Elaine, always curious about Morag's past, used this opening to ask a question or two of her own. "The plaid, the plaid ribbon," she was starting poorly. "Your home, do you ever miss it?" Elaine found herself staring into Morag's round, hazel eyes and heard her laugh.

"Miss it? My home in the Highlands? Oh, aye, there's days when I get a wee bit lonely. When I think of the heather and how the sea smelled of a morning, ah yes, I miss it." Morag stopped to look squarely at Elaine. "But," Morag shifted her bag to the other hip, "If I were pining for the old place when would I have time to enjoy what I have here?

If I were back near Aberdeen, there'd be no Ed. I'd not have Mary either. I'd have no time to tend to my own gardens and play with my babe and listen to the music shows on the radio. I'd still be herding some sheep, hauling water, caring for the house, catering to my brothers–the louts– and wishing my da would remarry–quick!"

Morag let out a bigger guffaw and used her free hip to nudge Elaine's thigh. They were in sight of the feed store now and it appeared that Ed was preparing his exit. "Here, let's just put these in the back of the pickup and I'll see if I can do my best to get Ed moving to his mother's place. I told her we'd be collecting Mary before too long. But Elaine, some morning if you like, why don't you bring your own wee boy to my house? You and Mary and I can count his toes and have some tea and maybe I can tell you more about my own coming to Mashkiki. Aye?"

Elaine grinned. "I'd love it, Morag. I'll call you first and see what day is good, okay?"

Morag nodded and then glanced back down the street. Ed was still loading his truck, and gestured that he would be another few minutes. Morag pointed at the one bench in the downtown area and asked Elaine to join her. For ten minutes she chatted about what she planned to do with the rest of her day, what she planned to fix for supper, what she hoped to catch on that evening's radio programs.

When Morag come up for air, the voices of the idlers standing outside Charlie's tavern could be heard more distinctly. Their simultaneous discussions of Negroes, women and old jokes chafed Elaine's ears.

"Well, I'm telling you, you know I was in the service in the Pacific Theater. Three years." It was Einar with that abrasive, raspy tone that held Elaine's attention now, much as she wished it didn't. "I never come across a one of 'em who had any ambition." He emphasized ambition as though it were the most important word in his vocabulary. It did, Elaine thought, contain three syllables.

"You got that right," Toots popped in. "When I was working for the railroad outta Chicago, it was hard to tell who was lazier. Those niggers or the beaners from Texas. A horse apiece I figure." All the men chuckled.

"Yeah, yeah,"came a leering voice. Recognizing Lloyd Defoe's voice, Elaine had a distinct thought: here it comes–a blend of women , sex, and color. Richard once remarked that if Lloyd ever had a sensible or kind word come from his mouth, Bud's father wanted to know about it.

Lloyd continued. "I don't have much time for 'em myself, but I sure wouldn't kick Lena Horne outta the sack for eating in bed." He began his own crude guffaw before the other men caught the lewdness of his remark. Since her aborted date with Lloyd, Elaine managed to steer clear of him. From the way he raised his voice, she knew he'd seen her and Morag across the street, and might be trying to get a reaction from the two women.

Elaine took in a breath, contemplating what she could say, what she could call across the blacktop that might shut those imbeciles up. Or at least make them more careful of where they voiced their ideas, of where they tossed their dirty words. Morag's hand closed around Elaine' s wrist. "Ach, I know you verra much want to say it, Elaine, but it willna do much good today. There will come the right day, ya know. What goes around, comes around they say. Come along with me now, Ed's here and we'll give you a lift home."

Chapter Twelve

July 1954

Elaine turned and smiled as Richard entered the lodge kitchen and looked around for an ample-sized mug. This was her first day back working at the lodge. She wouldn't be here at all except Lotty had an appointment and there was no one else to fill in until the late shift arrived. Bud had some billing and other paperwork to complete so he thought he and the baby would manage just fine for a few hours.

Maybe a few minutes alone with Richard would be her chance to get some information that would let her feel less like an outsider. Elaine set aside the full ketchup container and plucked a giant cup from the dishwater. She rinsed it and smiled as she poured some steaming coffee into it and set it before her father-in-law.

"Thank you, hon." He grinned his appreciation as he settled himself on a high stool. He stretched his torso and a slight grimace passed over his features. Must have been splitting some wood earlier this morning, Elaine thought. He mentioned yesterday that his back was acting up.

"You know you're welcome, Dad." Richard had told her to call him Dad as Olivia did and it pleased her. She turned back to filling the containers. "Can I ask you something? I know I sound pretty dumb sometimes.

Like when I ask something about things you Tildens have known about forever." She waited for his nod before continuing. "It's about that fellow that came in yesterday, the one who asked directions to the Little Trout campground. Perry called him a pulpcutter, not to his face, after he left. I got the feeling Perry didn't think much of him. Like 'pulpcutter' was a bad thing."

" Hmmm, so you think that I can be sweet talked with a fresh cup of coffee into giving you a local history lesson, do ya?" Richard asked before sipping his coffee. It was her turn to smile and nod. She knew how much he loved discourse, especially when the student was as willing and receptive as she was.

"Well," Richard continued, "Pulpcutters ... the name alone places these people in a distinctly different category than their predecessors. None of the glory and romance of the pine barons and the plaid Pauls of the Far North." He stopped to see if she caught his reference to Paul Bunyan. Satisfied, he cleared his throat, warming up to his subject. He looked around the kitchen area with a tiny squint in his eyes the same way one of her history profs did in a crowded lecture hall. Of course, here she was the sole pupil.

"The original logging companies in this area were from down river, on the Wisconsin where water power was more available. After they depleted the lumber value here, they left or folded up. Some years passed until the forest recovered as second growth timber. So now, in the last few years, the pulpwood industry began, which is when some smaller individual logging companies started. These companies are fairly small. You hear of the Ellsworths, over south of Rhinelander? No? Well, they're one of them. Family-owned, and they hire men for various operations, mostly cutting and skidding. Trees are cut with chainsaws, skidding's done with horses, or makeshift skidders, loading is usually some form of cable-operated jammer and the logs are mostly small, around 100 inches long. They're hauled by truck, again down river to paper mills at Tomahawk or Merrill and Wausau."

He sipped more coffee and let his gaze wander around the counter. Elaine knew she could keep him talking indefinitely if she fed him. She put the ketchup containers down, wiped her hands and lifted the door of the pie safe. "Small piece of apple here, if you want it, Dad." Richard grinned.

She found a fork and put the plate in front of her father-in-law. Richard took a healthy bite, savoring its taste. "Nothing like apple pie made with apples you tended and picked yourself," he declared. He took another bite and then resumed. "Now, your pulpcutter, your average pulpcutter if there is an 'average', is a family man, with young children, owns very little more than a chainsaw, is often off and on public assistance. Travels in a ramshackle truck or car. The guy stopped here yesterday was pulling a trailer, right?"

"That's right," Elaine acknowledged.

"Living conditions are bare minimum, no power, no water, except for the nearby state campsite wells. That's why that feller stopped in here for directions. Sometimes there's a run-down shack on the company land they can use 'til the job's done. Water's usually carried in run-down cars by the bucket. Sometimes the family might get an outdoor john, if the guy has a little extra energy for digging a pit and building the outhouse. Water for washing is probably a luxury; heat comes from wood in a makeshift barrel stove. The good firewood is sold by the jobber so only junk wood is used for heating."

Elaine was getting more details than she bargained for but she had to admit: her father-in-law was not only a font of local occurrences and history, but his deep baritone made listening to him easier than any stuffy history professor.

"But what if they have a child? Maybe more than a couple?" Elaine was curious.

Richard smiled affectionately at her. How did Bud manage to get one so smart and inquisitive and spunky? She sure was different than the local girls his son had brought home before Korea. Richard got up and slipped his plate into the still warm and sudsy dishwater before he refilled his mug. After hefting his tired self back onto the stool, he answered her.

"The family lives on the cutting, often a two or three year duration--- and yes, somehow they all manage to find sleep and shelter in that trailer. See, there is no home, no ownership or tax record, so schooling for the children is sketchy. An eight foot by twenty foot trailer like the one we saw yesterday is often all they call home. But there's an old house on Pearson's property–not much more than a shack–where they'll probably settle."

"Is that why Perry seemed to dismiss the man? Because he was kind of rough looking and his kids looked raggedy?" Elaine wiped off the counter and moved to the sink with the Ajax.

"Well, personal hygiene is secondary to survival so the kids are probably unwashed, most likely kinda smelly and none of them has an overabundance of fancy clothes." Bud's father sure loved understatement, but his last comment was the one which hurt her heart. "Since the family moves around a lot, there probably ain't a big chance for them kids to have lots of friends. In fact, most village mothers probably forbid their kids to play with those cutter's kids. They grow up pretty isolated I'm afraid. Sad."

"Sure it's sad. Some of those kids are right cute or could be if they got cleaned up proper," added Dorothy as she entered the kitchen with her accounts ledger. "And there's some of the adults who are pretty decent people, too. Just haven't gotten the breaks some of us have, right, hon?" She dropped a peck on her husband's cheek and moved to get a cup of coffee.

Elaine felt as though this were providence. Both her in-laws here alone with her, and the lodge probably wouldn't see any customers for another hour or so. Maybe Dorothy's presence would give her another chance to uncover some of Mashkiki's secrets and peculiarities.

Elaine turned to Dorothy. "Speaking of sad, what do you know about Mr. Cassidy? John Cassidy? Is that the name of the man who runs a little excavating service down on County D?"

"Yes, that's John Cassidy. Why?"

"Well, I always thought he was just crabby sometimes. None of us would say he's a favorite customer to wait on though he's fine when it comes to a tip. But Lotty told me that he's real mean to his wife. She says he locks her in the shed sometimes without shoes or a warm coat. Lotty saw her with some bruise on her face and thinks he's hitting her, too! She's such a tiny little thing! Can't somebody do something about that? What about a minister or even the constable?"

Richard set his cup down and turned to his wife. He appeared to be fighting an unsuccessful battle to keep a smile from his face and began to speak. "Now, Elaine, I don't know if –"

"Hush, Richard", his wife cut him off. "My turn."

"Fine with me" Elaine's father-in-law answered. "I'll just finish off this here pot of coffee. Okay with you ladies? You both had enough?"

Elaine looked from his face to Dorothy's. Had she missed something?

"I'm not sure why Lotty would tell you all that personal stuff about the Cassidys, Elaine, but if she insists on reporting, she needs at least to get the story straight."

Elaine colored. It seemed like she'd done it again. Maybe John Cassidy was a second cousin to Dorothy or to Richard. It was hard to keep all these family relationships straight. Maybe she had just insulted one of them.

"There is one thing where Lotty's right. When John Cassidy goes to work or takes himself a bath and there's no one else there in the house with Alice, I've heard he does hide her shoes." She mused a moment. "Slippers too, I'd suppose. Also heard he puts all the knobs from the stove in his pocket, too. But Elaine, he's not doing it to be mean or control-ling. See, Alice is sick. John's been noticing that she's been having trouble remembering things and sometimes she's just confused.

"His sister scared him to death and told him maybe Alice had a cancer, a brain tumor or something. So he took her to see a doctor in Wausau who sent him someplace else and what they found out is that Alice has something that's making her senile."

"Senile!" Elaine interrupted. "That doesn't sound right! I mean I remember discussing people who are senile in my health class at college and Mrs. Cassidy isn't old enough to be senile. I know she's not real young but she's not that old either."

Richard and Dorothy exchanged an amused look and Richard snorted. "Well, right you are, kid. Alice Cassidy went to school with Dorothy here. In fact she was just a year or two ahead of her. So yes, she's not real young but not that old either." He grinned at his wife and tipped his mug to her.

"Well, then that is way too young." Elaine was hoping to smooth over any age remarks and restore some good will back to the conversation. "Are they sure that's what it is?"

Dorothy retracted the tongue she stuck out at Richard and turned her gaze back to the younger woman. "I think John is pretty sure. He saw a slew of doctors and I think they did some tests. So that's the tragedy of it. Alice won't grow old with John. Eventually he's going to have to put her in a home. But until then he wants to keep her there with him. He's tried rearranging his work schedule so that he can be around if one of the daughters-in law can't. And Alice's sister lives down the road and sometimes she sits with Alice or takes her to her house.

"But sometimes he has to leave her alone for a short while and that's not been good. We've heard that recently Alice's started wandering off. Sometimes she doesn't know where she is. Last month John got a call saying someone had seen her walking and that she almost got sideswiped by a milk truck further down on County D. John went looking for her all up and down D, checking the ditches and couldn't find her. Spent several hours searching before going for the constable. They looked until the constable suggested John go home and bring his sons back with him to help look some more. And when he got home she was there. Old Mr. Nordstrom found her in his yard and managed to convince her to get into his car. He drove her back."

"But Mr. Nordstrom doesn't live on D does he?"

"No, he doesn't." It was Richard answering now. "He's over on Sommers Road. So that means she probably left D, walked through the woods, somehow got up and down that awful ravine and managed to get across the creek without drowning. John figured it was at least four or five miles Alice walked. And he was scared out of his wits it would happen again and next time she might not be so lucky."

"So the shoes," Dorothy clearly wanted the story back on track. "The shoes are what keep Alice at home. Ever since she's been a little girl, she never went barefoot with the rest of us in the summers. Her mama told her that girls going barefoot got big, ugly feet and Alice was real proud of those dainty little tootsies of hers. Size five. From what John says, she's fine with being home without shoes but she won't venture so much as an inch outside without them. So when there's no one to be there with her and John needs to be away, he hides her footwear and hopes for the best. So far it's worked. She might have some trouble keeping her marbles all in one bag but her vanity has remained intact."

"Ahh, so that's where Lotty got the shoe part of the story. If this comes up again I'll tell her the truth. Poor Mrs. Cassidy." Elaine shook her head.

Dorothy nodded. "That's the double tragedy here. Poor John. It kills him to see Alice slipping away more and more every day and it'll break his heart to put her in a home but that's surely where this is all heading."

It was quiet for a moment before Richard broke the silence. "Well, enough of this jawing in the kitchen. There's chores to be done! And pretty girls to be kissed!" He bussed his wife's cheek, winked at Elaine and headed toward the door.

Dorothy looked around the kitchen. "Well, looks like you didn't leave me much to finish up here. Thank you." She paused. "Elaine, do you ever miss not being in a college classroom? Not learning something new everyday?"

Elaine wiped her hands on her apron and hung it on the row of hooks where all the aprons hung. "No ma'am. Don't miss the classroom and as for the learning," she smiled at the older woman. "I do learn something new here–everyday!"

Chapter Thirteen

fall 1954

Elaine peered through the Suds 'N Wash windows and pushed open the door with her hip. Who'd've thought she would be frequenting Mashkiki's newest business so soon? Of course she'd used laundromats before; there had been one in the basement of her stodgy, sterile dorm. Today her own machine went on the fritz so Bud dropped her off and helped her carry in the heaviest and most overloaded of the two baskets while she went back for another. He directed a wave toward a group of ladies sitting at the back of the room and then was gone. Jimmy was being tended to at Madlyn's, Elaine had a book for company, and a promise from Bud to stop back for her in ninety minutes. She had seen Lloyd Defoe drive by and hoped she wouldn't have to contend with him today.

The last time she had seen Lloyd was when she and Bud were walking with the baby near the grocery and Lloyd had slowed his step enough to take a peek in the stroller. "Congratulations on the new baby, Elaine" he'd purred. "Cute kid, who does he take after?" She was mortified, convinced his remark was directed at Jimmy's paternity but Bud handled it smoothly.

"Thanks Lloyd," Bud rejoined, looking Lloyd directly in the eye. "Elaine says Jimmy is the spitting image of a couple of her uncles." Lloyd lost the smirk on his face, muttered "Hmm," and continued walking. Bud squeezed her hand and murmured, "Don't let him get to you, Lainie. He's just being his normal, cussed self. When he sees how happy we are, he'll stop his needling."

The laundromat had a nice warm feel to it. It was a pleasant respite from the briskness of the autumn air. If her machine's ordered part took more than a week to arrive, Elaine resigned herself to becoming even more familiar with the Suds 'N Wash. She pulled out her box of detergent and set her little leather change purse on the chair with her jacket.

Looking across the room, Elaine spied the custodian, Mrs. Mary Gunilda Swanson sitting in a corner surrounded by several chairs, curiosity showing on her plain broad face. Mrs. Swanson was a steady customer at the lodge restaurant, coming in every Wednesday for coffee and a bowl of Dorothy's Lodge Stew. She was among Elaine's favorite customers and the first regular to make Elaine feel welcome. When she and Bud married, Mrs. Swanson sent them a lovely wedding card to congratulate them.

Sitting next to her, baskets at their feet, were two Indian ladies who sat so still they barely seemed to breathe. They studied her with eyes black and shiny, like ebony disks she'd seen once in a natural history museum. Though she had never seen the pair of Indian ladies before she nodded at all three and was rewarded with a grin from the trio. Mrs. Swanson raised a huge thermos and tipped it toward a shelf where Elaine could see a few coffee cups stacked next to a box of sugar cubes.

"Get your duds going and then come and join us, dearie, "called Mrs. Swanson. "I bring a big, fresh thermos every morning and today only Mavis and Minnie here have elected to join me. There's plenty more for you."

Elaine had planned on reading and she wasn't sure what she could find to chat about with the older ladies, especially the Indian ladies. Dorothy had once said that the native women were pretty shy with strangers, but this invitation had been gracious. "Thank you, Mrs. Swanson, I'll do that."

"Call me Mary or Mary G. All my friends do. Mrs. Swanson sounds so old."

Ten minutes later found Elaine with diapers in one machine, darks in another, a third with all her lights. It might be nice to have all her clothes washed at once instead of taking the entire day as it usually did, washing one load, hanging it while another washed and then repeating the process until it was time to remove the garments from the line. And because it was such a damp and blustery day, she decided to splurge and brought enough nickels to use the dryers, something she hadn't done since she lived on campus.

She picked up a clean cup and deposited two sugar cubes in it before advancing to the three ladies sitting with jackets opened, ankles crossed, white anklets topped by chapped shins. The older of the Indian women had a round, chubby face and wore her thick, gray hair in elaborate braids wrapped around her head. Her companion, though missing a tooth, was slender and still a very attractive woman who definitely resembled the braided lady. Sisters for sure.

Mrs. Swanson had the thermos ready to pour her a cup of coffee.

"Thanks, Mrs. Swanson. That sure smells good today." Elaine extended her arm as she took a seat.

"Mary," Mrs. Swanson said again, firmly. "I wish you'd call me by my first name, Elaine. Makes me feel a little younger. Heard your washing machine broke down." Elaine marveled at the way even trivial news traveled the depths of the village. Mrs. Swanson grinned at the Indian ladies. "This here's Dorothy Tilden's daughter-in-law, Elaine, married to her boy Bud. That was him who carried in that bigger basket. Elaine, these two ladies are my friends way back from when we were girls at the old mission school near the reservation. They used to be the Brown sisters. Now this is Mavis Chapman and her little sister Minerva, Minnie, Soulier. Time was when the three of us used to be the prettiest girls around, right, Mavis?"

The sisters broke into a quiet cackle, one almost choking, the other saying "What do you mean used to be? Are you saying we couldn't turn a head or two even now?" At this all three women threw back their heads and laughed even more heartily. Mrs. Swanson slapped her thigh and wiped a few tears from her eyes. "Ahh, you two! Sometimes I have to look in the mirror and remind myself that 40 years or more have passed since we jumped rope and passed notes to the boys across the room."

"Oh, yeah, I know whatcha mean, Mary G.," Minnie spoke softly. "Sometimes if I glance over at Mavis quick, I think I'm looking at my Auntie Rosella. You remember her, don'tcha ?"

"Absolutely! She made the best fry bread! I used to love it when you brought an extra one for me."

"Yeah, well, you were the only white girl who had sense enough to taste them. Them other girls all turned up their noses at our fry breads. Ah, well, their loss, I guess."

The three older ladies all nodded and continued their visiting. Elaine sipped her coffee and let herself be lulled by the cadence of Mavis and Minnie's voices. Though she had seen Ojibwe people in the general store and grocery, she had never been part of a conversation with any reservation folk. From what she gathered from Bud, the Indian people kept pretty much to themselves with the exceptions being school and church. She got a kick out of listening to the reminiscences of the three older ladies whose faces shed decades as they recounted their youthful escapades. By squinting just a little Elaine could swear she was listening to some very young, teenage girls.

A pause alerted Elaine that the conversation had shifted. "So, how do you like married life here in Mashkiki?" It was Mavis directing a query her way. Their polite smiles encouraged her to join their discussion.

"Very well, I guess. I guess I'm just grateful these days that my little baby boy is pretty much sleeping better and giving me some rest. For a while I didn't ever think I was going to sleep through the night again."

"Oh yeah, I remember those days," Mavis ventured. "So does Minnie, I bet. Remember, Minnie, how one time after your Freddy was born I came over to help you and there you were out in the yard, hanging on to the clothesline like a pair of wet socks? You were snoring like an old bear, you were so tired. Kinda looked like an old bear, too if I remember right. I know there were days you smelled a little like one!"

Elaine glanced to see if the younger sister took offense but no, Minnie just smiled and nudged her sister's arm while Mrs. Swanson hooted and wiped her eyes again.

"Yeah, well back then, how many times a week could you sneak in a bath with three in diapers, another one not yet in school, and four that were. Much less water to haul and heat. Then there were those commodity lunches to pack and a husband who worked steady but was hard to get out of bed in the morning. You'd probably fall asleep when you had a chance, too." Minnie winked at Elaine over the rim of her cup.

"Did I understand you correctly, Mrs. Soulier? You had eight children?"

Minnie nodded, cup still at her lips. "You can call us Minnie and Mavis."

"Holy smokes, isn't that something!" Elaine couldn't imagine having eight little ones underfoot.

"Smoke, holy or otherwise, probably didn't have much to do with it," said Mavis. "More like that frisky husband of Minnie's." She turned to her sister and her voice took on an affectionate, teasing quality. "Does he still serenade you all these years later like he did when he first came calling or like he did when you were newly hitched? He did have a pretty voice. Musta sang some pretty convincing love songs to get him eight little ones, don'tcha think, Mary G.?"

Minnie stuck her tongue out at her sister much to Mrs. Swanson's amusement and turned her attention to Elaine. "Yeah, I did have eight and I loved every minute, every diaper I changed, every runny nose I wiped. The only piece of advice I will give you is to enjoy every day. They grow up way too fast." Minnie's next remark surprised Elaine. "By the way, I recognized your husband when you walked in. I know Bud from way back." The woman paused.

"Oh? Is that right?" Elaine felt there might be a "young Bud" story in the offing and hoped the woman would continue.

"Oh yeah, he and my youngest boy Willard were in school together. On the wrestling team." Minnie looked over at her sister and spoke a few words to her in what Elaine could only assume was Ojibwe.

"Ahhh," said Mavis. "Yeah, now I remember him. That Dorothy raised a righteous boy."

Elaine thought she could detect a faint smile from each of the sisters but they said no more. She looked at Mrs. Swanson for some clarification.

Mrs. Swanson met her gaze and seemed to make a decision before turning to her two old friends. "Elaine is a good girl but she's not from around here. She might have a need to hear your story, Minnie." Mary Gunilda poured a little more coffee into each cup as the older ladies all sighed and settled in.

Now Elaine's curiosity was beyond piqued. How exciting! Maybe she'd be able to surprise Bud later with some tidbits from his childhood. Perhaps some good teasing material. Sometimes lately it seemed they had little to talk about and she worried that Lloyd's remark made so long ago last fall might be right, that she was just a manifestation of Bud's role as a rescuer.

"Well," Minnie began slowly. "Bud and Willard were both on the wrestling team there in the high school. Willard was the only boy from the reservation to make the team. My husband wasn't really in favor of that. He was proud of the prizes Willard took with his art work and good grades but he didn't want Willard to get into any of those what you call contact sports. Willard was a good athlete, big and strong but my man didn't trust some of the coaches there at the high school. My man was at boarding school back when he was a boy and remembered when some of the white teachers didn't always do right by our boys, the Indian boys. Didn't give them the same respect a white boy might get. But Willard was determined to try it so we let him be part of the team."

She sipped some of her coffee. Elaine knew better than to interrupt if she wanted to be privy to whatever story there was involving Bud and these Indian ladies.

Mavis cleared her throat and made a little waving motion with her hand. Minnie blinked and continued her story. "Well, I'm not exactly sure what happened with Willard one night after practice but what I gathered was that there was some horsing around in the locker room. Maybe the coach left early. Maybe one of the white boys was showing off and got a little rough. All I know was Willard got the brunt of it."

"I was sitting home with one of my daughters when this truck pulled in by my house. Didn't recognize it. My husband was still out ice fishing and I knew it wasn't his truck so I kind of wondered what was going on. We didn't usually get too many visitors after dark. When I looked out the door, that's when I saw your Bud."

"Bud? What was he doing? I mean, why was– " Elaine was flustered; she hoped her question wasn't insulting these ladies.

"You're asking why was he at my place on the reservation on a dark winter night? No harm in you being surprised about that. I was too, truth be told. Bud walked right up to the stoop to meet me and he took off his hat all polite and said, 'Mrs. Soulier, I'm Bud Tilden and Willard got hurt after practice. I think his ankle might be broke. He wouldn't let me take him to the clinic but he did let me drive him home. When we pulled in he saw that his dad's truck is gone so if you want, I'll be glad to drive you and Willard back into town.'

"Well, when I poked my head inside the truck and saw how swelled up Willard's ankle was, I knew Bud was probably right and I went and got my purse and hopped right in. My daughter stayed there so's she could tell my husband to come into town to fetch us when he got back. Neither boy said much on the way back in but later when I got Willard alone, I found out that one of the other wrestlers had started bullying Willard, calling him names and shoving him around a little. Between Willard being the only Indian and no one wanting to get involved much at first, and the other boy being so big and looking for a fight, it wasn't long until there was a full blown punching match taking place. Willard got knocked down and then the other boy stomped on his ankle."

"Oh no, that's terrible!" Elaine exclaimed. "Your poor son!"

"I guess that's when Bud came back into the locker room. He'd gone out to warm up his truck and then come back. He broke up the fight and put the run on the bully. Then he and his brother got Willard out to the truck. He dropped his brother off on the County road near Tildens and then drove Willard out to the reservation."

"And your son? Was he okay?"

"Ankle was broke but not bad and it healed real well. You know how good young, healthy boys mend. He was done with wrestling but the coach gave him a letter anyway at the end of the season. It was a couple days before he got to go back to school on them crutches, but Bud brought Willard his schoolwork until then. I thought it was real nice of him to do that."

"What about the bully? Did that kid get punished? Thrown off the team?"

"Nah, Willard didn't want to say much and from what I heard by way of the moccasin telegraph, Bud shamed that Defoe kid plenty the next time they had a practice. I heard from one of my nieces that the jerk didn't mess with Willard anymore when my boy got back to school."

"The Defoe kid! Do you mean Lloyd? Was Lloyd Defoe the one who broke your son's ankle?" Somehow this revelation didn't surprise Elaine too much. Lloyd was an obnoxious man, it stood to figure that he probably had been a detestable youth as well.

"Yeah, that was him. My niece said Bud took a little guff from Lloyd for sticking up for the skin but Lloyd was too afraid to mess much with Bud."

"The skin?" Elaine interrupted the older woman.

"As in redskin," Mary Gunilda clarified. "Not a very nice label. Some of those town boys were pretty biased when it came to the Ojibwes. Some still are."

Elaine felt vaguely ashamed but didn't know exactly why.

Her friend's remark didn't deter Minnie from finishing her commentary. "That Lloyd Defoe could be a mean bastard but he wasn't completely stupid. He knew if he pestered anyone else, he'd not only have to take

on Bud, but probably Bud's brother and some of my nephews, too."
Minnie laughed a little at that possibility but her eyes were devoid of mirth.

"So yeah, we thought Bud was a little bit of a hero before all this
Korea stuff got known around here. I'd say you have a real warrior in that
man, Elaine." Minnie stood here and gestured toward the street. "Here's
our ride back to the rez, Mavis. We better hop to if we don't want to hitch
a ride home later. That'd be something, us out on the county road with
baskets on our hips, thumbs in the air. Nice talking with ya, Elaine. See
ya next week, Mary G. Appreciate the coffee. Miigwech."

—⟳

Later that night, after she put Jimmy down, Elaine thought she'd
see what Bud would add to the story she heard about him and Lloyd
and the Indian boy. When she mentioned meeting Mrs. Chapman and
Mrs. Soulier at the Suds 'N Wash, Bud only said "Oh yeah, I remember
her son, Willard Soulier. He was in my class at school. He was a real
talented artist. That kid could draw anything."

Chapter Fourteen

late October 1954

Hair looked good, no lipstick on her teeth, perfume not too overwhelming. Hmm, she told herself, looking pretty good if I do say so myself! Red swirls in the full black skirt of her dress looked like a fireworks display and exploded when she spun before the full length mirror. A wide scarlet belt accented her waist and made this Sears catalog version of haute couture more acceptable. Polished to a high sheen, her black leather flats were comfortable for dancing but still stylish and big city. Her entire appearance fairly sang out "ready for a good time!"

"Come on Bud, we're going to be late!" Elaine almost added, "Again!" but had promised herself that she was going to do her best to have a good time and that meant no hint of nagging or criticism. That Bud hadn't seemed too interested in much of anything social lately was not going to spoil this evening. Sunday suppers with the Tildens at Dorothy and Richard's followed by a few games of cribbage were fine but surely she was entitled to more of a social life than a weekly meal with her in-laws. Technically they were still newlyweds; surely a little more romance wasn't too much to ask. Was it? Would a hug or kiss on the street of Mashkiki Rapids spoil his hero image?

Now with the grand opening of the new American Legion Hall, everyone was talking about tonight's dance. Last week, she left Jimmy with Dorothy and had gone into town. She was waiting at the butcher's counter when she first heard that the event was a definite go ahead and tickets were on sale. "What do you mean, you didn't know about it?" This from Bertie Langholz. "Bud and Charlie are thick as thieves and it was all Charlie's idea, I heard. I know you can get tickets from him. Maybe you should ask Bud what's up."

Bertie's statement rang in her ears. "Maybe you should ask Bud what's up." Maybe Bertie needn't sound so smug. Was Bertie thinking that things were shaky with the Tildens. Things weren't shaky. Were they? Elaine admitted to a feeling of restlessness these past few months. Bud was still smiling every time he came in the door at night and he seemed truly in love with Jimmy and delighted in each new thing the baby boy learned. After straightening the kitchen and wandering into the living room, Elaine often found the two of them cuddled in the secondhand, overstuffed chair, absorbed in one of Bud's stories. Bud would tell Jimmy about his day spent in the woods and on the road even though the boy was not yet eight months old. His animation seemed to capture the baby's attention and she found herself listening attentively to this Tilden fairy tale.

Maybe she was jealous of their relationship. At times when she was holding her little boy, his eyes followed Bud. Jimmy seemed to prefer Bud to her. Shouldn't babies prefer their mothers? Did that make her a bad mother? Is this what made her so edgy?

No, it wasn't the baby. It was the two of them as a couple. Did she really know Bud? Looking back now, their courtship, if one could term it that, was so rushed. Did he really know her? Worse yet, did he want to know her? When he recalled his high school days, there wasn't much mention of any girlfriends. And Lord knows, her father hadn't allowed her to encourage any boys either. Maybe they were both late bloomers. Or was she, as Lloyd had implied, merely one of Bud's projects? Another soul that needed rescue?

Questions darted in and out of her mind like the minnows under the dock at Moon Lake. One idea moved quickly before another thought took its place. Did Bud pity her? Did he love her? Did she love him? After all, her experience with men was pretty limited. They seemed compatible. Bud was sweet and quick to compliment her, telling her she had a fine figure, reassuring her about what a good mother she was, and so on. But Elaine could swear there were times she felt Bud step back and, like a surveyor, measure her conversation, her values, her dreams.

His appearance in her life was something she first regarded as a kind of divine intervention–she hadn't lost all of her Catholic upbringing though the non-denominational church in the village served her spiritual needs just fine. From when she realized she was pregnant, she had prayed for something to enter her life and put it back on course. Last winter she had no doubt Bud was the answer to that prayer, but was he all of it? Could she be the answer to any prayer of his? She couldn't be sure. In any event, Elaine was determined that the two of them have a wonderful time at the dance. Maybe this was just what they needed, the chance to rekindle a little romance into the stew that was their marriage. Add a little zest to spice it up.

Ignoring Bertie's remark, Elaine decided to take matters into her own hands when it came to her social life–if there was to be a social life. She stashed her groceries in the truck, and drove to the Dew Drop Inn. It was too early for any serious drinking business but Charlie kept early after-noon hours, cleaning his tavern, making sure the glasses were sparkling clean, and stocking his cooler.

Others on entry might hear merely the clink and tinkle of the glass-ware as the bartender washed and stacked. Elaine's first thought was "tintin-nabulation." She always liked that word after first encountering it in a poem by Poe. Charlie's efforts were quietly rhythmic, and laid a lazy back beat to the music coming from his radio. He didn't seem too surprised to see her.

"I knew Bud would change his mind," Charlie told her when she asked about tickets. "I thought since he's made this decision not to hunt anymore that he needs to get out and take his mind off the upcoming season. I kept telling him he'd regret not being there but he said he preferred to stay at home on Saturday nights with his best gal." Charlie gave her his custom-ary dazzling smile. He swiped the surface of the bar and set the tickets in front of her. "Glad to see you changed his mind. Here ya are, Elaine. That's two-fifty for the pair of them. You want any tickets for the raffle, too? Twenty-five cents a piece, five for a dollar. Lots of good prizes. I think there's a couple for free wash and sets at that new beauty parlor in Minocqua if I'm not mistaken. My luck, that's the one I'll win!" He laughed easily and kept wiping down the bar.

Declining Charlie's offer of a soda, Elaine sauntered back to the car with two dance tickets in her purse, five raffle tickets in her jacket pocket, and a plan in her mind.

When Bud sat down to pot roast that night, the tickets were lying next to his plate. Elaine just smiled at him and pointed at the admission passes. He did have the good grace to blush, she'd noticed, and didn't say anything except, "Do you think my blue dress shirt will be good enough to wear that night?"

So here she was, ready for some real fun. Maybe a little romance, too. Maybe that was what was eating at her, the lack of spontaneity and reminders that she and Bud were still youngsters. Barely out of a honeymoon phase. Who knows what the night may bring? Village life here in Mashkiki was fulfilling for the most part, she had to admit. But for cripes sake! She could use some mashkiki, a little of that Indian love medicine. Bud didn't have to turn into a stodgy old man just yet, and she intended to remind him of his youth tonight! Only a few wedding receptions gave them much occasion to dance since they were married but she knew he could execute a decent waltz even with his missing toes. With the natural grace that all the Tilden men seemed to possess, she was fairly confident that an elementary jitterbug wasn't beyond his capabilities either. Tonight would tell.

Dorothy and Richard begged off attending the dance, "Next time, we'll be there for sure." Richard was still having some back problems after helping Bud and Perry with a couple loads last week. He told her his idea of paradise tonight was staying propped up on the couch with a hot water bottle, a couple of aspirin and the radio. Dorothy volunteered to treat by taking all her grandchildren overnight. She said her only payment was to hear a detailed account from Elaine and Madlyn the next day.

"Bud!" Elaine directed her voice to the back of the house and admitted there was a little whine creeping into her voice. "Please! I don't want to be late."

A gentle creak signaled the opening of the bathroom door, followed by the cadence of Bud's feet down the hardwood hallway. There was a skip in the usual pattern of his step. Was he executing a dance step? "Okay, okay. I'm coming." He walked into the room, hair combed and still wet, shoes tied, a whiff of aftershave following. A smile lit his face as he scrutinized his wife and slowly rotated his index finger. Skirt swinging around her calves, she completed a full turn before he uttered his verdict. "Wow. You look great, babe."

Color bloomed in her cheeks as she curtseyed and acknowledged his approval. "Thank you. You don't look too bad yourself. Now let's get this show on the road. What do you say, Jimmy?"

Bud directed his gaze at the baby lying on the blanket on the floor. "You ready for your first sleepover?" Jimmy waved his arms and gurgled at the attention from his father.

Twenty minutes later, they deposited Jimmy at his grandparents and were looking for a parking spot in the lot next to the Legion Hall. A full moon and a temperate breeze made for a perfect autumn evening. Strains of live music were audible and on key. Not quite Perry Como but respectable for the group hired from over Rhinelander way.

"Would ya look at this?" Bud sounded truly amazed. "There must be thirty, forty cars here. Looks like a decent crowd. No way I thought Charlie and his committee would pull this off."

They opened the door and Elaine noted the handiwork of the decorating committee: patriotic red, white, and blue streamers decorated the ceiling. Cardboard stars shining with glitter covered the walls and a mirrored ball hung from the center of the dance floor. Inside the door, Madlyn and Tommy presided over the box for door prize tickets and sold dance tickets to latecomers. Madlyn looked at Elaine's new outfit and nodded her approval.

Bud chatted for a moment with his older sister as Elaine stretched her neck and looked for their friends. She spied Olivia, Perry, Charlie and Bertie, and John Langholz seated at one of the larger tables near the center of the room. She was anxious to get settled and commandeer Bud out to the dance floor. Giving Madlyn a quick hug, Elaine steered toward Olivia who saved them places. Bud followed, got her seated and then started toward the bar. "Nice cold Coke?" he offered.

"Thanks Bud, but I'll have a nice cold beer, if you please. No getting up early with Jimmy tomorrow. Tonight I'm going all out! A glass of Millers will do nicely. Make it a big one, not one of those little sissy glasses." Covering his mild surprise with a nod of his head, Bud meandered off for the beverages.

"Well, woo-whooo, Elaine! A schooner of beer! We gonna have to roll you home tonight?" This from Perry. "And that dress!" A wolf whistle followed his remark.

Elaine saw Charlie grin. "Now leave her be, Perry," he said. "These ladies deserve to kick up their heels and not have to answer to the likes of you Tilden fellows."

Olivia scooted her chair closer. "Elaine, I told you that lipstick was the right shade for you; you look positively fabulous. And Per's right, your dress is really pretty. Is it new?" Elaine smiled and returned the compliment. The rich green sheath her friend was wearing was doing wonders for Olivia's appearance. Her eyes sparkled and her hair looked more lustrous. Heck, all the women looked wonderful, coiffed and dolled up. Not a one could be mistaken for the house fraus they were when chatting at Marge's Store or the grocery. Elaine's desire for a good time was reinforced.

Swiveling, Elaine saw Bud stop to talk with Lloyd and his wife, Fanny. She'd met Fanny this summer and had to admit that the new Mrs. Defoe seemed pleasant enough. Bud pointed toward their table but Lloyd shook his head and motioned to the other side of the hall where some welders and their wives were seated. She was pleased that Bud was kind enough to invite Fanny to their circle but was also relieved that Lloyd wanted to mingle with his friends from work. She didn't want anything to ruin tonight and having to put up with Lloyd's rudeness and jealousy might take the fun out. She could compare notes with Fanny another time.

Morag and Ed Gunderson entered the Hall and headed to their table. Bertie moved down so Morag would sit there and leave the men at the other end to gab about who-knows-what. The music made it hard to be heard, but they leaned close and worked up a mild shout if something was worth saying. Mostly they looked around, smiled, checked out the other women's outfits, enjoyed the music and sipped their drinks.

A busty, blonde woman joined the band for the next set and provided an above average rendition of "It Wasn't God Who Made Honky Tonk Angels" before teaming up with band leader Junior Corrigan for their version of "Eh, Cumpari." He invited the audience to sing along. Suddenly Elaine was giggling. Something about a bunch of backwoods Norwegians and Swedes, trying to sing like that handsome Italian Julius LaRosa struck her as very funny. Morag loudly added her Highland brogue to the chorus, and the rest of her group found it equally hilarious. They whistled and stomped their feet to sounds of each instrument mentioned in the song before thundering "tipiti tipiti tam." The song ended with a rousing burst of applause from the audience and a deep bow from Junior.

"Pretty good turnout, don't ya think, brother? Next time maybe we can get a bigger orchestra, bigger sound and really blow the windows out of this joint!" Bud nodded at Perry's remark. Elaine turned to looked at her brother-in-law and was surprised to see his gaze sweep over her face and lips, linger on her breasts and shoulders until he let his eyes return to the stage behind the dance floor. Morag kicked her under the table and leaned toward her best friend. The Scotswoman's voice was so low that Elaine had to strain her ears to hear. "Ah now, leave it to Perry to make sure he's ogled every woman in the place. Sometimes I don't know how Olivia can stand him!"

Elaine's eyes snapped to Olivia but her sister-in-law had been turned toward the men to catch a joke Charlie was telling Bud and Ed. Was Morag teasing? Surely Perry couldn't ignore his beautiful wife.

Back at the bandstand, Junior mopped sweat from his face and earnestly addressed the musicians. Then he turned to the audience and announced, "Here's one that we're playing for John and Bertie Langholz. We're told it's their wedding anniversary. John, you don't look any the worse for wearing the old ball and chain these past eight years. What say, the newlyweds start things off and then the rest of you can drift in. Here we go." With that "Red Sails in The Sunset" filled the air. The horns struggled just a bit but overall, the effect was good. Amid some modest applause, John had bowed to Bertie and led her to the middle of the floor.

Elaine looked at her husband and pointed at the dance floor. "Ah hon," Bud countered, "You know I'm no Fred Astaire. Next one, I promise ... or the one after." He tipped back his beer and continued to listen to Charlie. Hmmm, is Bud worried about his stability on the dance floor? He hardly ever shows any sign of a limp, but maybe his toes bother him more than I thought. I can wait. Elaine saluted him with her own glass and found it was empty. Ed was headed toward the bar and offered to refill her glass.

Perry threw an arm around his wife. "Okay, Livvie, guess it's up to us to show these folks here how it's done. We don't want to leave Bertie and John out there all alone!" Amid protests, Olivia let herself be pulled behind her husband. Perry was a smooth dancer; only Lloyd surpassed him on the dance floor, but it was apparent that Olivia would rather be listening than trying to follow her husband. Soon they were returning to the table as Junior announced a break.

Conversation and laughter dominated the hall until the band's return. This was wonderful. Live music and requests and dedications, even! Despite the fact that some of the lyrics were bobbled, the band knew a surprising number of dance tunes: "Unforgettable," "You Belong to Me," "The Blue Skirt Waltz," and "The Beer Barrel Polka." Smiles were abundant among the Legionnaires and their ladies this evening!

At one point, every male voice in the place joined in the theme song from High Noon. Even Bud. He smiled at Elaine and warbled along with the rest of the men in the Hall. "Do not forsake me oh my darling, on this our wedding daaaa–aay." Many had placed their hands over their hearts or swept off imaginary cowboy hats. Morag nudged her and used the pretzel in her hand as a pointer. "Would ya look at this now! They're all thinking they're bleeding Gary Cooper!"

It was a fine time. The only thing missing was a permanent dance partner. Ed, Charlie, and Perry took turns dancing with all the ladies at the table so Bud was off the hook, and Elaine got her turn on the floor. Was that her empty glass? Again? Before she could think about a refill, the band leader announced the upcoming tune. "Get ready to really move out there, folks. This tune is not for the faint of heart. Here we go with our favorite Hank Williams number–good old "Jambalaya"! Find yourself a pretty girl who can keep up, boys! One, two! One, two, three!"

A whoop came from Perry as he tried to pull his wife to her feet but Olivia was firm about sitting this one out. Elaine was already two steps to the dance floor before she realized that Bud was not following her. Her embarrassment was short lived when Perry saw her chagrin and jumped to her side, sweeping her along with him. His arms encased her, as he maneuvered Elaine to the floor.

Perry was fantastic; energetic and accomplished. He led her through what started as a fast-paced two-step and graduated into a more intricate number with passes, jitterbug moves and lots of spinouts. He commanded the steps so anyone could follow him, even a semi-tipsy city girl. More and more couples dropped back to watch the two of them, clapping their hands and stomping their feet.

By the end of the song, she and Perry were alone on the floor. He twirled her through the final bars of the song as the audience continued to whistle. Even the band was applauding their efforts. At the last line of the tune, every man in the place was shouting "Son of a gun, gonna have big fun on the bayou!" Elaine took note of their exuberance but bet some didn't have the foggiest notion what a bayou was. Maybe their high spirits were fired by the innocuous "big fun." It did sound a trifle naughty.

The music ended with another flourish as Perry lifted Elaine in a hug.

With her feet dangling he swung her around two or three times before marching her back to the table. Her group of friends gave them a standing ovation, with Morag standing on her chair, fingers in her mouth, whistling for all she was worth. Admitting to herself that she liked it, Elaine hoped they missed the discreet pat on the butt Perry delivered while navigating her toward Bud. What was that about? She glanced over her shoulder and saw a look in Perry's eye that stopped just short of a leer. Was he flirting with her? Why couldn't Bud be more demonstrative?

Olivia looked a trifle uncertain but acknowledged how her husband enjoyed his friends' praise. She ducked under Perry's arm to give her husband a quick squeeze. With no time to catch her breath, Elaine dismissed her brother-in-law's familiarity. All had heard Junior announce, "Last dance!"

Bud led Elaine to the floor and held her tight. He was not as proficient as his brother in the dance department—and there were his missing toes to consider—but he did well enough. The blonde singer was back and did a good job with "Deep Purple." Either Bud had one too many beers or he truly liked this song. Elaine could hear his rich baritone in her ear. "In the mist of a memory, you wander back to me, breathing my name with a sigh … ." Not a bad way to end the evening; Bud should sing more often.

The lights came up and the women searched for their purses as the fellows checked the sobriety levels of their friends. They congratulated Bertie on her door prize of four new bath towels. Groups lingered before the doorway until the men headed to their vehicles and pick up their spouses up at the door. Many of the women removed their high heels and stood wiggling their toes.

"Good night! Good night! This was great! Call me tomorrow. Good job, Charlie! I can't remember when I enjoyed myself so much! Thank you all for showing up. Good night!" Conversations repeated themselves and concluded a wonderful social.

As the crowd thinned, Elaine craned her neck to see what was keeping Bud. No doubt he was finishing his conversations with his buddies. In the darkened entryway she felt someone bump up behind her. Before she could turn or move aside, she felt herself being turned quickly around. Perry flabbergasted her with a quick kiss while Olivia had her back turned. It was definitely not a brotherly smooch, but one that left her lips feeling seared. His eyes held her, daring her to chastise him. Elaine turned from him and took a half step toward the door, but she did not scold Perry. No, she enjoyed that stolen kiss. Immensely.

Chapter Fifteen

early November 1954

It was still lovely out; daily customers and guests coming into the lodge commented on unseasonably warm weather. Everyone said colder weather was coming, but today's unexpected early release from the heat of the kitchen was a gift.

Elaine crossed the parking lot and looked down the gravel drive to the wood-splitting area. There was the shape of the old truck, sitting just beyond the tower of the woodpile, just where Perry said he'd be. The back door of the lodge slammed shut and the click of the lock signaled part of Richard's nightly ritual.

"Hey, hon," her father-in-law called. "I thought you caught a ride with Lotty and Oscar. If you wait while I lock up and check the windows, I'll run you home."

Perry poked his head out the window of his pick-up and tossed his cigarette as he addressed his father. "Aw, I can give her a ride, Dad. I just dropped these saws off here for tomorrow. I told Bud I'd be by in the early morning to pick up an awl but if Elaine needs a ride, I can kill two birds with one stone and get it now."

"Okay. See you both tomorrow." Richard waved them off. As Elaine climbed into the vehicle, her heart beat wildly. Perry glanced her way and grinned. "See that wasn't so hard, was it? Hardly worth the drama." He fished another cigarette from his shirt pocket and flicked his lighter, never taking his eyes from the road as he maneuvered around the potholes on the county road.

Elaine hadn't given Perry a definite answer earlier when he suggested giving her a ride home. Ever since the Legion dance, it seemed like it took all her energy to keep the flirting Perry exhibited every time he was in her presence a secret. Now, she admitted, this was thrilling. She was riding after dark, alone with a beguiling man. A man not her husband who would kiss her again if she gave him half a chance. How she knew that, she wasn't sure but she knew it was true. And she didn't have to do anything, anyway. Other women, modern women flirted all the time. And maybe Perry was just acting out some silly teasing of his own. Perhaps reading her thoughts, Perry's hand snaked over to her thigh and jolted her out of her reverie. He gave her leg a quick squeeze and rested his palm just above her knee, his fingers brushing her skin back and forth in a tantalizing rhythm. In the dim light she could see his nicotine stained fingers, feel his ready grin and smell the subtle scent of sweat.

She cleared her throat in a way she hoped would sound like Elizabeth Taylor in Giant. A small sputter had surely caught James Dean's attention. Instead, she sounded more like Richard using a small chisel out in the shed. Perry looked at her, concerned. "You okay, Elaine? You're not catching a cold are you?" So much for seductive behavior. She grimaced. "No, no, I'm fine."

Perry made a turn that led to the far side of Trout Lake. It was the road to Lover's Lane, away from more public spots at the beach. She debated saying something; like "Perry, did you miss a turn?" or "Perry, did you forget where I live?" No, a remark like that would be as transparent as newly-cleaned lodge windows.

Perry removed his hand and threw it around her shoulder. A tiny, electric spasm ran through her. Off to the side of the parking area she saw Oscar's Rambler. Was he here with Lotty? Oh! Perry parked the truck far over to the side of the lot, deep in the shadows, and pulled her toward him.

She thought about pushing him away or telling him "Stop." But his lips only grazed hers before she let him pull her out the driver's door.

Elaine's feet crunched on the gravel. Perry held her shoulders as she claimed her balance. He rubbed his nose with hers and laughed. "Come on," he said, taking her hand, "There's something over here I want to show you." Five quick strides and they were off the gravel and moving down one of the paths leading to the lake. Neither spoke. When they reached the tiny expanse of beach, they saw other couples further down the sand. Elaine squinted in the moonlight; she was fairly sure one couple was Lotty and her beau Oscar. No one appeared to take note of the Tildens' arrival.

Perry led Elaine behind him and suddenly she heard the lap of the water along the shore line. "Here we go, Elaine. Whadda ya think of that?" Elaine gasped at what she saw before her; a perfect sparkling reflection of the moon over Trout Lake. It looked like a movie set. Had the moon ever been this beautiful before? Before she could fully appreciate the balance of the moon and the curve of the beach, or the sweep of towering pines leading directly to the shoreline, Perry took hold of her again and faced her. He again drew her to him and kissed her. Softly at first, then with more insistence.

Good God! It felt wonderful and exciting. This guy, who charmed every female in the Rapids, wanted her. His hands were strong, his lips inviting and persuasive. She was falling into this. Her arms moved to Perry's shoulders, her fingers holding the back of his head, keeping his mouth on hers. Perry dropped his cigarette pack as his hands traveled the length of her back, rested on her hips, then gently kneaded her backside as he pulled her closer. His hard chest crushed her breasts, her legs parted to straddle his thigh. He kissed her with an insistence that thrilled and frightened her. The taste of him, foreign, rich with tobacco and beer, the feel of him pressed so tightly against her was addictive.

She felt him slowly, almost imperceptibly sucking on her lower lip, then her tongue. He kissed her full on the lips. The gentle sucking, the kissing, this act repeated, over and over until she began anticipating his moves and entered into this oral dance with him. She was uncertain how long they had been standing there, kissing and swaying, backlit by the moon, when she was jolted by a fine-grade sandpaper feel on her legs. Perry raised her skirt and moved his calloused workman's hands slowly up the length of her bare thigh.

All of this was so tantalizing, so wicked. Perry wanted her, and that wanting would soon translate into more. Don't stop, don't stop. Elaine's brain screamed; her mouth still melded to Perry's, her lips and tongue fused with his. Now! Now! Now? Now? Then what? Would she later teach this to Bud?

Bud. The thought of him was as real a presence as the moonlight.

"Wait!" Elaine pushed from Perry's grasp and moved a few steps back. "No, I can't—we can't do this." Her voice was a hoarse whisper. Perry grinned and moved toward her once more. His fingers played with her hair before his arm encircled her shoulders. So strong, almost primal. She heard a change in his breathing as he bent his face to resume caressing her mouth. "No, Perry! No. We can't!"

Palms flat against his chest, she pushed him away. The shove rocked him in the soft sand and he took a long step backward. For another moment they stood there looking at one another, breathing, surrounded by the sparkly reflection of the moon. Perry took a step toward her, retrieved his cigarettes from the sand and lit one. All the while his eyes never left hers. Good God, what was going to happen now? What was she thinking? Some of this had just been a silly notion, just a daring game she'd played with herself, but now! To think she could so easily betray Bud—and Olivia—where was her common sense? And what time was it? How was she going to get home?

Perry spoke first. "Okay." He took a deep drag from his cigarette. "Elaine? It's okay. Really. I was game for this, but you know I won't force you. No need for me to force any woman. Ever. Though I 'spose I could say there was a time or two when I was the one being forced." He chuckled at that and glanced over the water. "Let me smoke this here cigarette and then

I'll take you home." He appraised her with a practiced eye. "You might want to smooth your skirt and straighten your hair."

Elaine nodded and walked back toward the vehicle to wait. From the beach, she could hear the twitter of Lotty's nervous laughter and an answering rumble from Oscar. Elaine looked over her shoulder and was sure that her friend was giving her a wave. How was she going to explain this to Lotty? She told herself to just get back to the car; worry about her story later.

At the first step on the trail, Elaine heard the crack of twigs somewhere near her, just off the path. A deer, she thought as she continued. Then a distinct suppressed cough came from the pines and forest debris. A human cough. She gasped and her head swung in its direction but before she could call out, Perry was behind her, hand on her back, guiding her. She said nothing until they reached the parking lot.

"Per?" Anxiety replaced her earlier embarrassment. "Did you hear someone on the trail when we left the beach? Or was I imagining it? What if someone saw us and says something to Bud or Olivia?" She felt sick at the implications of that last question. What was she thinking?

"We're fine." Perry slipped in behind the wheel and started the engine. He appeared nonplussed as he backed out the drive. His calmness did nothing to assuage Elaine. Which was worse? Having Bud know and look at her with those Norwegian steely, blue eyes, sad and betrayed? Or having to face Olivia, her best friend, with the knowledge that Elaine had contributed to a mistrust that might already be a part of Olivia's marriage? What the hell had she been thinking? Why was she thinking only of herself?

She berated herself until she saw the sign for the lodge. They were half way home and her brother-in-law had not uttered a word.

"Per?"

Perry glanced her way. A few seconds passed before he spoke. "Elaine, I want you to listen to me cuz I'm only going to say this once. I 'spose I should say I'm sorry. You're upset, and if you are going to keep beating yourself up over this, then I am a little sorry, too. This was something I thought you wanted. Like I wanted it. Maybe I was wrong, but you seemed pretty interested a few days ago when you were flirting with me in the kitchen. Not to mention the Legion dance."

Elaine remained silent as he continued. "And so as far as I'm concerned, Elaine, it's over. You don't have to worry about me snagging on you again, okay? I'm cool with all this. Now, the noise, the cough on the path. I heard it too, but I don't think you have to get all bothered about it. Most likely it was some guy from the beach who wandered over to take a leak. Maybe someone else who was stepping out on a wife or hubby."

Elaine winced. How close had she come to "stepping out?" Per went on. "You think most of those folks on the beach want other people to know they're here? Think again. Think about Oscar and Lotty. Most of those people are there because they have nowhere else to go. They don't wanna advertise their whereabouts. And anyway, if anyone did recognize you, they'd think you were there with Bud. The old Tilden profile, the nose thing; the whadda ya call it against the moonlight?"

"A silhouette," Elaine supplied. "Maybe. I hope so." They were on County D now, almost home.

Perry swung the truck around the wide corner of their driveway. She saw the kitchen light on and heard the faint sound of WKAY's evening show coming from inside. It wasn't that late. Bob Farrell's program was playing, and Bud was no doubt lying on the couch napping after feeding Jimmy and putting him down.

Perry put the truck into neutral and set the parking brake. Elaine retrieved her purse as Perry got out and headed to the house. Surely he wasn't going to come in for a talk with Bud! Not tonight! Then she saw him lift the awl from the porch. So that part of his story would jibe when Richard, Bud and Perry talked tomorrow. They passed one another on the broken concrete of the little walkway. In the moonlight she saw a quick wink. "Nite, Elaine" and he was gone.

CHAPTER SIXTEEN

Elaine gazed skyward before entering the lodge's main door. Overhead was the mild honking of a small flock of Canada geese. Some days, from far away, they looked like specks of coarsely ground pepper scattered across the gray gravy of the early November sky. Today they dipped low over the dusty parking lot, slowing to land in a small lake down the road. She heard the beating of their wings as they fanned the air. Peering upward, she saw the individual feathers of their bellies. They were her favorite of all the big birds and Elaine could watch them for hours, had watched them all last fall while Bud courted her. She smiled thinking of those days. But now, she needed to talk to Lotty and put last night behind her.

Opening the heavy oak, Elaine took note once more of the fine workmanship on the face of the door. Her eyes flitted to the large window with its triple-paned glass. Streaky again. She'd remedy that as soon as she could. Her thoughts were scattered. Was she again avoiding entrance? Good Lord, go in and get this over with. A tug of the door and a few steps took her into the dining room.

The smell of Lodge Stew greeted her and she saw her mother-in-law seated at the corner window table, bent over the books, frowning at the ledger as she always did. Dorothy sometimes gave the appearance that there was a flaw, an error in those meticulous columns of hers but both Bud and

Richard claimed in all the years Dorothy handled the books, there'd never been a mistake, not even a penny's discrepancy.

"Morning, Mom," Elaine offered her customary greeting. She picked up an apron and hung her sweater with one fluid sweep of her arm. Dorothy caught the movement and smiled. "You don't waste much motion, hon. You do impress me, city girl." Both women laughed softly, companionably, and Dorothy returned to her pages as Elaine headed for the kitchen. Elaine hoped Lotty was alone in the kitchen, and there she was, finishing up the dishes from last evening. The radio provided background for Lotty.

Lotty glanced toward Elaine, and in her fine alto, resumed singing "Release Me" with Kitty Wells. Elaine waited for the familiar "release me and let me love again" before addressing her friend. Now, she told herself, do it now.

"Hey, Lotty," Elaine began, "Do you have a minute? I need to talk to you." She lowered her voice. "About last night."

"Sure." Lotty's hands were immersed in dishwater, her pans stacked near the sink. Always precise and methodical, Lotty finished the cutlery and glassware before tackling the heavier and greasier cookware. Elaine watched the blonde girl finish her chore. Lotty dried her hands and blushed suddenly–maybe she was reliving her own moments from the night before. Lotty giggled, a soft nervous titter, and blinked.

"Oh Elaine, I was so scared when we first saw other people at the beach. You know what a fraidy cat I am and then to be there... " Her voice became a whisper. "At that Lover's Point. I guess I was edgy. I probably seemed like a complete ninny to you and Bud. I just felt funny at being caught there. You know?" She looked at Elaine, her unblemished complexion colored by more than sink steam.

Elaine breathed a small sigh of relief and thanked God for Lotty's innocence. The girl believed she'd glimpsed Elaine and her husband last evening. All last night, Elaine thought about Perry's statement about the Tilden profile. It turned out Perry was right; maybe he'd been mistaken for Bud on other occasions.

112   *Mashkiki Rapids*

Elaine smiled and moved closer to Lotty, bringing additional glasses and cups with her. "Yes, Lots, that's just it. Bud was a little embarrassed, you know being a married man and all, at a spot where teenagers and new lovers come to spoon."

Lotty ducked her head and her cheeks turned an even deeper shade of pink. Elaine brushed Lotty's bangs from her eyes and leaned in conspiratorially, girl pals now. "Do you think you could keep quiet about this. Don't mention it to Bud, about seeing us there? I'd never hear the end of it from Bud for talking him into stopping."

Before she elaborated, Lotty broke in. "Oh. Sure, Elaine, no problem. In fact," she swallowed and resumed giggling, "I was going to ask you the same thing, about me being there with Oscar. If my ma ever got wind of me taking a ride, especially that kind of ride, with a Catholic boy, she'd send me away to Wausau, to my auntie's for sure." Lotty shuddered at the thought of being banished to God-forsaken Wausau.

Elaine hugged the girl to her. "Okay Lots, we'll just keep it between us. Girl stuff." She wiped and stacked the serving trays before casually adding, "You don't think Oscar will say anything to Bud, do you, Lotty?"

"Oh, no, Elaine, he's pretty shy around those older fellas but I can make him promise not to say anything." Lotty smiled into the sudsy water and then turned to Elaine. "I think he really likes me. In fact, I think he'd do whatever I asked him if it'd make me happy." She seemed pleased with this personal revelation

Elaine felt like a sponge, soaking up relief. Thank you, Lord. Thank you! I'll never do this again! Her girlhood training for prayers of thanks kicked in.

She didn't stop to analyze her relief. Was she worried about hurting Bud or regretting her cowardice with Perry? Or were those two notions blended? Maybe one and the same? Hmm. Right now there was work to finish. Grabbing a damp towel, she headed through the squeaky, swinging doors, to the streaky windows in the dining room. With luck she could get through today without seeing Perry.

CHAPTER SEVENTEEN

late November 1954

Bud opened the door and saw the bartender moving washed glasses to the drying shelf. "Good Lord Charlie, why can't I seem to do anything right these days?" Behind the bar, Charlie stood both hands deep in soapy water as he raised his chin in greeting. The brindled dog, roused by Bud's proclamation, elevated its head.

"Sorry, Hank, did I disturb your nap, fella? Sorry, boy." Bud reached down to pat the old mutt's head. By the time Bud reached a corner bar stool, Charlie set the clean glasses out to drain, dried his hands, drew a draft beer and refilled the peanuts bowl. Hank shook his head, his new dog tags clinking against his collar, and returned to slumbering on the floor.

Charlie glanced at the forlorn look on his friend's face and instead of offering sympathy, a deep laugh emanating like the slow start up of a Lionel train, filled the empty barroom. He rolled his muscled shoulders and shook his head, his clear gray eyes all but disappearing in the creases of his broad, handsome face. "What's the matter, Bud? Trouble in paradise? I'll be glad to take that smart, sassy gal off your hands for a day or two-or a night or two if you'd rather." Bud chuckled with the older man, knowing that had anyone else said these words to him, there'd be a fight brewing, female honor to defend. With Charlie, the statement merely noted the bond between the two men, not any disrespect directed toward Elaine.

Charlie scanned the bar's surface and then nodded his satisfaction. Its cleanliness passed inspection. He paused to light a Lucky Strike and patted the pockets of his freshly-pressed pants looking for his lighter. The knife crease of his trousers, his unwavering gaze and his no nonsense approach remained from his military career, of the days when Charlie was a quartermaster in General Bradley's army. There was a quick snap, a flick and the polished WWII momento was tucked in his pocket. He took a deep pull on his cigarette and blew smoke upward toward the ceiling fan. When he looked back at Bud, his tone was mock serious. "I keep telling you fellas, you backwoodsmen are swell guys but when it comes to the ladies you could all use a little ... "He paused significantly, "... finesse. And when it comes to finesse ... "Another pause, then, " I'm the man to see." He winked at Bud and laughed again. "Okay, what's the deal? What's going on now?"

Bud considered. After all, there were those rumors about Charlie and a lady librarian in Wausau, the one he supposedly kept satisfied for years with his weekly Sunday night visits. There were plenty of winks and innuendos when Uncle Roland asked "How did your weekend go?" A twinkle all around appeared when Charlie answered "Just fine, thank you." His uncle and the older men who frequented the tavern always seemed to defer to Charlie's opinions when discussing those of the female persuasion. Bud thought about it; maybe Charlie was an expert in these areas.

"Aw hell, Charlie, that's most of the problem. I don't know what's ailing Elaine. That baby is the sweetest thing on earth. Even Ma can't believe how good he is so I don't think it's that. And Madelyn and Ma and Olivia love to watch him so Lainie can have some time by herself. She says she's satisfied with having just the one healthy baby. And when I get a raise, I told her I'd buy her a new washing machine."

Charlie snorted. "Well, yeah, a washing machine is just the thing to keep the romance alive in a marriage. Things should be dandy then!" He looked at Bud and shook his head.

Bud took in his friend's teasing and sipped his beer. He averted his eyes from Charlie's direct, piercing stare. "Okay, I suppose that doesn't sound very romantic. But the romance part. Things between us, you know, things, always seemed to be fine. At least I think they're fine." He became flustered. "Oh hell, how does a guy know for sure if they're not fine?"

Had anyone else asked Charlie that, the speaker would be favored by a smart aleck reply. But when he looked at his friend's face, Charlie saw the pain there. The guy might be a war hero to the rest of Mashkiki but Charlie saw only an earnest, teenage boy. Charlie remembered the first time he laid eyes on this oldest Tilden boy. Back then Bud was a smiling, skinny, seventeen-year-old, eager to meet his Uncle Roland's army pal, Charlie, and show their guest the best spot to hunt deer. The barkeep set his cigarette in an ashtray, fiddled a moment with the flat, gold Woodsmen ring on his right hand and cleared his throat while he pondered a reply.

Bud kept on. "She doesn't ever nag me about money. And it's not like there was someone else for either of us, so why the sighs in the middle of the night or the way her spirits just seem to be dragging lately?"

Ah ha! Charlie kept his mouth shut, wiped the bar's surface and eyed the door. Now this might be something to consider. A picture of the Legion dance flashed before him. That of Elaine's shining smile and Perry whirling her around the dance floor. He recalled Bud laughing at his wife's delight and his brother's brashness, but there was also his recollection of Olivia's demeanor that night. A smile was frozen on her face, her eyes sad and resigned, and that night Charlie knew what Olivia knew. That Per, that young scoundrel, the guy rumored not to be able to keep it in his pants, was plying his charms with his brother's wife. Or thinking about it. No doubt Elaine was too smart to fall for him but it could account for the moodiness Bud was describing now. What to say to him? Surely Bud, as much as anyone in Mashkiki, knew what a rake his brother was.

Charlie saved his response as Hank emitted a low growl. Sure enough, the growl was followed by one sharp little bark. Charlie knew exactly who would cross the threshold next. A half second later Lloyd stomped through the entrance. The mill's day crew usually stopped in at a few minutes past quitting time at 4:30. It must be close to five and Einar and Toots would be right along as well as the other late afternoon regulars.

"Hush now Hank," Charlie stubbed his Lucky out and clapped Bud on the shoulder. A "we'll talk later" look passed between them. Charlie picked a clean glass and moved to the tap. "Afternoon, Lloyd. Hold the door there will ya so Hank can go out? What's new?"

The big man scowled as the dog passed by him and exited the tavern. "When you gonna get a new mutt? At least one that's not so mangy."

"Well Lloyd, as mangy as old Hank might be, he seems to be a fine judge of character. I notice when I let him out to do his business, that yours are the tires he chooses to piss on. Never seen him use anyone else's. Yessir, makes you wonder, doesn't it?" Charlie turned to draw a tap beer for Lloyd while Bud tried to hide the grin provoked by Charlie's remarks.

Lloyd grunted and picked up his glass as the door slammed behind him.

"Are you guys talking about Hank taking a leak on Lloyd's tires? I noticed that pooch was headed right for your truck, Lloyd." Einar entered and snuck into the conversation. "That's kinda funny, huh? Every time Lloyd's here that old dog has to make a trip to the parking lot and stake his territory. Never stops by my old beater. Just yours and nobody else's." Einar noticed Lloyd's expression and amended his statement. "Well, maybe it isn't so funny after all. I guess a fellow'd get tired of having his vehicle smell like dog's water all the time. I guess—"

"Shut up, Einar. A man's comes in here to relax after a hard day, not listen to some fool flapping his gums." Lloyd's mood wasn't improving.

Einar looked around and then focused on Bud. "Hunting season musta been a pretty busy time for all the Tildens, I suppose. Bet yer glad it's done, eh, Bud?" Maybe the best course of action was a subject change.

Bud rose. "You got that right, Einar."

"You do much guiding this year? Didn't hear much about you when those tourists were registering their kill."

"Nah, I left the guiding jobs to Perry and Dad. Didn't hunt myself this year, just pitched in to help Ma. Speaking of which, I need to get over to the lodge. Got some kitchen supplies in my truck. See ya, Einar. Lloyd." He looked at Charlie. "We'll finish this conversation another time."

When the phone rang later that night, it was Bud's turn to play counselor to his older pal. His conversation with Charlie was brief. With a set jaw and steely eyes he turned to Elaine. "I've got to run down to the tavern and help Charlie. He wants to know if he can bury his dog out here in our woods. Seems like Lloyd ran Hank over in the parking lot when he left tonight. No one saw it so it might have been an accident. Einar heard a thump and when they looked out Hank was laying there with Lloyd halfway down the road." Bud got his jacket and started for the door when Elaine heard him utter a single word. At first she thought he said "plastered," a reference to Lloyd's condition when he left the Dew Drop Inn. When the door shut behind her husband, she realized what she really heard was "Bastard!"

Chapter Eighteen

early January 1955

The entire clan gathered for Madlyn's birthday. The dinner table at Dorothy and Richard's was cleared and they all moved to the living room. The adults gathered to hear the rest of the story Richard had started at the table before Dorothy shooed them off. "Coffee and conversation before we have cake," she told them.

Elaine knew she had missed the introduction to Richard's recollection but if she listened carefully, he usually wound back to the beginning and she could easily catch up. He was talking about a visit from his father's brothers. Bud's great uncles, men now long dead. She perched on the arm of the couch next to Bud.

"Oh yeah," Richard was warming to the story, "that was an interesting situation I tell you. Imagine being a teenage boy here in Mashkiki. Not much in the way of excitement or romance except at the picture show. And then to have this ..." He waved his hand a bit, searching for the right word " ... drama dropped right in your lap. I don't know if my family just chose to ignore it, but no one else seemed to recognize what would happen ever' time all of us were together in the room."

"What was the deal, Dad? Those uncles let loose with some creative cussing or what?" Bud rose to give Dorothy his spot on the davenport. He folded himself onto the floor near Elaine, his hand resting on her foot.

Richard chuckled. "Oh, no. Curse words wouldn't've been enough to keep my attention. I'd heard all those words from half the lumberjacks who passed through here before I was in grade school. No, I'm talking about the tension that just sat there, a plunked-down, 'I ain't going anywhere' feeling in that room. It was like a maiden aunt asked out to a doings for the first time in months. It weren't going anywhere else." He paused to smoke his cigarette, and picked a small particle of tobacco from his tongue.

"Ennaway, when they came to visit, we'd have a big supper together. Usually the kids ate first but sometimes, depending on how many were there, the men would eat first and then go out on the porch for a smoke while the women and kids ate. Then my uncles would take chairs in the front room and after cleaning up, their wives came in.

"My Idaho uncles' wives were tall, big-boned, big-busted, long-legged gals with slender ankles. Real pretty. Sisters, looked almost to be twins, they was just a year apart. They didn't give in to no high-falutin' fashion stuff, either. Didn't make any difference to them that lots of modern women wore their hair short then. Botha them had long dark hair done up in these intricate braids and wound around their heads.

"Nice features, too. Long eyelashes and perfectly applied, deep red lipstick. I had a hunch some o'the women thought it was too red, too flashy or something. Made my grandma shake her head but I can tell you with their lush looks and those clingy dresses that didn't much hide those figgers, they made quite an impression on this scrawny, scraggly fourteen-year-old. Mmmm."

Dorothy coughed and flicked a finger at her husband's shoulder. Richard blinked and realized he was wandering off the course of his story. "What I'm talking about was the fact that even as a gawky, inexperienced kid, I could tell that these sister wives had married the wrong brothers. Now Myrna, who was Asa's wife, couldn't keep her eyes and sometimes her hands off Clifton." Richard paused to make sure all got his point.

"Clifton's wife, her name was Bea, was so smitten with Asa you could almost see the electricity bounce off. According to big sis Lovey, it had been going on for years. Ever since the day the four of them got married in a double ceremony on the girls' daddy's ranch. Regular little melodrama, that's for sure." Richard paused again.

"So Dad, did they ever do anything about it? I mean, you know, do anything about it?" Perry spoke, steadfastly ignoring his mother who was shaking her head. Maybe Dorothy had heard this story plenty of times and didn't want Richard encouraged to drag it out.

Elaine thought Perry sounded interested and a trifle amused. Her chest felt as though there was a girdle around it, squeezing her rib cage. She realized she was holding her breath. Refusing to glance in Perry's direction, she settled herself more comfortably and put her hand on Bud's shoulder. She gave him a gentle squeeze which elicited an ankle caress in return. She needed to keep her composure and act naturally around Olivia. That girl could pick up on tiny tensions better than anyone Elaine ever met.

Richard smiled and looked around at his progeny. "Well, Per, that's the melodrama, the not knowing. Kept Lovey and some of my girl cousins off balance for years. Ever' time the Idaho people made it this way for a visit—and they came regular every year for a week's visit until my grandmother died—it was like a new chapter in the saga. Lovey'd raise her eyebrows at the other girls and they would commence to studying ever' little gesture and ever' hitch in their getalong those Idaho gals made around the parlor and believe you me, they made plenty of walks. Myrna and Bea would volunteer to fetch more coffee or go in and check on a sleeping baby. All eyes would be studying them, including the uncles. Myrna'd make sure Clifton got an extra helping of dessert and Bea'd flirt a little and ask Asa if he wanted more coffee. For the rest of us, it was the not knowing for sure that kept it all interesting."

"Oh good night!" exclaimed Olivia. "That doesn't seem like anything too conclusive to me. Certainly not stuff that could keep people intrigued for decades." She looked at her in-laws to make sure she wasn't being offensive.

Richard laughed too. "You're probably right, Livvie, but remember this was thirty, forty years ago and heck, there wasn't even consistent radio service many evenings. This was the best entertainment we had, better than anything on WKAY."

A group laugh followed that remark. Elaine caught Olivia's eye and gave her a tiny eyebrow shrug, just letting her friend know that she too had a slight feeling of being an outsider with these dear people. Olivia looked thoughtful and Elaine saw Olivia's gaze move from Perry to Bud and back. Good Lord! Was she assembling a new version of family infidelity? Thinking about other possible betrayals?

Elaine cleared her throat and tapped Bud's head. "What do you think, Bud? Think we should call it a night? Or do you want another piece of cake?"

Bud patted his stomach and smiled at Dorothy. "No, thank you. That piece Mom served me was more than sufficient. Might be a good thing to hit the road; I want to get up early to check that fuel pump before it gets too dark." The rest of them murmured their assent. This was nice but they all had responsibilities to be shouldered come early morning.

Coats and children were gathered. Elaine hugged Dorothy and Madelyn, and looked to bid Olivia good night. She was talking in the kitchen doorway with Richard but her eyes were on Elaine. She smiled faintly at Elaine. "Night, Elaine."

Bud carried Jimmy to the car with Elaine leading the way. When she opened the car door, she heard Perry's voice. "Bud," he asked, "Are you in any hurry to get that awl back? If not, I'll return it when I'm done." Why, oh why did she turn? He was talking to Bud, not to her. If she had just kept her eyes on their car and not turned to look at her brother-in-law she would have missed the pursed little kiss he blew in her direction.

CHAPTER NINETEEN

February 1955

What was happening to her? Why wasn't she happier, ecstatic even, with an attentive husband, and a healthy toddler? Jimmy was napping. No crying heard above the rhythmic hum of the old washing machine. All quiet on the Western Front.

She glanced at the sink. Half a dozen plastic baby bottles jutted out of the soapy dishpan like the miniature bobbers near the beach at Trout Lake. Elaine looked around the kitchen. Was she finally finished? Was she doing everything right? Was Jimmy getting enough attention? Was Jimmy going to thrive because of her or in spite of her? Sometimes she felt so overwhelmed. Other times she just felt stuck

Just after Jimmy was born, Richard teased Dorothy that when her babies were sung a lullaby, they went to sleep out of self-defense. Elaine was aghast that her father-in-law would say something so harsh to his wife, and was ready to become indignant on Dorothy's behalf. Then she saw a light come into Dorothy's eyes, a spark that ignited the dual laughter from Richard and Dorothy's throats. A joke long shared between the two of them. Would she and Bud ever start speaking that effortless, private language that was second nature to her in-laws?

Maybe she should try being honest with herself. Maybe things weren't perfect with her and Bud but there was something else there. It wasn't just good old lingering, Catholic guilt that kept her from responding to Perry. And it wasn't only about hurting Olivia; although the thoughts of Olivia and Bud pulled her from lustful abandon that night at Trout Lake.

She wished she could be more wanton and cavalier, more modern, when it came to sex and desire, but when she indulged her fantasies, it was always Bud who had the starring role. She pondered this for a moment. Maybe the itch she felt with Perry was just a misplaced itch that only Bud could scratch. Was it really this simple? That she just needed to be more honest and assertive with her husband? No need for other complications? Maybe she should try a little sweet aggression with her man.

She could write some of her thoughts down. One of her college English instructors told Elaine that she possessed talent for shaping the written word. Hmmm.

—☙

This was a nice surprise. Early in their marriage, Lainie had left notes for him. Once she even put a note in between two slices of bread in his lunch. Bud recalled trying to chew what he thought was tough roast venison only to discover a sheet of his wife's stationery. Perry had a good laugh over that!

Bud lifted the note from the table and opened the pale blue envelope. There were three pages inside. The first said merely: "I wrote this a few days ago and couldn't decide if I could show it to anyone. And of course if I did decide to show it, that anyone could only be you, for it is in reference to you, Bud. Happy Valentines Day. Love, Elaine"

Smiling, Bud moved to the second page of his wife's fine, clear script.

"You know how you have favorite items in your life you will always keep, never discard? Souvenirs from past occasions or sentimental things. Things that might mean something to you alone. No one else would ever see the significance you attach to it.

I have a sweater.

Just a plain cardigan, solid color, no pattern or other yarns woven through it to disturb the block of color, just a basic sweater that will never go out of style because it has no style. It is older than anything else I wear but looks like it could have been bought just last year. A basic garment of the type that people wore for years and will continue to wear long after I am gone.

I keep it for a couple reasons. Not to commemorate the day I purchased it or some such thing as that. The color suits me, this ordinary woman whose eye color is picked up by the color of the sweater. It is very soft and feels good on me. The sleeve length is just right for this female whose arms are often too long for off-the-rack clothing.

But the main reason I keep it is because of the button. If you look closely at the fasteners on this plain sweater you'd see one button at the neck's closure. It doesn't match the color of the sweater and is pretty nondescript of any color at all. It is subtle, flat, almost unnoticeable, but made of some type of smooth shell. An antique button. Only in some lights can you see a hint of the iridescence deep inside it. Sometimes it looks almost black but at other times there is a tiny, microscopic flash of blue, violet, pink and green. Even if no one else appreciates this button, I love to look at it when I wear the sweater, love to run my fingers over its smooth surface.

If I lost this button, I doubt that I could find another like it. Of course, I could still wear the sweater, but I would have to replace the button or sew the buttonhole closed ... and then while it looked pretty much the same, it wouldn't be the same to me.

Bud, you are the button on the sweater of my life."

So this was what she was doing sitting alone in the kitchen at night after Jimmy fell asleep. Writing these words to him while he read or listened to the radio. He could feel a solitary tear trickle down his cheek, bouncing against the stubble of his beard like a big, silvery marble in a pinball machine. Damn, he didn't care if he had to humble himself and ask his father for a cash advance. He didn't care if he had to rearrange his whole afternoon schedule. He was driving to that fancy florist in Minocqua and buying that girl of his a half dozen roses. Maybe a dozen. They might have to eat hotdogs and canned beans for a month, but tonight! Tonight Elaine was going to be treated like the queen she was. He hastened his step and realized he was whistling.

Chapter Twenty

April 1955

Mid morning and the uncommon spring heat rid the grass of all dew. An aroma of sweet clover mingled with pine. Elaine paused at her mudroom's threshold and watched the flock of starlings in the distance swoop and weave through the sky. The screen door banged gently but not gently enough to keep the half dozen sparrows on her gravel drive from rising as one into the fresh spring air. They made a soft, chirping sound before moving to the low branches of the white pines bordering the yard. Blue-striped and faded, her soft, old cotton sundress topped with a sweater felt like the perfect apparel today. The sun on her back was like an old friend giving a backrub. She inhaled deeply; it was going to be a good day.

"Come on Jimmy, let's go look at your trucks in the sandbox." Though he'd been walking for several weeks, he was still unsteady so she took his hand as they maneuvered their way to the sandbox.

The tiny boy squinted upward at the sun's brightness before smiling and turning his attention to an old bowl and big spoon. Elaine watched her son sit carefully on one of the triangle seats Bud had nailed at the corners of the square structure. Pretty good balance for a 14-month-old. Jimmy spied a stray clothespin and held it up for his mother's inspection.

"Good boy! Thank you. Guess what? Morag is bringing Mary over to see us, too. Won't that be fun?"

Soon Elaine could see Jimmy filling a bowl with sand, dumping it out and spooning in more. She smiled; this could keep her young one occupied for most of the morning. She bent to pull some laundry from the basket and deftly scooped a few smooth wooden pins from her bag.

Lots of pins used today. Lots of small socks, little shirts and diapers. Towels and sheets. Some of her things. Bud had laughed when he saw her set of seven new panties, all different colored and embroidered with the days of the week above a leg band. "What happens if you cover your comely bottom with Sunday's pair on a Wednesday?" he teased. "Is this something you girls report to one another? Might there be a fine involved for wearing the wrong briefs on a specified day? And you think we guys are crazy when we talk hunting and fishing gear!"

Yep, six pair there. She had the Thursday pair on. Her eyes fell on the lilac pair. Tuesday. The color looked so appealing and feminine. Lavender and shades of purple were her favorites. A nice change from the standard whites she'd worn for years.

As Elaine was hanging the last garment, Jimmy looked up from the sand and squealed. Did he hear the approach of Morag's vehicle? Jimmy babbled and waved his spoon, excited to see the visitors.

Morag's friendship was one she treasured daily in Mashkiki Rapids. The old black Chevy pulled into the driveway, with little Mary waving out the window. Her strawberry, blond hair was smoothed back into long braids tied with ribbons. Five years older than Jimmy, Mary was old enough to be careful with toddlers but young enough to still enjoy playing with them. Elaine loved this sensible little girl, and Jimmy obeyed all her little commands and stayed close by when she visited.

"Hello there, sweet Mary," Elaine held out one arm as she balanced her basket on her hip. "Come give me a hug before you start making mud pies."

"Okay, okay Jimboy." Mary embraced Elaine and headed for the sandbox. Jimmy got a pat on the head from his older friend and a reassurance they would play farm this morning as well as assemble mud pies.

Morag jiggled a big paper bag in one hand and held the door for Elaine. "You wee ones play nicely for a bit. We'll watch you from the window now." Morag called to the kids, "I've got a nice surprise for you when it's lunch time, after I see Elaine's new kitchen. Be good babies now."

Elaine tucked the basket behind the door and wiped her hands on her apron. "What did you bring now? You are always spoiling my boy!"

"Achh, yes. And it's a good reason then for it lets me keep spoiling mine as well. Ed reminds me almost everra day now how big Mary's getting. I think she'll be tall like Ed's sister. Seems like all you Yanks are tall, even the girls! Though it's not bad to be tall." Morag quickly added when she remembered that sometimes Elaine was a bit sensitive about her height. After all, at a pinch over 5 foot 8 inches, she did tower over a few of the older men. Not like Morag's own sturdy five foot two stature.

Morag set her things on the table and surveyed her friend's kitchen. Things were always so tidy here. A large art calendar was the focal point of the wall space next to the refrigerator. She pointed at this month's offering: sunflowers and van Gogh. "Classy," she said. "Verra nice indeed. Your new paint makes the room look so cheerful, and bigger, too, I think. Just like a magazine photograph. You are a regular lass o'pairts!" Morag clapped her hands and executed a few steps of a jig.

"What was that you just said about my parts? Are you talking dirty, Morag?" Elaine teased.

"Achh no! Lass o' pairts—a compliment, silly! It means 'my talented girl'."

Elaine beamed. Perhaps having an art background was handy when she finally got around to redecorating. "Thanks Morag, I don't know what I'd do without you."

Morag looked solemn. "No, tis I should be thanking you. Without you and Olivia, I'd be doomed to be one of those old biddies, lurking outside Marge's Dry Goods, craning their necks to see who buys what." Her voice took on a croaky quality as she bent forward and imitated the senior members of the Mashkiki Falls Ladies Auxiliary. "Oh my, my, Selma! There goes that Tilden girl again, spending her husband's hard-earned money on frivolities. What? What! Is that a new tube of lipstick she's perusing there? Oh, the hussy! She just bought a tube a few months back. Not red enough for her? Oh my! The harlot, the hussy, that brazen big city woman!"

This monologue was delivered with rolling eyes and wringing hands. Elaine collapsed in a chair and checked the children from the window.

"Oh Morag, you're awful! What would I do without you? I want to run my proposal for the children's library by you before I show it to the Sorenson sisters at the library."

"Ahhh and isn't America grand to have free money for books and our kiddies? And am I not fortunate to have such a clever friend who gets some for us Mashkiki folks! You write the government and we get books for the kiddies and don't have to pay it back! I'm proud of you, I am, and so is your Buddy boy."

"I didn't really do anything so special," Elaine protested. "Rose Sorenson showed me a magazine article about small communities acquiring children's library collections. I just did a little investigating with the town clerk and filled out a few forms. Got them notarized. I was surprised when Rose told me that the Mashkiki Rapids Library was awarded $300. She was nice enough to ask for suggestions for books to purchase. Rose didn't really have to do that since she's the official librarian. Look in that folder there. Here come Mary and Jimmy."

Mary led Jimmy by the hand through the entry, then the little girl scooted past Elaine to Jimmy's little toy chest with the toddler hot on her heels.

Morag added a little sugar to her brew before opening the folder and scanning its contents. "A fine list Elaine. The kiddies will love it! And what's this notation for bitsy furniture?"

"Rose told me that not only could they buy books but what's needed in the children's corner too. She suggested some small round tables and chairs the right size for children not even in kindergarten yet. Maybe an adult-size rocking chair for story hour, too." Elaine tucked her hair behind her ear.

Morag clapped her hands. "Super! You're a smart one, Elaine. A perfect use of the money if you ask me. What else has been rolling around in that head of yours?"

"Well, I read another article and it mentioned this group of mothers in a small town who organized a reading hour once a week. We can do that. Say a Tuesday or Wednesday morning, everyone brings their children to the library for an hour or so's worth of stories and activities. Two mothers would stay and supervise the children while the rest do some shopping, get their hair done, whatever. We'd all take our turns with the kids, and depending on how many we get, we'd probably have to supervise once a month. We could post a calendar at the library as a reminder. What do you think?"

"Ahh my little sister, tis a grand idea! Grand! And I already know some of us who'd volunteer: you, me, Olivia, Fannie, Madlyn for sure. All this energetic talk makes me hungry. Shall we feed those little rapscallions of ours?"

Jimmy and Mary, with faces and fingers washed, gathered around the table for soup and crackers with Morag's brownies for dessert. Dishes done, Morag left with Mary and as a bonus took Jimmy with her ("I'll have him back before your evening tea.") Elaine was delighted with some time to herself. Okay. Gather the clothes, sprinkle a few shirts of Bud's and you can curl up with your book for an hour.

Back in the yard she moved steadily down the line, unpinning, folding the small articles of clothing and placing them in the basket. Afternoon sun highlighted the wooden half barrel where the yellow and purple pansies were ready to explode into the warm air. Dorothy had predicted they'd be early. Elaine could hardly wait to see the deep magenta petunias she'd plant next.

When she reached the last row of clothing she noticed something amiss. There was an empty space in the middle of the line. One lonely pin was still attached to the rope. Its mate was lying on the ground at her feet. She glanced at the garments still on the line and checked the ones in the basket. Her silky lilac Tuesday undies were missing.

CHAPTER TWENTY ONE

Elaine swung open the massive, oak door of the Last Resort. Her eyes and nose were immediately assaulted by the smell of warm, homemade biscuits, and the sight of the bright, new tablecloths Dorothy had finished stitching yesterday. Wednesday evening was church night, so the usually brisk and loud conversations were minimal. Only a few customers remained as she headed to the kitchen with the package of butter Dorothy had requested. On her way to the kitchen, she spied a family in the far corner of the room.

Mrs. Clarkson, the pulpcutter's wife, and her four children sat there, quiet and solemn. Two small boys and a girl, faces freshly scrubbed, had packets of crackers and glasses of water in front of them. They were surreptitiously nibbling them while their mother sipped her coffee. All of these younger children shared the fair, sunburned skin, blue eyes and blond hair of their mother.

An older boy–what was his name? Donald? Daniel? No, Donnie, sat slouched at the end of the table. Elaine guessed his age at 16 and wondered if he was of mixed blood. He had straight black hair, penetrating dark eyes, and the complexion of the nearby Ojibwe residents. He wasn't particularly striking in the looks department and Elaine wondered if he might improve with age. His eyes were closely set and his rare smile was slightly buck-toothed. He sat, pushed back from the table, hands folded in his lap, his eyes downcast. There were no packets of crackers at his place.

When Elaine passed, he glanced at her briefly, his gaze sullen and hostile. His hand went to the pocket of his jacket and tucked something inside. What was he so intent on concealing? Was he stealing sugar packets or crackers? There was no need. Dorothy knew they were munching her free saltines.

Only Elaine had been present in the almost empty dining room a month or so ago when the Clarkson brood appeared. The woman seemed hesitant to let Dorothy seat her family. She told Dorothy she wasn't ordering a meal but was it alright if the children had a glass of water? Dorothy told Mrs. Clarkson that she was welcome to bring her children into the lodge dining area and take a table as long as she ordered something off the menu. "I don't care if it's just a lone cup of coffee. You order and pay for something and that makes you a customer, Mrs. Clarkson. And if your children choose to sip some water and eat a cracker while you're enjoying your coffee, that's just fine with me."

When Elaine brought up what she'd seen and heard with her mother-in-law, Dorothy dismissed her admiration. "Those poor kids can't help it if their father is a reprobate. That woman works hard, too. Did you see her knuckles? I know that she gets occasional cleaning jobs from some of the church ladies but you can be sure it's chores they would never think of tackling themselves. Cleaning out the henhouse, moving shelves and jars around the root cellar, stripping floor wax, that sort of thing. Probably only give her a quarter here and there. Doesn't cost me much to let those kids have a few crackers and some jelly. Mrs. Clarkson told me that she has plenty of dry soup mixes—she just has to add water—out there in that ramshackle house so they aren't starving, but sometimes I think kids need some civilization and a chance to practice manners as much as they need food."

And so it had become an infrequent social hour for the entire Clarkson family, minus their father. Apparently Mrs. Clarkson had pride going for her and didn't take advantage of Dorothy's generosity often.

Something niggled at the back of Elaine's mind as she breezed through the kitchen entrance but she dismissed it as she greeted the kitchen crew.

"Hi, Mom. Hello Rachel. I've got your butter. I'll put it in the fridge for you."

Dorothy looked up from the stove, waved away a bit of steam and pushed her hair from her face. She moved the pot with tomorrow's soup to cool and motioned to the prep table where Elaine could see the remnants of the last pound of butter. "Looks to me like you timed it perfectly, Elaine. Thank you, hon. I really need it for tomorrow's breakfast. Take a seat and we'll taste my soup while you tell me what's new. Saw Morag earlier and she told me she was out to your place today with Mary. Said she liked the way your new kitchen was shaping up. I told you that shade of blue was perfect! Sit down while I run to the ladies' room."

Elaine removed her jacket and sat at the large table. Things were slowing down at this time of the night. Only Rachel was still here, finishing her duties in the kitchen. Dirty dishes slid from Rachel's grasp into the sudsy water in the oversized sink.

"Hey, Elaine!" Rachel checked the doorway where Dorothy exited and then moved closer to Elaine. She and Lotty were careful with passing along any scuttlebutt when the boss might be in earshot. Dorothy told the waitresses that she wasn't opposed to gossip but "not on my time!"

"Umhmm." Elaine knew if she acknowledged Rachel once in a while, the hired girl would get her duties finished and be out of here on time. Then Dorothy could get home to Richard and their favorite Wednesday night radio program.

"So what do you think, Elaine?" With a practiced hand, Rachel wiped the table and replaced the salt and pepper shakers. "Don't you think it's a little creepy? Someone stealing ladies' drawers right off the clothes-lines? Who is it? I could be serving an honest-to-God pre-vert here some morning and wouldn't know it! Yechhh!"

"Umhmm." Elaine headed for a bowl, intent on sampling tomorrow's featured soup. Sometimes she was just too tired to keep up with Rachel's sudden shifts in conversation. But, wait a minute. Wait just a minute! "Did you say ladies' undies, Rach? Someone is stealing ladies' undies off clotheslines here in town?"

"Well yes! What did you think I was talking about?" Vigorous toe tapping on Rachel's part accompanied this remark.

"My goodness!" Elaine didn't have to pretend interest now. "How many thefts have you heard about? Several?"

Elaine's attention switched from almost nonexistent to full blown intensity and Rachel hadn't missed that. Now that she had Elaine's consideration, she intended to keep it. She drew herself tall and leaned toward Elaine. "Hold on, hold on, Elaine. Like I said, when I stopped at the drugstore, I talked to Bertie. She lost a pair on Monday. And one of the Sorenson sisters, too. Same day. I saw Madlyn when I was walking to the post office and she heard a lady in Marge's store yesterday say the same thing. We got someone stealing ladies' smalls right under our noses!"

Elaine considered potential thievery in her own back yard and a niggling at the back of her brain bloomed into vivid acknowledgement. She flashed on the Clarkson boy, moments ago, shoving something in his pocket. She'd thought it was a handkerchief. Now, recalling the gesture, she was sure the patch of cloth she glimpsed was pastel, a lavender shade. Not the color of kerchief that an almost grown boy would use even if he was without any other hankie. Far too girly. That sneaky rascal had her underwear!

Before she blurted this out to Rachel, she needed to be sure.

Anger fought with disgust as she turned the revelation over. She could just ignore it and warn her friends to be more vigilant. Was this some silly new pseudo-sexual rite of passage now for teenage boys? No! No! Darn it—those were her new underthings! What did this little twerp have to say for himself? Elaine marched out into the dining room, over to the table where the Clarksons sat. They were preparing to leave when Mrs. Clarkson saw Elaine approach and gave her a weary smile. Then she placed a dime near her saucer to cover the cost of the coffee and tip. A small wave of uncertainty flitted across her face as she glanced about the table. Maybe she was counting the number of empty cracker packets left in her children's wake.

"Evening, Mrs. Clarkson. Could I ask you something before you leave?"

The woman nodded as the two little boys and their sister looked at Elaine expectantly. It dawned on Elaine that perhaps not many people engaged their mother in conversation. They were curious. Donnie looked at her from the corner of his eye and scuffed his boot along the floor. "Donnie," his mother murmured, a caution about his lack of courtesy before focusing on Elaine. "Evening to you, too. What can I do for you? You need help cleaning that house of yours?" Her voice sounded hopeful.

"No, thank you, Mrs. Clarkson, I'm managing just fine but I do need some help with my woodpile. Bud's been keeping up as best he can but with the added delivery runs he and Perry are making this month, it's easy to get behind. I was wondering if Donnie could swing by late tomorrow afternoon for about half an hour, forty five minutes?" She swung around and fixed him with her stare. "I'm not Rockefeller but I will pay you," she added.

"That's real nice of you," his mother interjected. "He'll be there tomorrow, won't you, Donnie?"

If the boy was puzzled by Elaine's offer of employment, it didn't show. He stared for a second at Elaine before taking his mother's elbow.

"Come one Ma, we don't want to run into any wildlife on the county road so we'd better get moving. If we step lively we can be home in ten or fifteen minutes."

The family moved to the door, leaving a slight sour smell in their wake. The littlest boy turned his gaze on Elaine, shot her his own buck-toothed grin, and waved.

CHAPTER TWENTY TWO

Donnie'd shown up in her yard just after three. He worked for nearly an hour and it looked like he was in the final stages of tidying up. He wasn't terribly tall but had a good set of shoulders on him; it appeared he was used to hard work. Maybe helped his father haul some bigger logs from the cut areas. Though he had the muscular body of an almost grown man, his face, when he wasn't scowling, was all boy. His eyes were clear, deep brown, and penetrating. Elaine could now clearly see the sign of Indian heritage in his features. The flash of his smile showed when Jimmy toddled over to show his sandbox spoon. So the teenager liked smaller kids, too.

Elaine sat down on her back steps. Two old wooden chairs, bought at the church rummage sale, sat before her. She'd sanded and primed them with Morag's help and since the day was sunny and cool, she was administering a last layer of varnish. They looked good. She waited until her task was completed and Donnie was finished before offering him a cup of coffee with his pay. He looked at the coins she placed in his palm and nodded before tucking them in his pants pocket.

Last night she turned over in her mind the best way to approach him on the subject of the stolen underwear. At last, she decided that direct but nonthreatening confrontation was her best strategy. The boy took a seat on the step below her and stretched out his legs. When he took a sip of coffee, she spoke. "Donnie, I saw what you tucked in your pocket last night. What's going on with you?"

It surprised her that he didn't bother with a denial. There was a slight hesitation and another tentative sip before he looked up at her and blurted, "They weren't for me! And they weren't taken because I'm a retard or some kind of warped person. Someone who goes around sniffing ladies' briefs. That ain't me." His chin lifted; his stare was slightly defiant.

"Okaay." Elaine drew out the syllable. "Then tell me–why did you steal them?"

Donnie started as though the "stolen" concept was foreign to him and again hesitated. Perhaps he realized his admission and was now concerned about possible punishment. "I ain't saying I did steal them. Did you hear me saying I did?" His voice lost its edge and something replaced the hardness in his face. Maybe an onslaught of tears? He saw her scrutinizing him.

"Damn you!" He spat the words at Elaine and tossed the remnants of his coffee into the yard. He lurched to his feet but did not stalk off as she expected. Instead he stood, his back turned to her, hands on his hips, his face scanning the road.

Well! Maybe not tears; maybe anger building again. Perhaps she should be fearful of this strong, young male. No, something told her that wasn't necessary and besides Donnie no doubt knew the reputation of the Tilden men and wouldn't chance crossing them or theirs. What was that quote she remembered from a college literature class? Discretion is the better part of valor? Elaine remained silent as the boy struggled to calm himself. He blew a sigh before continuing.

"What if I told you it was me who took them underpants? What would you say then? Would you turn me in? Give that fat ole constable Jeff Warner a call? Make my ma pay a fine to get me out of the hoosegow?" He took a few more paces away from the steps, his shoulders hunched, his chin resting on his chest.

Elaine replaced the cover of the varnish can and smoothed her faded pedal pushers against her thighs. "I'm trying to understand, Donnie. I'm just trying to figure out why you took them in the first place and why you're ... " she searched for a word, "collecting them. Seems you took a pair from about every woman in the village."

The boy snorted and turned again toward Elaine. "Aw, damn you! I'm not collecting anything. And I'm not putting anyone out much. That's why I only took one pair at a time. So nobody would get too riled up. Who's going to call the law over one lousy pair of panties? And some of them weren't even very new." Was he smiling at that last remark? When he smiled his slightly buck toothed grin, he lost his manly demeanor. Then he was all boy and a mischievous one at that.

"I'm just trying to understand, Donnie. What did you do with them? Was it part of some prank? Do you just toss them?" Elaine patted the spot next to her, indicating he could sit there too. Jimmy had climbed into her lap, thumb in mouth, eyes closed.

Donnie stood, looking first at Elaine, then away toward the road. No further sound came from him. Much as Elaine wanted to continue her gentle interrogation, she waited him out. Finally he took the seat she offered, most of his fire burned out.

Elaine looked around the yard and inhaled deeply. The fragrance from her barely budding wild rose hedge filled her nostrils. Donnie followed her glance toward the roses.

"My ma likes flowers too. When I was little, maybe three or four, Ma and I stayed with one of my ma's aunts. Aunt Royanne. Ma had a job at a canning factory, so she worked during the day and I stayed with Aunt Royanne. This was after my pa, my real pa died. I was real little so I don't remember him much. But before long, Ma met Mr. Du-ane Clarkson at that factory and married him." He dragged out the pulpcutter's full name, no affection in his voice. "So anyway, Aunt Royanne had a garden. I remember my ma coming home after work and after she cleaned up, we'd sit on a blanket in the yard and she'd throw her head back and just take the biggest sniff of that flower smell and give me a big smile. Told me someday we'd have our own flower garden." He let out a derisive snort. "Don't see that happening any time real soon."

What to say to this boy? This lonely troubled male who was, for all his posing, just a boy. Middle ground might be the best and safest path. "Well, when you go home, I'll cut some of those daffodils for you to take her."

"Oh yeah, that'd be just dandy. Somebody'll see me walking from the village toward our shack and the next thing you know, they'll want to be lynching me for posie theft." He managed a half smile at that and kicked at the hard dirt under the lowest step. He picked up a small twig and began to snap it into small pieces. He found Elaine watching him with frank appraisal. "Well, if you mean it, it'd be nice, I guess. I mean my ma would appreciate the flowers. You have a jar I could put them in? Then she could set them on the table. Spruce up the place a little."

As they listened to the chirping of a solitary bird, Donnie extended an index finger and gently traced a wispy curl on Jimmy's head. "Do you like little kids?" Elaine asked. "I've seen you walking and talking with your sister and little brothers and they seem real happy to be with you. And you look like you enjoy their company, too."

Donnie's head whipped toward her at the mention of his siblings. Maybe checking her sincerity? He studied her expression for a minute. "Yeah, I guess so. They can be pretty funny. You know how little kids can say the goofiest things? My littlest brother, Joey, he knows the deputy's name is Mr. Warner and I think Joey is impressed with uniforms. Every darn time Joey sees some guy in a uniform, the postman or a bread delivery man or that older kid who works at the Shell station, he says ' There's that other Mr. Warner.'" He smiled at the thought and shook his head.

"My ma is cooped up and stuck with them most of the day so I try to give her a break later in the afternoon. Seems to make the old man a little happier when he can crack a beer and talk to her alone. Unwinding he calls it. I call it staying out of his line of vision until supper's ready. So he comes home, ma starts our meal and the kids and I take a walk. Sometimes we come into town and just look around. My sister Martha doesn't have many friends so she likes to walk with me. That way, when I'm around, none of those asshole boys from her school dare make fun of her."

A frown creased his brow. Snippets of Elaine's conversation with Richard about the pulpcutters came back to her. She remembered her father-in-law saying that other children sometimes shunned the children of the pulpcutters or teased them.

"What about you, Donnie? Do you ever go to school when you move around so much?" Elaine hoped she hadn't overstepped the boundaries of their conversation; but Donnie seemed to relax and respond to her attention. There was something about his posture, the way he looked in her direction that told her he liked being involved in this conversation; never mind the way it began.

"Nah, not reg'lar. Depends on how much work there is for us. Sometimes the old man gets work for me, too. Usually, he lets me keep a part of my daily wages. And mostly the school people and truancy officers don't bother us. I'm almost 17, old enough to be done with school, so they don't ask. Around here they prob'ly think I'm from the rez and not their problem. Nobody can miss that I'm Indian. At least part."

Elaine continued her questioning. "Do you miss it? Going to school?. Being with other kids?"

A harsh bark came from his lips. "Hell, no! Get enough crap from the old man when he's a mind. Don't need any more from any of those snoots in my class! Don't need their guff and sure don't need those asshole remarks about Injuns or half-breeds. I stick by myself." A sly look came into his eyes. "I saw you once on one of my walks."

"Oh? When was that?"

"In the fall. Right after we moved here. I was sitting on the beach at Trout Lake, looking at the full moon and all these couples started showing up. Seen you with your hubby. I even started to follow you back to the parking lot."

Oh good Lord! He was referring to the time she was there with Perry! How much had he seen? At least she knew who'd made the sound she heard on the way back to Perry's truck. She looked sharply at Donnie. "Why did you follow us?"

"I heard about him being a big hero and all and I wanted to shake his hand," he explained. "I chickened out at the last minute. I figured he'd think I was a bother."

Thank God for teenage insecurities! And that Tilden profile. How close had she come to being found out by this strange boy? Another reminder that she had to deal with Perry. Her life in this mundane little village was getting too complicated. Would Donnie ever mention this to Bud if they should meet?

"Bud's pretty touchy about his hero status. He doesn't like to talk about it much but if you're here sometime when he's around, he'd be glad to meet you, I'm sure." She needed to change the subject. "Sounds kind of lonely not being around other kids at school. What about basic learning?"

"Ya don't need to look sorry for me! I'm caught up in math and last school I was at I got a C+ in English so I'm doing okay with learning stuff. And besides, I got a plan for myself. Sort of." His words stopped abruptly.

A few more moments passed and the only sound was Jimmy snoring gently as Elaine rocked him on her lap.

"Yes?" Elaine prompted Donnie. There was a tinge of pink barely visible on his dark cheeks but easily discerned on the tops of his ears.

"Ahh, it ain't much. Nothing much to tell. And why would you want to hear it anyway?" He picked up another twig.

Why indeed? She wasn't sure, but this conversation was giving her some satisfaction. "Hmmm, I don't know. I guess I remember what it was like to have some plans, some dreams and nobody to discuss them with." Her response was honest.

"Your old man was ornery, too?" He gazed at her expectantly.

"It wasn't really like that. I was an only child and my mother died when I was very young so I don't remember her much. Like you and your dad. We had a housekeeper who was around until I was around ten or so. But as for other kids—we lived at the edge of town so there were no close neighbors. I do remember feeling lonely sometimes." Donnie looked directly at her, listening to her story.

"One summer, I guess it was the last summer I had a babysitter with me all day–when I got to be about 12 or 13 my dad figured I could manage alone–but then I still had a babysitter. She was earning money for beauty school or something in the fall. She used to style my hair. I think I was her guinea pig. Anyway, she listened to me and I told her all kinds of things about what I wanted to do when I grew up. Probably didn't entertain her very much but I felt good just saying some of those things out loud."

Silence fell between them. Maybe she had revealed too much. She wondered how long since Donnie had a one-on-one conversation with someone outside his family. One that didn't involve a chore for the money Mr. Clarkson negotiated.

The boy took a few steps from the stoop before he spoke.

"The aunt with the flower garden? She wasn't married when my ma and I lived with her. When we moved, I wasn't happy about leaving her. I cried a lot and hid out in the tool shed when Mr. Clarkson showed up. But Aunt Royanne told me she was getting married and leaving that place, too. She said I could come back and live with her when I got older. She said it was her promise to me and I remember she crossed her heart and the whole thing. Yep, she was set to marry this older feller who was a widow man when we showed up. Aunt Royanne put him off to help us out. So when we were leaving, he sent for Aunt Royanne and she moved to Nebraska.

"There are some years, if we're in a spot for a while, my ma sets up a post office address, and eventually we get a letter or two from Aunt Royanne. She and that guy have this little ranch or farm place. They raise chickens and cows, and they have a horse. She's got gardens and her husband has a little business, too. Don't know what it is, but I think he's kinda old so it can't be too strenuous, I think. He sounds handy.

"Every time Aunt Royanne sends my ma a letter, she does two things. She sends Ma a money order for twenty dollars and she adds a P.S. It says 'Tell Donnie I'm waiting for him to turn up on my doorstep one day.' That's how I know she meant what she said when I last saw her. She wouldn't keep including a mention of it if she didn't really mean it, would she?" His voice carried a hint of concern in it.

"No, I don't think she would. She sounds pretty nice. But what about your sister and little brothers? Would they be okay alone with–I mean–" she stumbled over the query.

Donnie tossed the last of the twig he was snapping away from him and turned to face Elaine. "Oh, you mean Mr. Clarkson? You think he's abusive or something? With my ma or with us kids? Knocks us around?" He waited for her answer.

"Well, yes, I guess that is what I meant. I mean you described him as ornery and you have to admit he doesn't seem very sociable."

"Sociable!" The boy's laugh was a snort. "Boy, that'd be a stretch for him, oh yeah! No, m'aam, Mr. Clarkson isn't what you'd ever call social. But abusive? No, that's not him either. I never saw him lift a finger to my ma or Martha or the little ones and I don't think he ever would. Oh, you're probably thinking me, ain't you? You're asking if he slaps me around? Because I'm not his, you mean?"

"I guess that's what I meant, Donnie. I think some men might not be as accepting as–as they could be." Somehow she doubted Mr. Clarkson was as loving toward Donnie as Bud was toward Jimmy.

"I don't pretend that Mr. Clarkson's ever been thrilled with having me around but my ma's a pretty strong woman even though she's not real big, Mrs. Tilden. I think she made it pretty plain to him from the get-go that having her meant taking the two of us part and parcel. So if he wants her to stay–and he does, that's real plain–then he has to put up with me until I leave. I'm just waiting till Martha gets a little older."

Puzzlement danced across Elaine's face and the boy took note of it. "In that shack the old man's got for us? It only has three little sleeping spots. The old man and ma have the biggest one, off the kitchen. The little guys and Martha have what's probably supposed to be a storage room near the back of the place. There's two small beds in there–one for the little guys and one for Martha. I have this dinky area that ma and I worked on. We tacked up a flimsy little wall so it's big enough for an old army cot. But Martha's almost 13 and I figure she's gonna need some room to herself soon because ... "He looked at Elaine, struggled to look grown up, but lost the struggle and blushed furiously, his dark complexion a deep rosy brown. "Well, you know what I mean, girls need space for themselves. Privacy and stuff."

Elaine nodded and kept herself from smiling at his embarrassment. Donnie wanted to be regarded as a grown up and she would try to oblige him. "Martha sounds lucky to have you around. Looking out for her and knowing she needs a room for herself. But if you left, she'd probably miss you."

"Yeah, well, maybe." He was pleased with this assessment. "But if she had some confidence, some notion that she deserved that kind of stuff, then maybe she'd get along better at school and maybe make some real friends and who knows, maybe later meet a nice boy. And maybe when we're all growed up I can come and visit. Maybe someday be someone's Uncle Don. That's what I'd like to think anyway."

"It sounds nice, Donnie. I think your plan sounds good. I think—" And then it hit her. Good Lord, didn't Richard always tease her for being smart about figuring things out? Didn't Bud always give her an extra squeeze in his good bye hugs and tell her "I am so proud to be married to a gal who's just as smart as she is pretty!"? She was grateful those Tilden men hadn't been privy to this conversation with the Clarkson boy. They'd certainly rescind any vote of confidence in her intelligence today!

"The underwear from the clotheslines! You did take them, didn't you? And I'll bet dollars to doughnuts, you gave them to your sister, didn't you? Washed, clean and pretty underwear for her to have for school. Don't you shake your head at me, young man. I know I've got it right."

A smile played on his lips and gave birth to another full blown laugh. "Well, good for you, Sherlock Holmes!" His face was full of pride. Elaine laughed, too.

His look turned sober. "Are you going to tell anyone? We get some clothes from a church now and then. And sometimes ma buys some things at a yard sale but no one ever sells underwear and Martha says the really pretty ones in the stores are pricey. Too pricey for us when sometimes we're—you know—watching our pennies.

"So Martha's down to two pair—two pair only! And she washes them out every night by hand so's they won't, you know, smell for school. Then a week or so ago, she cried and told me sometimes the other kids pull pranks on her. On the playground they lift her dress up so's her drawers show. And she's ashamed because her underpants are so gray and worn. And one pair is almost see through. I told her not to let them see her cry. Soon, it'd be different. I promised her." He looked to see if Elaine understood the significance of what he was telling her.

"So I started looking for when you ladies started putting out lots of laundry with plenty of socks and underwear. I'd watch and make sure no one was around and then just take one pair. I had to guess about sizes and I only picked families that didn't have no girls Martha's age at school so that no one could point at her and say she was wearing stolen drawers. She's got a half dozen pair now so I think that's enough and two pair of un-holey white socks. No one seemed to mention the theft of a sock or two. Guess that's not as exciting as the underwear angle."

Elaine was studying her shoes, quiet, not knowing what to say. The boy was not looking for absolution and she'd only wanted to understand why he took them. She could feel his eyes on her and looked up.

"Those undies I took yesterday? Which ones were yours?" His gaze matched his voice and was unwavering.

Elaine cleared her throat. "They were lilac colored and had 'Tuesday' stitched on them."

"Lilac, hmmm? That's kind of purple-y, I suppose? Sort of a light purple?"

She nodded.

Donnie hesitated. "Yeah, okay. So, you want them back? I can bring them over or stick them in your mailbox or something." He took the coins from his pocket Elaine had given him for pay. "Maybe I could give this back to you? To pay for them?"

Elaine shook her head. "Not necessary."

Again, hesitation and then a tiny smile floated across Donnie's face, giving Elaine a full glimpse of the more attractive man he might become someday. "Well, okay then, Mrs. Tilden. I appreciate the job and would be pleased to come back for more chores if you'll have me. And if you meant what you said, I'd be grateful if you'd cut some of those yellowish flowers for my ma. Thank you."

CHAPTER TWENTY THREE

early May 1955

Something had to be done about Perry. Especially since things were going so much better with Bud. Her husband was definitely more spontaneous and romantic in their day-to-day interactions. Things weren't perfect but since her encounter with Perry, she had realized how much she loved Bud and what they were building together felt strong and secure to her now.

Still, family functions made her nervous. She was constantly looking over her shoulder to check Perry's reactions or worry about accidentally brushing against him in the kitchen. She was attracted to him, flattered by his attention but she could never risk a fling and hurt Bud or Olivia. And if she were honest she knew that was all it could be-a fling. Perry was no more enthralled by her than she by him. They'd let themselves be swept up by some clandestine excitement. A diversion was all they could ever be to one another and at what cost? But she had to confront him very soon so she could stop avoiding him. It was bad enough trying to avoid Lloyd.

Last week she had rounded the corner in the grocery store only to bang her cart into Fanny's. Elaine greeted Fanny and turned her attention to Fanny's little boy. Four-year-old Davey smiled from the well of the shopping cart, holding cereal boxes and quietly humming.

"Hello, Fanny. Hi there, Davey. What a nice little boy you are, helping your mama this morning. I hope when my little boy is bigger he'll be a good helper like you." Fanny smiled proudly but before she or Davey could respond, Lloyd appeared with packages wrapped in butcher paper and insinuated himself into their conversation.

"Yeah, the little mutt's okay most days. Be nice if he looked more like his mother, though, instead of ... ." His hand gently ruffled the boy's hair before Lloyd's glance took in the contents of the cart. His eyes shifted to Fanny. "Are all those items from our list or did he talk you into something extra?"

Fanny colored and her eyes were guarded. "Only some pudding, Lloyd. And you like that as much as Davey so I thought it'd be fine."

Lloyd locked his gaze on his wife but swiveled toward Elaine before answering. "Got to keep an eye on the budget. Job pays good but the ole lady here knows how to spend it fast, too." He reached down and chucked Davey under the chin. His voice gained volume. "Ain't that right, sport? Your ma's real good at spending my money."

The little boy looked uncertain as his eyes shifted between his mother and the loud man before him. Elaine intervened. "Well, it looks like she's doing you proud, Lloyd. Nothing says prosperity better than a well-fed family. Looks like you've got that. A beautiful wife and a well-mannered little man to help his mother. No wonder you look good. Nothing enhances handsome more than living a satisfying life."

She felt as if she were rambling on out of control, but her words cut off Lloyd's bluster. The big man blinked and studied Elaine. "I believe you're right." He allowed himself a pleased grunt and a pleasant nod, preening a little. He threw an arm around Fanny and herded her forward, a little strut in his step. Fanny tossed Elaine a grateful look before heading to the checkout.

Delighted she'd caught Lloyd off guard and overcome her own nervousness, Elaine congratulated herself. An argument was deflected.

Lloyd left without being snide or surly, was even momentarily pleasant. A minor victory!

Now her thoughts returned to her present dilemma. If only dealing with Perry could be as easy as dealing with Lloyd. Almost on cue, Perry's truck swung into the yard. Perhaps he was here to return Bud's tools. Elaine met him at the door, and handed him freshly brewed coffee. He grinned. "Nothing stronger, pretty lady? Bud's not here, we could loosen up a bit."

Elaine refused to let him fluster her. "I know you're teasing, Perry. Bud called a few minutes from the lodge office and he told me you'd be stopping by. He'll be back himself in twenty minutes so you're just talking big, but Perry?" She waited for his full attention. "This flirting with me has got to stop. Now. Today."

She could visualize Perry's charm going into overdrive. He leaned across the table toward her. "Now Elaine, no need getting all flapped. You told me last fall that you weren't interested in anything real physical but what'd be the harm in a kiss here and there? Keeps things interesting, don't you think?" His eyes twinkled.

Elaine shook her head. "No, Per, I don't think so. And what you're leaving out is Bud and Olivia. Even if this stayed as innocent as you think it could, don't you realize how devastated Olivia would be if she knew what you were doing? And what about Bud? Bad enough if his wife makes eyes at another man but his brother? Adds insult to injury there, Perry. And there's another thing to consider, too."

Her brother-in-law sipped his coffee before he spoke. "Okay, I'll bite. What's the other thing?"

"The truth, Perry. And the truth is I love my husband, and I'm willing to bet that you love Olivia, too. I can't imagine why you tomcat around when I know deep down you adore that girl. I know you do! If you didn't there's nothing to prevent you from leaving her. So I'm guessing there's something here more complicated. There's got to be a reason she hasn't given you the heave-ho." She paused. In for a penny, in for a pound, Elaine took a breath and continued, "Doesn't she like sex?"

Perry's eyes flickered and she knew she had hit a nerve with her brother-in-law. He stood and looked at his feet. Then slowly he raised his head. He wasn't smiling anymore. "No Elaine, that's not it. If you must know, Livvie is a wonderful partner in that respect. And you're right, I do love Olivia. That's not it at all. It's more like fishing. You ever hear of catch and release? Well, you see… ."

His explanation was cut short by Bud's arrival. Her husband swept into the house, bouncing a laughing Jimmy and supplying a menagerie of animal noises.

"Hey brother," Bud greeted his sibling as he sidled toward his wife. Bud set Jimmy on the floor and wrapped his arms around Elaine, surprising her with a lingering kiss full on her mouth. He'd never been that demonstrative with others present before her valentine note. Maybe he was taking this intimacy thing seriously. Good.

Perry's eyes took in the kiss his brother delivered to Elaine and pretended he was chagrined. "Whoa! Time for my exit before you guys embarrass me." He paused at the door. "Nite, you lovebirds!"

Chapter Twenty Four

late May 1955

Curiosity bubbled within Elaine like the broth in Dorothy's famous Resort Stew Extraordinaire. It was so unlike Olivia to request a meeting. Not that Elaine minded the summons. Olivia and Morag were the paste that kept her bonded to the pleasantries in Mashkiki Rapids. But Olivia's wish to meet here, alone, in the picnic area past the resort, where they wouldn't be overheard, piqued Elaine's desire to indulge in some girlish, secret, sharing.

When she reached the oft-painted roughhewn tables, Elaine spotted her sister-in-law. Leave it to Olivia to choose the most select spot for a talk. The table was situated close enough to catch a puff, a baby's breath of breeze from the lake and provided just enough shade to shield them from the ever-present scrutiny of the women driving past en route to the Ladies' Circle. It was a perfect spring day. Gleefully Elaine noticed the wicker basket Olivia had placed so precisely in front of her. No doubt it contained some sandwiches made with fresh Scandinavian rye, some of Livvy's watermelon pickles and maybe a shorty bottle or two of Coca-Cola. Lord, how she loved the sweet behaviors of her favorite in-law.

"Hi sweetie." Elaine's greeting to Olivia produced a grin, an acknowledgement of the closeness of the two Tilden women. "What's up? I'm dying to know." She smiled back at Olivia and experienced a tinge of alarm. Olivia was nothing if not calm and selfless, but her smile faded as quickly as it was flashed. She began to gnaw a bit at her lower lip, avoiding Elaine's gaze.

"Olivia, what's wrong? What is it? Come on sweetie, talk to me." Elaine sat beside her best friend and put her arm around Olivia's shoulders. Olivia drew a steady breath and looked Elaine squarely in the eye.

"Elaine, I need help and you're the only one who can help me pull this off."

"What do you need, Livvy? You know I'd do anything for you." What could be plaguing Olivia? Elaine gave her a slight squeeze and felt again how fragile, how wren like Olivia was.

"It's Perry. I need to talk to you about Perry." Olivia looked sad.

Elaine's insides turned icily frigid. Not the pretty crystalline ice that dotted the walkways on a crisp January morning, but the ice that hung like daggers on the backs of the wheel wells on Bud's trucks. Oh no, not this. Oh God, I promised I would stop and I did! Please, please. I never wanted to hurt Olivia. Please don't have her ask me for details on what did and did not happen between me and Perry. Horribly uneasy, she concentrated on what Olivia was saying.

"... and I know the talk around town about Perry. I have for a long time. I know there are some of the Rapids women–maybe you, too–who wonder if I know about his running around, if he is running around. And if I do, how do I stand it? Well, I do know it and I do care. But ... " Olivia brushed away Elaine's protesting sigh. "There's a reason I put up with it."

Olivia's directness seemed to desert her here, like the remnants of an afternoon shower in August. Elaine waited, still not sure where this revelation would lead. Olivia cleared her throat, a soft rumbling sound emanating from her.

"The thing I want most, and what Perry really wants too, is a baby. What most folks don't know–you're the first, Elaine–is that Perry and I went to a doctor in Milwaukee last year. When all of you thought we were on a second honeymoon, gallivanting at the state fair, Per and I were with a doctor who specializes in ... this kind of stuff. Fertility." Olivia's cheeks looked like Oriental poppies now and tears started to seep from her eyes. Elaine took her hand.

Olivia rushed on. "We found out the reason we can't have a baby is ... is ... Perry." And I think that's why he takes up with other women now and then. All of this started up when we came back from Milwaukee. I think he can't bear to think about all this. I know he loves me, Elaine, but it's like he needs to prove something to himself. Like if all these women want him, he's still a real man." Olivia's voice trailed off.

She swallowed. "And that's where you come in. You and Bud. I want to adopt a baby but Perry is so proud and he won't talk to me about it. I got information when I was in Milwaukee but he won't listen, but I know he'll listen to you and Bud."

Shame washed over Elaine like the tiny lake waves she could see from the corner of her eye. Looking directly at Olivia was impossible. Could they start this conversation over. She knew she must refuse her best friend. How could she and Bud speak to Perry about his sex life, about what was private between Olivia and Per? Olivia was right, Perry was nothing if not proud with a capital P. And if she let Bud take the lead? What was to prevent an embarrassed Perry from flying off the handle and saying too much? Perry might think Bud was lecturing him about other women. What would prevent Perry from blurting something about Elaine and her indiscretions? Before guilt could transport her to that night in Lover's Lane, Elaine felt a tiny talon's grip on her hand. It was Olivia, weaving her fingers with Elaine's.

"Besides ... I don't know how to say this ... but I've got to somehow." Olivia looked teary but there was no quaver in her voice as she locked eyes with Elaine. Olivia took a deep breath. "You owe me, Elaine."

Oh boy! Elaine had not felt shame like this since her last conversation with her father. She couldn't meet Olivia's eyes. She knew! Olivia knew her husband was flirting with his brother's wife, with her best friend, and had said nothing. How horrible that must have been for her! What to say to her now?

"Livvy, you need to know ... I didn't ... we didn't ... it's not what you think ... ." Nothing was coming out with any coherence.

Olivia reached for Elaine's hands. "It's okay Elaine, really. It's okay. I don't care how far it did or didn't get. That's not quite true. I do care but I don't believe you betrayed me. Not ... " She struggled for a word. "like that. I know you and Perry too well to believe that."

"Livvy, it was a kiss. Just a kiss ... a stupid kiss. Livvy, I would die rather than hurt you. You've got to know that. I ... we ... couldn't hurt you or Bud." Perhaps she was being generous with the "we." If she could keep Olivia from hating her, she could afford to let the woman think that Perry practiced restraint as well.

"It's alright. I know it sounds like I'm blackmailing you, and you must think I'm terrible! But Elaine, that's how important this is to me! I want a baby so bad and if this will enlist your help, I have no pride. Just tell me you'll do it."

Tearing up, Elaine reached for Olivia. No more words passed as two of them cried until Elaine thought she would crumble. Finally, she held her sister-in-law at arm's length. "Okay Olivia, yes. I'll do it. Whatever you want, I'll try and help."

Elaine thought about how much she loved Jimmy. How much Bud loved him too. What she would do if she lost either of them. She thought about Olivia's generous spirit. Was this what the nuns meant by atonement? Handling things with Bud would be hard, but how to handle Perry?

CHAPTER TWENTY FIVE

Jimmy was busy at play and gave Elaine the peace she wanted while she listened to the music from the record player. She gathered the ingredients for tonight's special dinner on the counter and sang along with the recording. "Smoke Gets in Your Eyes" was a beautiful song. Maybe she'd play it later for the two of them.

Bud generally was later getting home when he finished this run from Wausau. She'd give Jimmy an early bath and put him to bed before tending to herself.

An hour later, Elaine heard Bud drive into the yard. She turned on the record player, checked her hair in the small mirror by the kitchen door and lit the candles on the table. She remembered to dab on a little perfume. She knew Bud would notice that fragrance as well as the hearty and inviting smell of meat loaf coming from the kitchen.

"Hey, Babe." Bud stopped and hung his jacket before proceeding to the kitchen. He sniffed appreciably at the aroma of the meal in progress. One glance at the candles and the table set for two made his smile to bloom even more as he looked at his wife. Elaine moved toward him and rested her palms on his chest. "Hey, yourself sweetheart. Are you ready for a quiet evening with just the two of us?"

Elaine heard the laugh she loved so dearly. Bud kissed her cheek and drew her into a hug. "I'm not sure what the occasion is, Elaine, or what it is you may want, but after I get my belly filled with that delicious meal you fixed, I'm all for waltzing us right into the bedroom. Leave the dishes and let me rub your feet. Maybe something else? What do you say?"

Elaine thought this was a great idea; a prelude to the talk about Olivia and Perry. She laughed and kissed him back before stepping toward the stove. "Let's have a leisurely dinner first and maybe I'll let you convince me." The Platters were singing again about that smoke, Bud was humming and Elaine was jubilant about her strategy. What could be better? An unrushed meal with time for an intimate conversation that didn't include childish chatter, some much needed alone time later with her loving and interested husband, and an opportunity to keep her promise to Olivia.

Later, Elaine stood at the kitchen table, hands on her hips, a dish towel draped across her shoulder. They had finished their meal and she'd said her piece. To his credit Bud listened attentively without interruption, slowly sipping his coffee, now and then nodding his head. She wanted his reaction to all that Olivia requested of them.

Bud stared at the table top while she spoke, then slowly raised his eyes to meet Elaine's. He threw a watered down smile her way and shook his head. "No, darlin'. No. There's no way I'm getting involved in my brother's sex life, love life, whatever. No sir. No can do."

"But Bud. Come on! I promised Olivia and you know she's never asked us for anything before." Elaine slipped into the chair next to her husband and laid her hand on his muscular forearm, taking care not to let any hint of a whine be evident in her voice. Her fingers stroked the hairs on his skin. "Bud? She needs us."

A not entirely unsympathetic chuckle came from him. "Us? I would wager she asked you, Elaine, not me. Am I right? Uh huh, I thought so and anyway, I don't know as I can talk to Per about adoption." Glancing at his wife for some understanding Bud continued. "Come on, he'd know I was somehow privy to all his medical stuff and dang it, Lainie! Us Tilden men, well, we just don't do that."

Elaine squeezed his arm. "Bud! What if it was us? What if we didn't have our baby? What if you didn't have Jimmy? Isn't that sort of the same thing? We don't talk about it and your name is on his birth certificate, but it's like you adopted him, right?"

Bud's surprised expression turned thoughtful as she hurried on. "Yes, I thought so. Don't you want your brother to have that in his life too? Olivia says all they have to do is meet with a social worker in Wausau and that'll get the ball rolling."

Bud moved to the kitchen counter, carefully pouring and stirring his coffee before turning back to her. "Now Elaine, first off, you know I love Jimmy! I'm not saying I'm not sympathetic and I didn't say I'm indisposed to what Olivia is asking, I'm just saying there's definitely another way to go about this." Bud shut his eyes and after just a heartbeat or two, a wicked grin crept across his lips.

Elaine clapped her hands in anticipation. He'd thought of something she hadn't considered. "What? What, Bud!"

She waited for him to sit again. "There are two things about my brother that are unshakable. One is I know with 100% certainty that he never, ever breaks his word. If he promises he'll do something you can take that to the bank. I've never known him to break his word." He looked at his wife for agreement. At her nod he continued.

"The second thing," and here the wicked grin returned. "I've never known him to pass up any opportunity to flirt with a pretty girl. If he can make her blush, he moves into phase two. If he can steal a kiss, all the better. It's kind of like a game to him and he fancies himself the Lew Burdette of love!"

Elaine was uncomfortable. Was this Bud's way of telling her he knew about her indiscretion with Perry? But when she swung her gaze to his eyes, she found no guile or hint of duplicity there. No recrimination, just one fellow stating facts as he perceived it. Another thought was scratching at the back of her mind. Was this the catch and release thing Perry had referenced and Bud had explained? She'd never considered the idea that if she hadn't halted the action with Perry, maybe Perry would have. Maybe he was all about the chase, the pursuit. Did Per felt the same way about Olivia as she did about Bud? Perhaps she wasn't as sophisticated as she thought! This was getting more complicated and she forced herself to focus on what Bud was saying.

"So," he continued, "I figure the only thing we have to do is expose him to a little of that flirting closer to home. If Livvie plays her cards right, she'll get a promise locked down. It's not as though she's without feminine charms of her own!"

Elaine mulled this over. "Could work. How do you propose we do that?"

Bud spun the coffee cup in his saucer and turned his gaze toward Elaine. "I figure that's up to you ladies. If the two of you put your heads together I bet you could conjure up some gentle treachery. You can think of all kinds of female traps to snare Perry. Maybe some soft music, new perfume, a pretty dress with a neckline down to there. Throw in a little S-E-X and that boy stands no chance; he's a goner. Use some of those smarts you have, city girl!"

A laugh burst from Elaine's throat. It had been a long time since he called her that. And maybe Bud was right. Lord knows that a little active initiative on her part had helped her own marriage.

A matching laugh, full and throaty erupted from Bud. "I hope my brother knows what a lucky man he is. Probably the second luckiest in the entire world!"

Elaine smiled, taking delight in her husband's exuberance. It took a few seconds for her brain to catch up. When his words did register, she laughed along with him.

"Yep, the second!" he declared. "That's because I'm number one!"

She set the dishcloth on the drainboard, took the coffee cup from her husband's hand and pulled him to his feet. They laughed like kindergartners and raced to the bedroom.

Days later, Elaine awakened from another satisfied, post-coital sleep. Slivers of the early morning sun poked their way through the tiny spaces where the curtains didn't quite meet. Every inch of her skin felt glowing and refreshed. She glanced over at Bud and gently, gently removed the leg he had flung over hers.

She thought about the week-long chats she'd been having with Livvy and Bud about "Project Perry." Mmmm, sharing these intimate plans had done wonders for her own love life. Wonder if last night was as satisfactory for Olivia and Perry? Last night the blush on Olivia's cheeks was rosier than the sunrise over Trout Lake and how absolutely gorgeous her sister-in-law appeared after Elaine helped her with a little primping and advice. If Olivia followed through, today might bring the first of many small miracles to the Tilden family.

She swung her feet from the bed, donned a robe and headed to the kitchen to answer the phone. Not yet 6:30 on a Saturday morning. A call this early could mean trouble. Bud was here with her, but Richard ... or Dorothy? Her head cleared quickly as she grabbed the receiver before the next ring.

"Hello" she tried to keep any anxiety out of her voice. "Hello?" A sound came from the other end. Was that a woman weeping or laughing?

"Elaine!" It was Olivia and she was definitely laughing. "Can you take over my library hours next week? Perry and I are going to Wausau!"

Chapter Twenty Six

June 1955

It was late afternoon and Elaine was walking to her vehicle, Jimmy slung over her shoulder, when she passed the Suds 'N Wash. She looked through the window, and noticed Mary Gunilda was nowhere in sight but spied Mavis Chapman and Minnie Soulier in their customary spots. Bud had gone into Minocqua with Richard to help haul weekend supplies, and she needed to be at the lodge to pick him up. She knew she had time for a visit if she didn't tarry too long.

"Boozhoo." Elaine entered and spoke to the laundromat's sole visitors. She took pleasure in greeting the Indian ladies in their own tongue. She heard little Ojibwe spoken in other public places but loved to listen when the sisters conversed with one another. Mavis and Minnie returned her welcome. Minnie reached out for a sleepy Jimmy and with little fuss transferred the toddler to her own shoulder.

They exchanged pleasantries as Elaine sat and checked her shopping list. Her eyes stopped at aspirin, my everyday medicine.

"You know Mavis, when we visit, I've never taken advantage of your knowledge. I've wondered so many times about the origin of this town's name. I know Mashkiki means medicine in Ojibwe but no one has ever been able to tell me what the medicine is, specifically. Bud always tells me I'm too curious but I want to know. Is there a certain root or herb that had particular healing powers? Maybe something found here along the river or near the falls?" Elaine looked expectantly at the sisters, wondering if they considered her questions too nosey.

Mavis studied her and turned to her sibling. She spoke to her quietly in the language Elaine thought sounded ancient and primal. Minnie listened and responded with a lengthier answer. Mavis remained silent for a moment and then grinned.

"Yeah, you're right Minnie, I had to think about that one." The older Indian woman swiveled to face Elaine. "Had to check with the family expert here. Minnie really understands the language better than I do but I'm better at explaining. First of all–this is what I had to check with Minnie–the translation for mashkiki doesn't exactly mean medicine, although that's pretty close. Ojibwe is a complicated language and sometimes it takes longer to actually say a word than it would take to draw a picture. See, our word for coffee is muckadaymashkeekiwabu which is literally "black medicine water." You can hear the medicine part in there–the sound of mashkiki, right?"

Elaine was hearing more of an explanation than she bargained for but also understood that she was getting a glimpse into the culture of these ladies. She wanted to respect that. Besides, this was pretty interesting. She limited her response. "Right."

There was a pause and a quick consultation with Minnie before Mavis continued. "So one translation of mashkiki might be more on the order of "that which heals" which is how the white man and some Shinnobs interpret it–as a thing, as a medicine." She looked at Elaine to see if she was following.

"But isn't that kind of splitting hairs? 'That which heals' is a pretty accurate definition of medicine, isn't it?"

"Ahh, you missed what Mavis just said," Minnie piped in. "The white man interpreted it as a thing, and it can be. But what Mavis is trying to say is "that which heals" could also be a person."

Elaine beamed with understanding. "Ahhh." Of course, this definition was far more enriching than simply "medicine." Underneath their wisecracks and good humor, these women were very wise. When she left them she always felt enriched. A glance at the clock on the wall told her that she needed to move quickly if she were to pick up Bud at the time they had agreed.

"Thanks ladies. I'll check back in next time I'm here and maybe we can share some coffee." She shifted the sleeping Jimmy back onto her shoulder and started to the door. Their shared conversation and something undefinable made her show off what she had learned in a book from the library. She knew they'd get a kick out of this and struggled to keep a straight face. "Giminadan Gagiginonshiwan." It was nice talking to you. She hoped her pronunciation was passable.

Four obsidian eyes widened and Mavis started to cackle as Minnie smiled and nodded at Elaine with frank approval. "Gigawabamin nagutch. See you later."

～♋

"I don't know," said Richard, sliding into the kitchen with a sturdy cardboard box, bulging with grocery items. His legs were bent at the knees. Elaine looked past her in-laws and spied the back of Richard's well-traveled truck. There were at least six additional boxes in the vehicle's bed along with two hefty, fifty-pound flour bags. She saw the familiar blue, plaid sleeve of her husband's shirt on the other side of the truck as he hefted another large box. Handing Jimmy to Rachel who did better at babysitting than she did at organizing, Elaine went into the kitchen to assist.

She and Lotty unloaded boxes as the men hauled in the foodstuffs. Dorothy took inventory, counting each extra-large can. Finally the task was finished and everyone took satisfaction in the neatly lined shelves, filled to capacity with what they would need for this busy week. Elaine handed Bud and Richard a cup of coffee and took up the thread of her father-in-law's conversation. "What don't you know, Dad?"

"Aw, this parade thing that Lovey dreamed up. Here in Mash-kiki? You heard about this?" Dorothy gave him a sidelong glance as he continued. "Sure, I think it's a good idea to have a commemoration of Independence Day and it might keep more of the folk here instead of having them skedaddle to Minocqua to eat their meals. I'm just hoping Lovey knows what she's doing. She's drove Roland just about crazy with her details. I stopped there yesterday for coffee and she has a list— a list—on a clipboard! Roland's been taking his lunches with him instead of coming home at noon. I wouldn't wonder; she looks like a banty hen version of George Patton marching around her kitchen command post. All she needs are some pearl handled pistols strapped to her apron." He chuckled with the others as they pictured Lovey at work.

"Well," Lotty seemed anxious to contribute, "Oscar told me that the Minocqua Chamber of Commerce ..." She was interrupted here by a snort from Richard. Dorothy gave her husband a playful slap and encour-aged Lotty to continue. "... that they kind of snubbed the Mashkiki folks last year. The Williamses and the Robertsons were all set to have a small float and no one called them back to say if they were welcome or not. And then when the Drum and Bugle Corps did show up, that snooty parade master said they couldn't march because they didn't have proper uniforms. Oscar wasn't very pleased about that!" All nodded assent, assuring Lotty that her interjections were noted.

"All too true Lotty, but I don't know that letting my sister organize her own separate doings here is going to come off any better. I just hate to see folks disappointed is all." This from Richard.

"Richard Menard Tilden, you stop that right now!" Apparently Dorothy had enough of this if she thought using Richard's middle name was warranted. Elaine had a hunch this was a continuation of an earlier discussion. Dorothy moved the box of Fels-Naptha to its place on the highest shelf, picked up a stray spatula and turned to address her husband. "If you're really worried that folks might be disappointed then maybe what you ... " She paused and glanced around the small group assembled in the kitchen, motioning with the spatula as though conducting a small orchestra. " ... what we need to do, is help Lovey. I think a Fourth of July celebration right here is just what we need to put a little pep back in the village. What could it hurt? Business wise or just showing a little support for Lovey. Could be a keeper."

Richard rocked back on his heels, a Tilden trait, a mannerism Elaine noticed Bud perform as well, and grinned at his wife as though they were alone. "Good Lord woman, I love it when you get feisty! That mood gonna last all day? Maybe into tonight?" He lifted his eyebrows expectantly. Everyone but Dorothy burst into laughter. Dorothy tried mightily to glare, but after a moment her lip began to quiver and the magical lyrical laugh that Elaine found so enchanting rang above the rest.

Dorothy joined her husband at the sideboard, put her arm around his shoulder and said only, "Oh, you!" When the atmosphere in the kitchen returned to normal, Richard hugged Dorothy before he rose to his feet. "Okay, I've got a bag in the truck yet that Lovey asked me to pick up for her. When I take it over, I'll ask about helping out with her danged parade. Satisfied?"

Chapter Twenty Seven

July 4, 1955

"Okay, so is everyone ready to pro-ceed?" This from Perry who in nervous excitement tapped his foot and pulled on his earlobe. He leaned against the newest of the vehicles from Howard's Motors. He was designated to lead off the festivities by driving the Parade Marshal, Aunt Lovey. She sat in his passenger seat, bedecked in new hat with pearly, pink gloves to match. A cluster of grapes presented to her at the lodge pre-parade breakfast, adorned her best dress.

Richard looked about him and saw his entire family ready to help initiate the first Mashkiki Rapids Independence Day Parade. "I think everyone is here but Everett Hobson. He's the guy from Sayner with the convertible that I'm using to drive the guest of honor."

Bud balanced Jimmy securely on one hip, and reached for Lainie's with his free hand. "Looks like the entire town has turned out for this. Maybe half of Pullette too," Bud murmured. They walked two blocks through a few dozen people and then headed toward one of the long, wooden benches in front of the feedstore where Morag waited for them, Mary in tow. Maybe in scope it couldn't compare to some of the parades in Madison or Chicago but Elaine couldn't remember being more excited about attending any urban cavalcade. Already she heard the band playing just beyond the curve of the street and knew they would be advancing shortly.

"Here we go!" Bud said to Jimmy,"you can sit here with Mommy. I have to go back to march with the soldier men and then I'll come back to be with you. Okay? Come on, Mary, I'll see you to your unit." The boy smiled and Bud turned to Elaine. She ran her fingers over the rows of campaign ribbons and checked the tie of his dress uniform. He gave his wife a quick peck on the cheek, exchanged her hand for Mary's and hastened to join the others from the newly formed Veteran honor guard.

Morag smoothed her skirt and looked at her friend. "All this is really rousing, eh, Elaine? I can hardly wait to see Ed in his uniform. He was wearing that verra same uniform the first time I saw him. He looked so handsome, I was positively gobsmacked at the sight of him!" The Scot wrapped her arms around herself. " We've gone to some of the celebrations in Minocqua in years past but this is my first American parade in Mashkiki. When it's over, we that wants head to the cemetery and then the park for our picnic? Have I got that right? Maybe the fireworks later?"

Elaine nodded. "There'll be a short prayer at the cemetery and a laying of the wreath. If this goes well then maybe next year we'll have a separate parade and ceremony for Memorial Day. Wouldn't that be something! The wreath is placed by the honored guest in the last car, whoever that is. Lovey and Richard are pretty hush hush about it. There'll be a gun salute and then on to the park. Bud is bringing horseshoes and a few decks of cards. If we get there first I'll have Bud save you a spot."

For a few minutes they occupied Jimmy by counting flags, and pointing out people they knew. Elaine noticed Mr. Cassidy with his wife seated across the street. Alice Cassidy sat smiling, holding her husband's hand and occasionally peeking down at what looked like new shoes. Elaine was glad to see them, this must be one of Mrs. Cassidy's good days. At a gentle tap on her shoulder, Elaine turned to see Minnie and Mavis followed by an assemblage of children and grandchildren. A few little ones pulled up short to see what their grandmas had to say to this stranger.

Most headed directly toward a shaded spot down the block where several other reservation vehicles were parked. "Nice day for a parade, Elaine. Have a good time."

"Thanks Mrs. ... Minnie. Hope your day is good, too." Elaine smiled at a pair of twins holding hands who looked to be about five. They smiled shyly and ran ahead to join an older, native girl herding all the youngsters. It looked like all of Mashkiki was out for the festivities.

Elaine squinted down the street to see if there was any activity. Spying Fanny and little Davey across the street, she and Morag waved until Fanny shyly waved back. Fanny made it a point last week in the grocery to turn from Lloyd and congratulate Elaine on the article in the County Gazette announcing the grant money allocation given to the Mashkiki library due to Elaine's efforts. Though Fanny's comments were warm and sincere, Elaine could feel resentment seething from Lloyd. Undoubtedly he saw this newest Tilden attention as another indignation he had to endure. His bitterness and sullen demeanor seemed to have no limits.

"I do like seeing that girl getting out once in a while, Elaine," Morag pronounced, "but of course her being over there probably means we have to put up with viewing that jackass of a husband when he joins her. Ach, well."

Just then they saw the motorcade heading out. "Look Jimmy! Here comes Uncle Perry! Way down there in that blue car. See, he's driving Aunt Lovey. She's the big cheese here today."

Jimmy frowned until he could make out the familiar face of his dad's younger brother. Then the boy was all but bouncing off Elaine's knee. They all waved wildly as Per slowed the big Merc down and tooted the horn at Jimmy. Aunt Lovey blew him a kiss before Morag redirected the little boy's attention. "JimBoy, ya do na want to miss your da coming. Look at those flags a fluttering now JimBoy! See, there he is and Ed, too!"

And sure enough, the recently formed marching contingent of the American Legion of Mashkiki swung into view, all eleven of them. Six of them, the youngest fellows and Charlie, still fit in the uniforms they wore in World War II and Korea. Elaine was pleased to note that two of the soldiers were from the reservation. Max Stewart, Killian Donahue and Severin Gustafson, World War I vets, now late middle-aged and a little thick around the middle, looked smart in their black trousers and new red jackets. Names were embroidered over the left front pocket. Bud said in the future that all of the town's vets might be dressed alike. Elaine was glad they didn't have the funds as yet. Bud looked so gorgeous in his Army uniform, much more handsome than Alan Ladd in any of those war movies she'd seen.

Now the group was directly in front of Jimmy. The three, older men led the group bearing the flags: American, State of Wisconsin and the new one: American Legion Post 126, Mashkiki Rapids, Wisconsin. They were followed by two rows of three servicemen each, all carrying rifles and stepping in unison to Charlie's pronouncement "Left, left. Left, right, left." Those in uniform also wore black arm bands to commemorate their fallen comrades. Elaine admitted that as obnoxious as Lloyd Defoe could be, he looked quite handsome in his uniform. The tallest and broadest of all the men, his eyes were clear and his bearing regal. She was glad for Fanny that Lloyd looked so admirable today. If only his demeanor was as sterling as his handsome good looks.

Ed Gunderson was pushing forty and could still get into the clothes he wore at twenty. Morag liked to brag that he could still fit into his wedding coat while she patted her own ample thigh and proclaimed "No one'd accuse me a that, now would they?"

Elaine watched Morag rise and blow a kiss to her ramrod straight husband. She also watched Ed twitch his cheek just a little as if he caught it. Morag giggled and waved animatedly in appreciation of a husband who played along with her frivolity.

Elaine helped Jimmy stand as she placed a hand over her heart. She was delighted to see that Jimmy did as well. The soldiers were moving by them and she glanced up to see Bud's deep blue Norwegian eyes dart toward them, saw that he glimpsed Jimmy's efforts at patriotism. A small smile played over his lips as the Legion moved on. She noticed how wide her son's eyes appeared and wondered if he'd remember his first parade. Bud wore only a few of the campaign medals he was entitled to wear, though he had given in and let her affix the Distinguished Service Cross to his uniform. She was determined to ignore the image of Lloyd's scowl and squinted eyes as she beamed at her husband. No pettiness on Lloyd's part would ruin her day.

The fledgling city band advanced toward the front of the feedstore. Their brass was polished to a high gleam, hats squarely placed on each head. Only 14 musicians but their rendition of "On Wisconsin" wasn't half bad—on key and fairly lively. She was surprised to see that the oldest member was the town librarian, Rose Sorenson, marching along quite sprightly and playing a flute. Today was chock full of tiny surprises.

There was a short lull, a gap in the lineup, before the tractors appeared. Two spiffy Allis Chalmers rigs followed a pair of John Deeres and huffed their way down Main Street. All farm vehicles had ribbons tied to their exhaust pipes. A few ribbons were scorched by the heat emitted but looked festive nonetheless. Last was Oscar's father on his big, golden Minneapolis Moline. Sitting on the fender, one hand holding onto the light assembly for balance was Lotty, her feet braced on the seat. She wore a new red and white, checked blouse and a huge grin. Her white-blond hair was tied back and Elaine thought with the blush on her cheeks. Lotty never looked prettier.

As the monster tractor moved by at five miles an hour, Lotty removed one hand for a quick wave and call to Jimmy. Five tractors chugged by, with signs lettered on white cardboard and fixed to the drawbars. "Remember Our Veterans" and "You are Not Forgotten." This was one purpose of the day, Elaine reminded herself. She swallowed and noticed Morag swipe her eyes before their attention was drawn to the oncoming units. Morag leaned in close and whispered. "Well, I suppose we should be grateful the parade committee decided not to grace us with any decorated manure spreaders." That was Morag, dispelling any teary emotions with her droll commentary.

A float fashioned by the church ladies auxiliary was next. Half a dozen choir members, complete with robes, sang with gusto. Earlier drowned out by the tractors, they were now pouring forth "God Bless America" to everyone in earshot.

A 4-H float with members holding small livestock followed close on the choir's heels. Their sign proclaimed, "We Are Your Legacy." The boys were dressed in pressed, white shirts, the girls in their best Sunday dresses and patent leather shoes. One of the boys looked straight ahead while he snaked a hand over to nudge the girl beside him. Rewarded by a shy smile, he pretended not to acknowledge the girl's response. Big city or tiny village, the games of adolescence and novice flirtation were the same everywhere.

Next came a string of cars from Howard's Motors in Sayner. Lovey'd agonized over the parade lineups and concluded that one way to stretch out the spectacle was to involve local merchants. Lovey asked shy husband Roland to speak to Mr. Howard and see if he wanted to be part of Mashkiki's parade. Realizing there was no parade entry fee and free advertising was involved, Mr. Howard was soon won over. He promised eight, clean, quiet vehicles, beribboned and decked out with patriotic slogans. Lovey not only acquired a unit guaranteed to capture the interest of any male over the age of 12, but one to make the length of the parade more impressive.

Next was the float crafted by the Senior Ladies Quilting Circle. All the women had the same hairdo: curls tight to the head with some poof at the ends, courtesy of Toni Home Permanents purchased at the dry goods store during Marge's pre-parade sale. Some coiffures were topped by church dress hats; most ladies were bare headed to showcase their modern hairstyles.

The quilters surrendered the spotlight to a crowd of little girls following them. Here was Madlyn trying to keep the Twirling Tots in straight rows. With her was her assistant, Olivia, pushing a stroller. In it, fast asleep was a two-year-old girl. How lucky for all the Tildens when Perry and Olivia had been told at the Wausau agency that if they would consider an older baby instead of a newborn, that a child was available. Here was the evidence, Annabelle Tilden, nicknamed Punkie by her proud new father.

Virtually every little village girl aged five to twelve was present in this group, each grasping a shiny silver-shanked, white-tipped baton, courtesy of another sale at Marge's Dry Goods. Some were fairly coordinated, but only a few managed to master any wrist movements. All were trying their best to look like a budding Miss America by marching in unison, some smiling toothless grins at friends and parents along the way. Wild applause greeted the little girls as they moved down the street. Olivia was right. It didn't matter how well they performed; this unit was an unabashed hit with the viewers.

Morag nudged Elaine and waved at her daughter. "Ach, now I dinna think my little Mary would look so bonnie among those older girls, but Elaine, my babe's the beauty of the lot is she not now?" Elaine threw an arm over Morag's shoulder and gave her a quick hug. "She sure is!" Bud agreed as he and Ed joined the women. Their part in the festivities was over until the gathering at the cemetery. "Looks just like her mother!" Ed added as he sidled over to his wife.

Cars belonging to local merchants followed, hand lettered signs advertising "Markeson's Food Mart Celebrates Independence Day" and "Feed at Good Prices for 40 Years, God Bless America!" fastened on the trunks. Waving crepe paper streamers of red and blue, merchants' children hung from the car windows.

Finally the group Bud and Elaine had anticipated drew within sight and hearing. The Drum and Bugle Corps, complete with starched white shirts, white gloves, new blue and gold striped ties and best of all, new hats with bright, blue plumes, marched toward them. As soon as the color guard was visible, all those sitting stood. Every spectator could hear Oscar calling out a cadence "Hep, hep" as the drums accompanied his vocals.

Elaine was grateful the group stopped where Jimmy could see them. She didn't realize this placement was no accident until the Corps executed a smart right turn and focused as one to where Bud stood. The group gave a salute and pointed their horns and drum sticks in his direction. They were honoring him! Elaine often forgot that despite Bud's humility and lack of bravado, that Bud was a bona fide war hero to their friends and neighbors, perhaps the only one Mashkiki could ever claim.

Bud was clearly embarrassed but acknowledged their courtesy with his own smart salute. At a signal from the drummers, the group stopped marching in place. With a flourish from Oscar, all buglers lifted horns to their lips and began to play.

Elaine had heard them practicing near the lodge every night for the last two weeks and realized that their efforts had paid off. The screeches she heard days earlier were gone, the notes now clear and deliciously sweet as they began "The Caissons Go Rolling Along," the tune Bud often sang to Jimmy, the theme song of his unit in Korea. Teary-eyed, she watched the young members play with no slips that she could discern. A pair of short toots on Oscar's whistle and the corps turned and continued down the block.

Elaine turned to her husband with pride. He winked and mouthed "I love you." How like him to deflect the attention from himself. Inexplicably, Elaine felt a chill and lifted her gaze across the street. The frown on Lloyd's face was unmistakable; he was most definitely not pleased that Bud was singled out. Why couldn't he just enjoy the day like the rest of them?

Just then a melodic car horn sounded and all eyes turned to the last car in the lineup. Driven by Richard, a bright sky blue convertible rolled slowly their way. "Whooo!" Bud exclaimed. "Ed, what is that spiffy jalopy there?"

Ed eyes roved over the vehicle with obvious appreciation. "Well, Bud, that there is a brand, spanking new Dodge Firearrow convertible. Look would ya at that chrome grill and those concave vertical slats. They're the air intakes. It's got a V8 and all manner of gears and whatzits. Didn't think I'd ever see one except for pictures in the Sunday supplement. Man, oh man, that is some automobile! Look at your old man grinning! Wow, would I like to peek at that engine!"

While their husbands discussed the Firearrow's finer points, it was Morag who first noticed the "Gold Star Mother" sign on the car door and the identity of the woman sitting tall in the passenger seat. "Oh look wouldya now, Elaine! Sure and it's Mrs. Swanson sitting there like the queen of Sheba." At first Morag's words didn't register but as the car drew closer and stopped, Elaine recognized the Gold Star Mother. It was Mary G., the Suds 'N Wash custodian!

Her usually mousey hair was stylishly arranged and her hat the most stylish seen today. Face powder, and a shade of lipstick that matched the soft peach-colored dress and jacket she wore complemented her appearance. Upon her breast was a small corsage of white roses. The wreath for the cemetery sat perched on her lap.

Most surprising was the confidence Mary Gunilda Swanson exuded as she scanned the crowd, making eye contact here and there, gracefully waving a peachy gloved hand. There was loud chatter and applause as she passed Minnie and Mavis. The Indian youngsters jumped and cheered as they spotted their grandmothers' friend.

Elaine turned to her husband. "My goodness Bud, Mary Gunilda looks terrific! So this is Dad's surprise. How did this happen?"

Bud wrapped an arm around his wife's waist. "Well pumpkin, Aunt Lovey told me that the other ladies initially pooh-poohed her idea about our parade. As you heard yourself, they fussed about no floats and no bands. When Lovey commandeered those, they still didn't shut up. 'What about banners?' they asked? 'What about the cemetery?' 'What about the Gold Star Mothers?' The parade in Minocqua always has at least one Gold Star Mother. Lovey got pretty sick of their whining and Roland and Dad and I told her not to worry; we'd help her with all that. And we did. We got everything lined up except our own Gold Star Mother. Had the convertible promised but no one to ride in it.

"Then Dad remembered a day last winter when he delivered some firewood to Mrs. Swanson. He stayed after unloading and had a cup of coffee while the house heated up. Somehow, I got the idea pie was involved. Anyway, she mentioned her son who died years ago, "in the South" and asked Dad to look at her boy's picture.

"Everyone knew she came here to live because she was a widow and inherited that little house free and clear. Knew she had a child who died too, before her husband did, but I guess no one bothered to ask any details about those tragedies. When Dad saw the young fellow's photo, all spruced up in his Navy blues, with the black ribbon draped over the corner of the frame, he realized he'd misheard her.

"She hadn't said her son died in the South, what she said was he died in the South Pacific. Turns out it was Guadalcanal. When Dad left, he spied the Gold Star hanging in the kitchen window. Last week, he remembered that visit so he sicced Lovey on Mrs. Swanson and voila, Mashkiki's very own Gold Star Mother."

Before gliding forward, Richard honked that luxurious horn yet again. Mary Gunilda Swanson turned, waved and regally dipped her head in Elaine and Morag's direction. And they all applauded, and laughed, and celebrated with Mary G. when she heard a call coming from one of the Indian children. "Hey, Mrs. Swanson, we know you! And you look really pretty today!"

Chapter Twenty Eight

August 1955

Elaine pulled the Chevy into the yard and slid next to Perry's pickup. She sat unmoving behind the wheel of the car, and stared at her hands, sunburned and chapped, her knuckles white from their grip on the wheel. A glance around the yard told her Bud had mowed earlier. Moisture stained the concrete under the planter of bright violet lobelia; Bud had watered her plants, too. Faintly, the voice of sports announcer Earl Gillespie came from the house, his baritone, baseball patter laying background for Bud and Perry's conversation who were listening on the kitchen radio.

"Elaine, Elaine." Olivia's murmur from the passenger seat pulled her from her reverie. "Remember we've got to stay calm, though I'm not sure I can." The smaller woman hoisted her sleeping daughter to her shoulder and reached for her door handle. She squared her narrow shoulders and turned to her sister-in-law. "We've got to tell them, though. I know I won't be able to keep myself from nightmares and having Perry know will help, I think. You, too, with Bud—don't you think?"

"You're right, Liv," Elaine asserted. "We have to try." With that she opened her car door and removed a picnic basket from the back seat. She fell in step with Olivia, feeling like a soldier who gathered strength from his comrades.

Their husbands were seated at the kitchen table. They heard the car's approach and looked up from their gin rummy. They always played while they listened to the Milwaukee Braves. This season they were cheering for pitchers Warren Spahn and Lew Burdette, and outfielder Hank Aaron. A small floor fan oscillated. Olivia was still shaking as she handed their sleeping girl to Perry. She smoothed the hair on Punkie's head and gave it a gentle pat before taking a chair.

Bud looked out the window toward the quiet yard but Elaine answered his question before he could form the words. "I left Jimmy with your mother so Olivia and I could talk to you." Her voice held a quiver and her lower lip trembled slightly.

From the twinkle in Perry's eye and the number of empty beer bottles on the table, it seemed inevitable that a smart, slightly boozy remark was forthcoming from the younger Tilden brother. That remark died when he looked at his wife, saw her tightly clasped fingers, and listened to her ragged breathing. Had she been crying? Per observed his wife's eyes pooled with worry, tension, something. He saw the grim look on her face mirrored on Elaine's countenance. He swung his gaze toward his older brother. Bud usually handled things better.

"And now the windup," proclaimed announcer Earl Gillespie. At the look from his brother, Bud rose, turned the radio down and steered Elaine to a seat. Hand on his wife's shoulder, he fixed her with his clear blue eyes. "What's wrong? Elaine?" His gaze moved. "Olivia, what's going on?"

Olivia opened her mouth to speak when a low wail came from Elaine. Like a lilac bough succumbing to a May hailstorm, she slowly bent her head to the table until her forehead rested on the smooth finish. Within seconds her wails grew more fierce.

"What?" Bud jumped to his wife's side, knocking over his chair. Its clatter momentarily shook Punkie from her toddler slumber but she settled back in Perry's arms as he soothed her. Bud knelt beside Elaine, encircling her shoulder. "Lainie, what's wrong?" he asked again.

"I'll start," Olivia began when it appeared Elaine could not. But before she could say more, Elaine's head jerked up. Tears coursed down her cheeks as she looked first at her husband and then at Perry.

"That son of a bitch! That rotten no-good son of a bitch!" Her voice was loud. Bud's eyes widened and he tightened his grip on his wife.

Perry and Olivia studied Elaine. Neither of them heard her curse before; not even a damn or a hell. Her vehemence commanded attention.

"Who? What?" The questions came simultaneously from the men.

"I hate him Bud, I hate him!" Elaine continued. "I wish I were a great, huge, mean man so I could hurt him bad! Pound him! Just pound him!" Her fist was clenched and she banged it hard against the table's surface.

Bud shook Elaine gently, and finally, she looked him full in the face and let her crying overtake her. Her words were lost for a moment in wet, gulping sobs. She lay her head on Bud's shoulder as the men turned to Olivia. "From the beginning, please," Perry instructed her, and then more firmly. "The beginning."

Olivia's chest heaved. She reminded them how some Mashkiki women gathered a few times a week during this summer's heat to cool off with the children at Trout Lake. At first they met informally but now had a more regular time established and some "rules" for their charges. Any child caught rough housing had to sit out for five minutes, regardless of whose mother caught them. Morag was the general enforcer. Graham crackers were shared with everyone. None of the bigger kids who swam could go out near the raft without Fanny or Bertie Langholz.

"They're the moms who can really swim well. Not just dog paddle like the rest of us but strong swimmers who could help a kid if there was trouble." Olivia paused to take a long pull on Perry's bottle of Blatz. Bud and Perry met one another's eyes and noted this with a raise of their eyebrows. First Elaine swearing, now Olivia guzzling beer. What the hell was going on? Olivia took another swig and wiped her mouth with the back of her hand, her gaze unfocused for a moment.

Bud thought they were getting more back story than necessary but didn't interrupt. Olivia seemed to read his thoughts and continued.

"Okay, I'm getting there. You know we usually we meet during the week, but today was such a hot afternoon and most of the husbands are doing what you guys are–listening to the game and trying to stay cool. So we decided to go and hope the tourists weren't too thick and hogging the good spots on the lake front. We lucked out, most of the beach was deserted. So we had our normal spot to ourselves."

Olivia paused to take a breath. "Sometimes we splash in the water a little with the kids. Most of us try to get some sunbathing in." Her eyes suddenly pooled and Elaine took up the story.

"But never Fanny. She always wears a bathing suit with an old white shirt of Lloyd's over it. She told us she burned easily ... ." Her voice shook as she looked at Olivia and again burst into tears. Bud patted her and nodded at Olivia to forge ahead.

"So today, after all the kids splashed for a while, we made them get out and come in the shade to rest. The sun was so hot and last year Mary Gunderson had that little bout of heat stroke so Morag makes us all take a time out. We had a big blanket in the shade and Elaine herded them all up from the sand.

"I was handing out some crackers and a few green grapes when Jimmy started pointing and trying to talk. He was excited and had a mouthful of crackers so none of us knew what was going on at first." Now Olivia's voice cracked but she looked at Perry holding his gaze as she continued. "And then Perry–oh I'm so sorry, this was my fault!" Olivia swallowed and continued. "Then Morag screamed and we all looked toward the water and there was Punkie, our little pumpkin, running straight down the dock! Her fat little legs were churning and you'd have thought she had a destination in mind! I don't know how she got away from me! I thought she was sitting right there next to me but you know how fast she moves. And then–Oh Per–I saw her run straight off the dock, into eight feet of water! I didn't even have time to yell stop. She just disappeared. Boom, like that!" She snapped her fingers and drew in a deep breath.

"And then, before I could get to my feet, before any of us could, there was Fanny running toward her. Like a sprinter in a track meet. She covered that ground faster than I thought possible. I could hear Fan's feet slapping the planks and I saw Punkie's head pop up for just a second before she rolled over face down. She was at least ten feet out from the dock already. How could she get so far in that instant? And just when I thought I would die, when I saw Punkie go under a second time, Fanny dove in."

Olivia's voice speeded up. "And just like that, Fanny's head came up, and she raised Punkie up in her hands, held her over her own head and started to kick her way to shore." Olivia choked and reached across the table to grab the hand Perry extended. Her crying was less tumultuous than Elaine's but the look on her face just as compelling. Her eyes moved back and forth from Perry to the tiny girl slumbering so peacefully on his chest. "Oh God, Perry, it was so awful!" She dissolved into another bout of tears.

Elaine sat straighter. "All of us were at the shoreline by the time Fanny carried Punkie in. It wasn't more than a minute, start to finish, but it seemed like years! Punkie was coughing a little but by the time Olivia got her wrapped in a towel that little girl was more mad than scared. She shook herself off and tried to push away from Olivia. 'More,' she kept saying and pointing to the water. She wanted to go back."

Perry's hand left his wife's long enough to wipe his own cheeks. Then he placed his fingers back atop Olivia's and patted her gently. "It's all right, hon. Okay? It wasn't your fault, okay? I'm sure it seemed scary but look! Punkie's fine, isn't she? And she won't even remember what happened. It ended fine. Thank God for Fanny. I didn't know that scrawny little wife of Lloyd's was so athletic. Wait 'til I see him!"

"No!" Olivia jerked her head up, her eyes taking on a fiery look. "It didn't end all right. There's more!" She looked at Elaine to continue.

"Oh no," Elaine spat bitterly. "It gets worse. After we made sure that Punkie was okay and quieted all the other kids' crying, we took turns hugging Fanny. Olivia had a death grip on Punkie so I think I was the first one to see it when I moved toward them from the back." Her tears started once more.

"See what?" asked Bud. "What was so bad?"

Elaine took a deep breath and struggled to get her voice under control. "Fanny. Fanny's back. When she got out of the water, that white shirt of Lloyd's was plastered to her back. And right there on her shoulder was a snowflake, a red bumpy snowflake, plain as day."

"A snowflake? What do you mean, Lainie?" Bud was puzzled. He'd never seen his wife so riled up and frankly, though she and Olivia seemed to understand the import of what she was telling him, it didn't make much sense to him. From the look on his face, Per wasn't having any better luck at comprehension.

Elaine's voice picked up volume. "Do you remember last winter that Fanny helped out in the lodge when Lotty was sick? Dorothy really needed the help and Fanny thought the extra money just before Christmas was a Godsend.

"Your mother just started some holiday baking and had a big plate of rosettes on the kitchen table for the help when they took a break. Fanny'd never seen or tasted a rosette and so she was asking Dorothy all about how to make them. Your mom explained how they were basically Scandinavian–Norwegian treats and all that–and showed her the pastry iron and told Fanny how to make them.

"Showed her how the iron you used could be all kinds of shapes: flowers, butterflies, different things. Told her how you use the iron and heat the oil. Told her about the batter and the powdered sugar dusting. Dorothy offered to give her the recipe and Fannie borrowed the rosette iron that looked like a snowflake."

"Ah hell!" Bud rasped as recognition registered on his face. He looked at Elaine and then Olivia to confirm what he pieced together. He glanced at his brother, looking sick to his stomach.

"What! What!" Perry was almost shouting now and Punkie began to stir in earnest. "What? What am I missing?"

Elaine took a deep breath and looked at Perry. "What you're missing is the story I got from Fanny when I walked her to her car. She didn't want everyone else to see what we saw. What Olivia and I saw. She threw a beach towel around her and took Davey by the hand. We walked with her to the boys' toilet. While he was in there and she was sure he wouldn't hear, she spilled the story."

Elaine's voice sounded sharp and insinuating. "Seems she was making her rosettes when Davey was asleep one night and Lloyd came in real late. She didn't have his supper on the table. He started yelling at her and gave her a push. Maybe it wouldn't have happened ordinarily but Fanny chose that moment to get a little backbone and told him to hold his horses. She didn't realize how many extra beers he'd drunk.

"She knew he was mad but she didn't think that he'd do any more than yell a little more. Maybe give her a little slap her if he accused her of sassing him. She wouldn't have been surprised at that. Told me that had happened before. But no, no. The son of a bitch ... ." Elaine searched for something stronger. Olivia interrupted.

"That rotten son of a bitch!" Olivia's voice was venom saturated. "That filthy rotten son of a bitch grabbed her. She kept moving and he pulled her sweater off her shoulder. She wouldn't stand still and when he saw her bare skin, he grabbed the rosette iron, and branded her."

———

Elaine waited until mid afternoon Monday before driving into the lodge parking area. This was the time when Dorothy chose to do the books and Elaine could count on her being alone to listen. Bud and Perry were such a disappointment after she and Olivia told them about Fanny's burn.

Both looked sickened by what they heard but neither had any ideas to offer about Olivia's pleas to "do something about Lloyd!"

Perry looked sad. "What do you want us to do? Get the law involved? Is that what Fanny wants? I'll bet you dollars to doughnuts that if we got old Jeff Warner out to their place, she'd probably stick up for him. Maybe even deny it."

Before the women could protest, Bud spoke up. "I think Per's right, ladies. Maybe the best thing you can do is just keep on being friends with Fanny. Lloyd's temper is fierce but he always straightens up when he realizes what he did wrong. A burn is a terrible thing, but maybe the two of them have patched things up. It happened more than six months ago. Maybe we'd do more harm than good by interfering now."

Elaine thought about Fanny protesting that Lloyd wasn't an evil man. That after he saw her skin, he broke down and cried, ran to town and got some burn salve for her, had been extra nice to her and Davey since. Dorothy was the person to talk to. Since filling in at the lodge, it was apparent Fanny had developed a deep respect for the Tilden matron. If anyone could figure this out or get through to Fanny, it was Dorothy.

Dorothy listened without comment to Elaine's story of the day before. She pursed her lips and slowly shook her head. "I don't know, Elaine. Maybe as bad as this is with Fanny and Lloyd, maybe this is better than what Fanny had before. Did you ever think of that? We don't know much about Fanny's past. Hard as it may be for us to imagine, maybe Lloyd was a good thing for her. Maybe he can grow to be a better man. Unfortunately, that's not up to us. That's up to Fanny. All we can do is just stay friends."

Elaine thought about it. Maybe Lloyd was just a smoldering volcano, and his future potential for destruction could lie dormant forever. She'd like to think that but deep down she believed differently. It was only a matter of time before Mount Lloyd erupted again.

Chapter Twenty Nine

October 1955

The shot glass shattered near the front door of the bar.

"That's enough, Lloyd! Get your change off the bar and don't let the door hit you in the ass on the way out!" Charlie's voice was no nonsense as he headed down the bar toward the tall man now swaying slightly, his hand locked on Toots' upper arm. Charlie's eyes were fastened on Lloyd's, whose arms hung at his sides, his fingers moving of their own accord into fists.

"You think you can make me move, Charlie? You think you can make me? Last time I looked you were no cock of the walk anymore. You're no spring chicken, old man. Maybe wrinkly, old poultry but no cock of the walk!" Lloyd grinned and looked around to share his joke and bravado with the other welders who'd been taking turns buying beers with their overtime pay. His sneer died when no one else laughed. The other men were silent and avoided his eyes. Confused, Lloyd turned to the bar's owner.

"Whaddya think, Charlie? Think you can take me on? Think you-"

Lloyd's bullying was interrupted by Bud's appearance at the door. He took in Charlie's reddened face and furrowed brow, and saw Lloyd drop his hand from Toots' shoulder to glare at Bud's approach. Only muted sounds of Hank Williams and the crunch of glass were heard as Bud advanced toward the bar. He noted a few shards on the floor. Unlike Charlie to have debris lying around. Unless ... hmm, some kind of trouble here?

Bud reached to pull out a bar stool and too late, registered Lloyd moving toward him, a broad, sickly smile on the big man's lips. Too late, Bud saw a fist gloved in the dirty, gray suede of a welders glove swing toward him. Just before Lloyd's punch connected, Bud saw Charlie launch himself over the bar. He had a millisecond to wonder at his friend's middle-aged agility before hearing the bones of his nose crunch. Then all was black.

—ᏩᏣ

Bud's head jerked from the odor in his nostrils. "Whoa now boy, stop your head! It's just smelling salts. Lie quiet now." Charlie's voice was near him. Bud's head was on fire. Pain! His head jerked head again but his movement was limited. After blinking, Charlie came into focus. The bartender knelt on the floor, holding Bud's chin in one meaty hand, a small bottle in his other. Charlie moved the bottle once more to Bud's face before Bud swatted his friend's hand away. "Whad?" he could manage no more.

"Just smelling salts. Keep a first aid kit behind the bar. Didn't think it'd hit you so strong, what with your busted nose. Oh yeah, it's busted. That horse's ass! Here, now just lay still for a few more minutes."

Bud blinked and noticed Toots also on the floor next to him, a lumpy bar towel in hand. "Ice, Bud? Think you want some ice here for your schnoz?"

"Gentle now, Toots." The pitch of Charlie's voice rose from mother hen to drill sergeant. " I 'spect that hurts like hell!"

"Okay, okay. Oh, Bud. I'm sorry, man, I am just so sorry!" Bud's eyes shifted to the little man as he lightly dabbed blood from Bud's face. Toots' hand trembled as he mopped Bud's cheek. "I am just so sorry."

Bud tried again. "Whad?" He sounded like he had a cold. His eyes sought Charlie's.

"Aw, hell! That goddamned Lloyd decided to spend his overtime pay here. I shoulda been watching him better. But, ya know, I don't like to cut them guys off too early on a pay day, Bud. A man like me has bills to pay, too. I shoulda been watching better. Lloyd was putting 'em down pretty fast. Who knows, maybe he had a snort or two somewhere's else before he blew in here. The next thing I know he's got Toots here by the arm and threatening to break it." The bartender shook his head and peered at Bud's pupils, assessing further damage.

Toots picked up the story. "Yeah, I didn't think I had done much to set him off. I just asked him if he was wishing on a cold day like this if he'd rather be playing softball. You know I was talking about warmer weather, and the next thing I knew he asked me if I was being a smart ass about last season. You know, the win he thinks you and Perry stole from him with that nifty double play and ... ." Toots' voice drifted off.

Charlie picked up the narrative. "Lloyd thought Toots was ribbing him about his lack of prowess as a big time batter. Next thing you know, Lloyd was wrenching Toots' arm, challenging him to a fight and throwing a shot glass. I told him to leave and–"

Toots interrupted. "And then in you walked, Bud. Like I'd planned to rub Lloyd's nose in it, kinda like we rehearsed it. I am just so damn sorry my mouth started this." He paused before again wiping the blood running down Bud's cheek.

Bud closed his eyes and tried to take a deep breath. His efforts resulted in a stab of pain and bubble of blood. Nose wasn't working. "Zo, whud–"

Another blast of cold air and angry words rushed toward him. Bud refocused and saw his brother and Ed standing over him. Both looked him over before turning to Charlie. Perry took the iced towel and nudged Toots from Bud's side. He put the towel to Bud's nose, eliciting a yelp from his older brother.

"Easy now, Per," Charlie continued, studying Bud. "When all the action started–and ended–the other fellows grabbed that stinkin' lunk and tossed him out the door. Einar said earlier that he saw Perry talking to Ed at the feedstore so he went there to fetch 'em. I'll admit I was a trifle worried when your eyes rolled back and you blacked out. Your head hit the floor pretty hard and I think your nose's busted so I thought having Perry and Ed take you over to the doc's might not be a bad idea."

Bud attempted to sit and almost threw up. Whether it was inertia or blood that gagged him he didn't know, but Ed's suggestion to "Take it easy a little while" sounded good. Ed placed a hand on his chest and pushed him back to the floor. "We'll get you all taken care of in a few minutes."

"That's not all we're going to do!" Perry spit out. "We'll get Bud taken care of and then I'm going to find that asshole myself! From what Einar told me, Lloyd presented you with one helluva sucker punch. Dumb ass!" He looked at the other men. "Bud probably didn't even see it coming!"

Toots shuffled his feet and started his litany once more. "I am purely sorry, Bud. I didn't know I was going to set Lloyd off like that."

Bud waved his hand at Toots, took the towel from Perry and pressed it to his nose. Once the thrill of pain passed, the cold registered as soothing. His head began to clear. He reached a free hand to Ed and was pulled to sitting position. In another minute he indicated to Perry that he wanted to stand. "Home," he said.

"Yep, home," Per agreed. "But we're stopping at the clinic first and having the doc look at this." Bud's protests were cut short as he was led out by Ed and Perry.

Charlie called after them. "I'll clean up here, Bud. Toots will help me—and check on you later. Per, I'll call you later tonight, alright?" Charlie was still in charge. What he didn't tell the Tilden brothers was that he also planned on running out to Bud's house. Someone needed to prepare Elaine for this.

Chapter Thirty

December 1955

Elaine heard Jimmy's playful shrieking and looked to the snow pile Bud had shored up for just this purpose. Jimmy, Mary and Madlyn's girls were having a great time with their sleds. Morag and Madlyn were doing Christmas errands and Elaine gladly offered to watch their girls–payback time. Besides, these older children kept Jimmy occupied so she could get a few chores done herself.

Jimmy's fair hair was tucked inside the dark, red, knit woolen cap. He looked bulky in the plaid jacket and new snow pants Dorothy had made from one of Richard's old logging jacket. His cheeks were rosy with the cold and exertion of helping pull the sleds up the incline. How much she and Bud delighted in his daily accomplishments.

Only a week until Christmas, a week to complete my "to do" list. Elaine wanted to get her cookies baked and stored in tins, and finish the tree skirt she'd begun sewing. She'd already convinced Bud to drive with her to Minocqua tonight and finish their Christmas shopping. Dorothy offered to take Jimmy and Bud promised to be home by 4:30. Judging by how little light was left of the day, she guessed it was nearly that time now.

Ahh, the Christmas season! She went through her list again. She had finished sewing flannel pajamas for her son so all that was needed were socks and some mitts. Perhaps a new truck from Santa. She had her gifts for Bud hidden at the back of the closet: a bathrobe sewn with Dorothy's help and the new Perry Como record. Maybe she's splurge on some aftershave for him, too.

Thinking of shopping made her forget how frustrated she was with Bud. After his nose mended-thank God it wasn't broken—he told her he'd deal with Lloyd. She wasn't sure what she expected. She didn't want Bud to provoke a fight but what he told her seemed so, so ... anticlimactic. "We talked, Lainie. Before I could say too much he apologized for being such a horse's ass. Stuck out his hand and told me he was going to lay off the beer for a while. What more was I supposed to do? We've known each other all our lives and this is how we settled things in school. With an apology and a handshake. It's over."

Maybe for now. She held her tongue but didn't have much faith that the peace would last forever.

She should move past this. After all, it was Bud's nose and his pride. It was the season of forgiving but the memory of Fanny's rosette scar made it hard to do. Poor Fanny, how could she live with that man?

Back to more pleasant thoughts. Back to her list.

What else? A box of chocolates and bottle of Mogen David for Richard and Dorothy? She reminded herself to talk to one of the Ojibwe ladies at the laundromat. They often had wild rice for sale. How much Richard liked that rare treat! She'd probably look for floral handker-chiefs from the dime store for Morag and Olivia. She looked forward to exchanging those inexpensive gifts: hair ribbons in a special shade, a bag of angel food candy, some variegated yarn, a magazine on gardening.

This year she'd include Fanny in her Christmas shopping. A nice headband for Fanny's long, pretty hair would be just the thing. She liked Fanny and Lord knows the poor girl didn't have many friends.

After the bar fight Elaine used her mother in law as a sounding board when Bud refused to discuss it. "What is going on between them, Dorothy? I don't understand why Lloyd hates Bud so much, and why he seems to go out of his way to be rotten to Bud!" Then she added somewhat adamantly, "And why Bud doesn't do more about it! We know what Lloyd's capable of." She couldn't hold her anger and disappointment.

Dorothy shook her head and turned troubled eyes on Elaine. "Ahh, Elaine. Sit down here, hon." She patted the table in the lodge kitchen and poured coffee. "Lloyd's cussedness with the Tildens goes back a long way. There was always his competitiveness in sports. Lloyd wasn't satisfied he was one of the best athletes in the class; he wanted to be the only good athlete. Every time Bud or Perry or one of the other boys did well, he acted like they were on the opposing team. He was so spiteful and jealous." Dorothy paused. "Maybe his anger pushed him to try too hard."

"But that's what I don't get! Why was he so angry with Bud and the rest of you Tildens?" Elaine interrupted.

Dorothy paused a minute. "I don't think the anger started with Bud. It started when Lloyd was much younger. Lloyd's mama was born somewhere up around these parts, but she left and lived out west. I think Lloyd was born in California. His father died in a car accident when Lloyd was a baby so he and his mother moved back. She had some cousins around here. Made it plain she didn't like being here; that she wouldn't be here if she had another place to go; she didn't relish raising a child alone, and so on. She didn't have the best disposition–Lloyd took after her in that department."

Dorothy sighed. "There were also a few men who hung around her. I think she thought one of them would marry her and when those guys moved on, she was pretty bitter. It was easier to blame Lloyd's presence for their departure than admit to a fondness for drink and her sour attitude. Sometimes when he was younger, around eleven or twelve, he hung around with the boys, going fishing and so on. He could be real sweet and just soaked up attention, especially from me. I always liked him and felt kind of sorry for him. Once in a while he brought me some wildflowers he picked on his way over. I always made a fuss over them, had a feeling that maybe his mother didn't do that. When his mother finally did get remarried–Lloyd was 15 or so then–she made it known that when Lloyd graduated, her duties as a parent were over. She and her new mister were moving south. Alone. That probably made Lloyd anxious, so he took his rage out on the playing field."

Elaine nodded. "But that still doesn't explain how the Tildens-"

Dorothy held up her hand. "Well, there's more. There's the thing with Madlyn."

"Madlyn! How does she figure into all this?"

"When Madlyn graduated, she took a job in the high school office. She was a whiz in her secretarial classes and with her experience at the lodge, she was a shoo-in when an opening came. Tommy was in the service and they wrote regularly but there wasn't any promise or anything between them. Not that Richard and I knew about anyway, but Madlyn didn't seem too interested in anyone else.

"Lloyd took to coming into the school office early in the mornings just after Madlyn got there. Always a question about something. Pretty soon Madlyn figured out he was coming in to see her. Thought he was lonely with so little attention at home and such. Sometimes at the end of the day he just happened to be pulling out of the parking lot when she was walking out. More days than not he'd offer her a ride. Sometimes after practice, he'd have Perry or Bud with him so it didn't seem too obvious. But later on, it was apparent Lloyd had a thing for Madlyn. What do the kids call it? A crush." Dorothy paused and shook her head.

"Richard and I missed it. We had two teenage boys ourselves and should've known how easy those hankerings could develop. It all seemed harmless until Madlyn came running in when I was alone here doing the books. She was hysterical, crying.

"The day before, Lloyd'd given her a ride. Just her. He stopped the car a ways down the road and said he wanted to talk. Then he tried to kiss her. When she pushed him away and said she wasn't interested, that she was waiting for Tommy, he called her a cock tease or some other vile thing. She told him to go to hell and got out. She thought that was that. But Mr. Lloyd didn't like being on the short end and wasn't about to let it go." Dorothy's eyes closed and a sigh escaped her.

"What happened then?" Elaine asked.

"That next day Lloyd followed her walking home and pulled ahead of her. When he got out of his truck and got close enough, Madlyn smelled beer on his breath. He must have been drinking after school. He wanted Madlyn to get into his truck. She told him to keep moving and tried to walk away, but he wouldn't let her loose. Kept pushing her back to his truck. There was no one in sight and she was terrified."

Elaine felt herself blanching. Too familiar, this brought back the fear she experienced back on that county road with Lloyd years back. That skunk had a pattern! She refocused on Dorothy. "Then what happened?"

"What happened is that my girl remembered what I told her! Tromp on his instep, or if you can, plant on fist in his privates! When he turns you loose, run like hell! That's what she did. When she got through telling me about it, Richard came in the door with the boys. One look at Madlyn and they knew something was wrong. I told them what happened and Richard just stood there with that vein in his jaw bouncing. He put his arms around Madlyn and asked if she was alright.

"Then he turned to the boys and said 'Come with me.' They left and didn't come home for an hour. Richard never told me exactly what transpired and the boys never talked about it either but Lloyd missed the next day of school and when he showed up he was sporting a black eye and moving pretty gingerly."

"Did the authorities get involved? Didn't you call the constable?"

"That was my first thought, too but the more I thought about it, Richard's approach was right. Lloyd would've denied it; maybe tried to intimidate Madlyn again. And who's to say what people would believe? Madlyn would have been embarrassed at being the object of everyone's gossip. And she was worried about what Tommy might think if he got wind of it. I'm not sure what was going through everyone's minds." Dorothy got up to get a refill for her cup. Then she finished her story.

"I don't condone violence, Elaine, and Lord knows Bud hates the idea of ever turning on another human again. No fighting, no guns, no hunting. At the time, those men of mine convinced Lloyd that he needed to leave Madlyn alone for good. And he did." She paused to sip her brew. "Now I hear about Fanny and those occasional foul moods of Lloyd's she puts up with. I keep hoping that somewhere along the way maybe Lloyd grew up but I'm not convinced. I'm sure happy that she has you and Olivia for friends."

—⌒⌒

Elaine dismissed the memory of that chat with her mother in law. She donned her jacket and moved out on to the porch to shake the kitchen rug and check on the children.

Tonight was going to be so much fun. She'd be ready to go as soon as Bud changed his shirt. Then off to Minocqua. They'd grab a sandwich and soup at the Main Street Diner and then be off on their little shopping spree.

In her yard, the children were having so much fun in the snow. "Why are you laughing so hard? Are you getting excited for Santa? Just a few more days!" She ignored the older girls who rolled their eyes at mention of Santa.

Mary chirped up. "No, Elaine. It's Donnie. See he's making funny faces and singing Frosty!" She pointed a mittened hand behind her.

Sure enough, there was the Clarkson boy walking from the road into the yard, a large paper bag in each of his hands. "Well, so it is," Elaine agreed. "You kids go inside and get warmed up. I left some cookies and milk for you on the table. Put your wet mitts on the heater to dry. I'll be right in, OK?"

Donnie reached the porch and set his paper bags on the bottom step. He pushed his cap out of his eyes. "Evening. Well, almost evening. Anyway, beautiful night." A shy smile and a downward glance. He was trying hard at adult conversation.

"I'm waiting for Bud to get home. We're leaving Jimmy at my in-laws and then doing some Christmas shopping. Looks like you got a head start there!" Elaine's eyes took in the bright wrapping paper peeking from Donnie's parcels.

Donnie smile broadened. "Oh yeah, this shopping is fun alright!" he admitted. "I hitched a ride into Minocqua this morning with one of those truckers at the lodge and ran some errands for Mr. Tilden—your father-in-law—Mr. Tilden, that is. I sure appreciate you putting in a word for me for that job at the lodge. He pays pretty good and gave me a little Christmas bonus so I could look in the stores. Bought a few things for Ma and the kids. Not too fancy but they'll like it anyway. And ..."

He emphasized the last word to gain her full attention. "With money left, I took your advice and opened a savings account. I've just about run out of places to hide money at our place and this way the old man can't get his hands on it and drink it up or whatever. Like you said, this way I can make some interest on it."

There was an unmistakable degree of pride in his voice. Elaine smiled at him. "Well, that's great, Donnie. Real smart, I think. I'm proud of you."

She thought he'd welcome her approval and was momentarily puzzled at the serious look on the boy's face.

"Aww geez!" He stammered. "I know you're a married lady and all that but if I don't give you this little Christmas present from me I'm going to bust!"

Ahh, the poor boy. He had a crush on her. Not too crazy really, she supposed. He wasn't in school so he wasn't meeting girls his own age and if he did would their fathers let them keep company with a pulpcutter's son? A pulpcutter's Indian son? She knew the answer to that one. She smiled, forming a remark to give him if he presented her with a dimestore Christmas brooch or something else from one of those bags.

Instead he handed her an envelope from his jacket pocket. A Christmas card! "The lady in the store said a nice card for a special friend is always in good taste. And like it or not, you're my only friend in Mashkiki."

She took the envelope as he moved toward her. He placed his hands on her shoulders and administered a quick, tight-lipped kiss on her lips. It was over, too speedy for any reaction from her, too hurried for any indignation. And in truth, it was too chaste for any objections. Donnie stepped back, his hand resting on her shoulders. "Merry Christmas, Elaine." He'd never used her first name before. "Thanks for all you've done for me." He stepped back to retrieve his parcels.

Elaine laughed out loud. A pained look supplanted the smile on his face. Elaine shook her head. "No, I'm not laughing at your kiss. I'm laughing at this nice surprise! You're going to be a real lady killer someday, Donnie Clarkson. But no more practicing on me, ya hear?" She noted his loopy grin and the blush. He looked unsure of himself so Elaine reached out and drew him in for a hug.

Poor boy; caught in that infernal place of adolescence and despite his size, not nearly a man. So much a little boy yet. How he'd changed from when she first met him! He was smiling more and had confidence. He wasn't ashamed to display his affection for his mother and sister and little brothers. She'd seen that on more than one occasion. Bud teased her and called the boy one of her projects but all she knew right now was this felt good! This Christmas mood was catchy!

Elaine released him and turned to go inside to the children. A toot and the sound of tires slowing on the snow stopped her. Donnie was already heading down the road and waved at a passing vehicle which had slowed to a snail's pace. Aunt Lovey!

The car jerked to a full stop at the drive. Elaine could see Bud's aunt's mouth moving at breakneck pace. What was she excited about? What had this scene looked like, those last thirty seconds before the car's horn blared? Despite the innocence of the situation, Elaine supposed it could be interpreted differently. It could be described as a man-sized fellow kissing Elaine before she pulled him back for another embrace.

Lotty, on her way to choir practice, was in the passenger seat, with wide eyes and an open mouth. Next to her, brow furrowed and lower lip extended, driver Aunt Lovey shook her finger at her nephew's wife before accelerating down the county road.

Chapter Thirty One

the next day

Dinner was, well, funny. Not ha ha funny, but weird funny, odd funny. Elaine knew Bud had heard the Aunt Lovey's news broadcast. As she drained and mashed the potatoes, she heard him on the phone with Dorothy. "Gossipy old woman!" His voice rose as he followed with "She told you what?" Then he'd herded Jimmy to the table, laughed with the little boy, and told Elaine her pot roast was delicious.

After supper, Bud bathed Jimmy and read him a story before bed. Half an hour later Bud joined Elaine in the kitchen. "All quiet on the Western Front," he reported.

Elaine moved to finish washing the pans but Bud placed an arm around her waist and intercepted her. "Dishes can wait," he said. Her anxiety increased when he gently steered her to a chair. He took in a deep breath, puffed it out and plunged in.

"I'm guessing you're upset with Aunt Lovey and what she blurted to the Ladies Circle." He waved off the first syllable of her reply. "If it's any consolation to you, my ma is ready to kill her. Don't look so surprised. You know Dorothy Tilden thinks the world of you and sometimes gets a tetch fed up with Aunt Lovey much as ma loves her, too. So don't get all worried about the other ladies; ma'll take care of that gossip. But that does leave the two of us, doesn't it?"

"Bud, I can explain what was going on," She tried for a gentle laugh. "It isn't really what you think at all. I just—"

"Why would you think I need a big old explanation? You think I don't trust you, Lainie?" His eyes locked on hers, intense and deeply blue. "Or do you think I'm such an old fuddy duddy I can't remember what it is to be a teenage boy who considers himself a stud and is smitten with a pretty woman? You think I'm gonna lock you in this kitchen and then go out and whup that boy?"

Elaine was confused. For once she couldn't read her husband's face. What was he thinking? Was he angry? Baffled or indifferent? In truth, he looked amused.

Bud's gaze swept her face before he turned to the window and focused outdoors. "I'm having some trouble with my words. Maybe the best way's to talk to you about Korea. Is that all right with you, Lainie?" He peeked at her over his shoulder.

Korea? How did this relate to Korea? She folded her hands on the table top. Her mouth was open but nothing came forth. Bud continued. "I know I haven't been too forthcoming about that time. Sometimes you must be curious and I appreciate the fact that you haven't bugged me with too many questions about what happened there. I'm glad you never got all caught up with all this Mashkiki hero stuff either. So." He straddled a chair, forearms leaning on its back. "Can we talk now?"

Elaine nodded, letting herself get lost in the Nordic blue depths of his eyes. She wasn't sure what this had to do with Donnie's crush but she was glad her husband was cool and didn't seem fazed by Aunt Lovey's allegations.

"When I left for army training and Korea, I'd never been further away from home than Milwaukee for a basketball tourney with Perry. Can't say it inspired any wish for travel in me. First time I really saw much of the world was when I started training at Camp McCoy. Can you believe it?

That old and that's the furthest I'd ever been from home. From there to Frisco was by train and then a troop ship overseas where we were flown to a base near Seoul. I'd never been on a train before; biggest boat I'd ever been on was the 20 footer MacKenzies put in every spring at Trout Lake. A plane ride was never on my "to do" list.

"What I'm trying to tell you, Lainie, is that even though I was a little older than most of the boys I shipped with—most of 'em right out of high school—I wasn't all that much more worldly. A real hick from the sticks. Basically I was just a backwoods fellow who knew when he enlisted that he'd miss his ma's cooking and hanging out at a bar with live music playing, but I felt this obligation." His eyes took on a faraway cast.

"When I was a little kid, I remember the Pearl Harbor broadcast and later hearing FDR's fireside chats. During most of the War, I was in high school and promised ma I wouldn't sign up early to fight, that I'd graduate first. Well, you know how that turned out. May 1945 arrived and Germany surrendered while I was getting fitted for my graduation gown. It was over in the Pacific by the end of summer. For years I'd heard my uncles and Charlie talk about the troops and the country's sacrifice and later, putting war behind us and settling into peacetime.

"We thought our lives were getting back to normal, and then all this foolishness in Korea started. And it was my turn. Perry inherited Dad's flat feet so he was exempt. When I got called up, I felt ready. That sound crazy to you?"

Bud waited for Elaine to nod her head before he went back to the thread of his narrative. He took another big breath.

"What I didn't count on was how strange all of it was. It didn't take many days after I got to Seoul to get assigned to an infantry unit. Not too long after that I saw my first dead body. Then a lot of bodies. Suddenly I was the old man in a unit of 18- and 19-year-old boys. Mostly 'cause I listened and kept my mouth shut, I got promoted quick. Then whoa! All of a sudden, I was the one in charge of getting these guys home to their mothers and sweethearts. So I tried to push down my own fears and not let on that I was a mess inside. I never ran from my duty, Lainie, but I swore that when the North Koreans surrendered—and we dreamed every night that the next morning would be the day—that I'd be the first to pack my gear for home.

"It wasn't the parades at the end I remember most. You know that. It was earlier. Even now, I can sometimes hear those guns at night, and the lieutenants yelling directions, and the Chinese and Korean gibberish floating from enemy lines that we'd hear when it got quiet. Sometimes I was afraid to wake up. Thought I'd see another frozen corpse. And Lainie, I don't wish that on anyone! Sometimes a new guy would wake up and forget where he was. If I saw that lost look in his eyes, I cussed 'im out good so he'd snap to and not do something dumb enough to get him killed before morning chow. If there was morning chow that day."

His eyes filled with tears but Elaine was afraid to touch him lest his revelation stop. It was important to get this out and she'd be damned if it was her that shut him up! She'd waited so long for him to confide in her. He took another breath.

"So yeah, eventually I became that big brother soldier. I had to if us Wisconsin boys were going to get back to the pinery, and those Kansas boys were going to head back to their little farms and ranches. Got to know a couple Indian fellows from Arizona and they were lonesome for the desert and wanted back there. We did the best we could and hoped we'd have the same number waking up tomorrow as we did today.

"And then Chosin reservoir happened. Ma let you read some of those newspaper accounts and some of my letters? Okay, you know most of it. We marched, dug in and tried to stay alive. The long and short, we came under heavy fire and I got hurt. Not as bad as some of my platoon, though. It was pretty cold and maybe I was more used to that early morning numbness. Maybe that cold kept my wounds from bleeding so much, I don't know. All I recall is with all the artillery and the scream-ing, I didn't feel like I was hurt too bad. Even with my leg wound, I could move okay. So dragging a boy back with me and going with the medic for a few more wasn't a big bravery issue with me. I didn't give it much thought. I just had to bring them back, same's I'd hope they'd do for me."

Bud rose, walked to the sink and plucked a clean glass from the drainer. Elaine watched the muscles on his back tense and relax as he drank the water and went on. "Somehow I ended up in an aid station and after they looked me over, they got me to a MASH unit, the field hospital. My leg wound wasn't as much concern to them as my foot. My toes were pretty black from frostbite and they thought I'd lose 'em.

"They hurt plenty. And they kept on hurting. Lots of us were thawing out and the pain from getting that blood recirculated was terrible. They gave me some narcotics and that helped until it was getting in short supply and they took it away to give to those more severely wounded. And that's about the time my leg wound got infected. I developed a fever and was out of my head for a while." He took another long drink from the glass and Elaine could hear his swallow across the kitchen. He wiped his eyes as he straightened his shoulders and turned to her.

"You wondering what the hell this all has to do with that pulpcutter's kid kissing your pretty mouth and my Aunt Lovey thinking she was seeing the ruination of this Tilden marriage?" He tried a smile but it was an effort.

Elaine had kept her eyes dry during Bud's recital and returned his smile.

Bud drained the glass and set it in the sink. He leaned back and crossed arms and ankles. "So in the middle of my little piece of hell, slowly the fog started to lift. The pain seemed better but could still bring a yell up from my belly if I got moved suddenly. And then I began to hear a voice. At first I thought I was dying and my life was flashing before me, like you see in the movies. Then I thought it was ma calling to me. But gradually I saw, and heard, that it was one of the nurses.

"First thing I noticed was her bright red hair. And her ton of freckles. Covered her face and neck. Hands, too. She had real pale blue eyes, kind of cracked looking, like a doll's. She took my pulse and checked my forehead for fever. She'd lift my head to give me water and a pain pill when they had them. Whenever I woke up, she was there.

"I 'spose if I was real honest, I'd say she wasn't the most beautiful of women. She was pretty short and a little thick around the middle. And except for her eyes, her features weren't too remarkable. Later, when I thought about it, she wasn't even in the ballpark of what I'd consider young. She was probably pushing forty. But Lord, Lainie, she was so clean! She smelled really nice and she was so kind to us. To me, she was the most gorgeous creature God put on earth. Her name was Bernadette.

"I was in that unit for four or five days while they amputated my toes and tended the infection in my leg. I knew I was there until I could be airlifted to the American base outside Tokyo. When other guys settled down for the night, she'd stop by my cot and talk to me. She checked on the guys from my unit, the ones I helped bring in, told me who made it and who wasn't so lucky. Got me to chat about Wisconsin, my family, anything to get me to forget the pain and my fear that I was going to lose my whole foot. It was cold in there and pretty smelly, with me probably contributing a good part of the stink with my infection. But when she trained those eyes on me, I was grateful, and I'll admit it, after just one day, I was goony in love.

"I probably looked and acted like every soldier they brought in. All gaga over the first American girl we'd seen in a while. Last night I was there, I asked if she'd kiss me. Part of me believed I was gonna die and having this woman kiss me was of utmost importance. She laughed and told me she was too old for me. Told me she had an army sweetheart she planned to marry when their hitch in Korea was over.

"When she realized I was gonna bawl, she took pity on me and administered the sweetest kiss I'd ever got. It was just a quick peck on the lips, then she patted my arm and moved on. I believe part of that kiss was pure love, like what the Indians out on the rez call love medicine, real mashkiki stuff 'cause it made me determined to get strong and get home. And for those few seconds, I didn't feel lonely or unloved. I felt good, Lainie. I felt so good; better than any dopey heartsick kid had a right to feel in that place, at that time. She made me feel better about the boys we lost and those other boys. All those other boys–American or Korean or whatever.

"So what I'm telling you, Lainie, is that I can guess what that Donnie kid was feeling. Sure, it's not wartime now and he's not wounded or anything. Not in the flesh anyway. But from what I see, he feels as removed from having anyone truly care about him as I did when I was in that MASH unit. Maybe you're his Bernadette, Lainie, and if he's as lonely as I was in that hospital ward, I reckon I'm glad he was able to steal a kiss from you." He turned and she could see his quivering grin. "Poor kid. Had to grab it unawares from an old Mashkiki house frau in faded dungarees, probably wearing one of my old shirts."

Elaine knew his remark was intended to lighten a serious conversation. Probably the most serious talk she'd ever had with Bud. She left her chair and in two fast steps traversed the kitchen and flung herself at her husband while he moved toward her. Her arms twined his neck as he wrapped his arms around her back. She lifted her feet, and let her legs encircle his waist. She moaned as she crushed his lips. The kiss lasted a good, long time until she buried her head in his shoulder. She was laughing, crying, breathing in her love for the man holding her and laughing with her.

Chapter Thirty Two

mid January 1956

Saturday night and Jimmy was in bed. Gentle snores came from his bedroom. Elaine glanced at the clock. Almost 8:30 with good roads and no more snow, Bud should be no more than 35 minutes away. Maybe she should take a leisurely bath. Hmm, might be nice to greet Bud at the door with freshly washed hair, smelling like that fancy bubble bath Dorothy gave her for Christmas. Time to shed this heavy sweater and the old dungarees. Time to shuck off her heavy woolen socks and clunky shoes.

She gathered a book, her robe and started toward the bathroom. Reflexively she glanced in Jimmy's room as she passed. Bud always teased her about the nightly checks on him, but ... No! What? Was someone standing outside the window? Maybe she was imagining it. She stood still and listened. Only quiet, then the distinct sound of heavy booted footsteps, crunching on the snow.

Threatened, like a mama bear with cubs, she charged to the porch, door slamming behind her. She could hear breathing and knew before she turned that Lloyd Defoe was coming around the corner of the house toward her. She mustn't show that yahoo any fear. He'd feed on that. She took a few deep breaths and straightened her shoulders. Be firm. This was her property.

She backed up a little but abandoned any notion of retreat. She'd never get inside and lock the door quickly enough if he followed. And she wanted him as far from Jimmy as possible. She touched the wall of the porch, her hand seeking something: Jimmy's little snow shovel, anything. The moon moved from behind a cloud revealing Lloyd's swollen, drunken face and uneven gait. It was so bright she could see the rip in his shirt pocket, the scattered little holes in his trousers, trademark of a welder.

"Hey Lainie," his use of Bud's nickname sickened her. His words were only slightly slurred; but Elaine could hear the alcohol in his laugh. Then his statements became exaggerated in their precision. "I was just in the neighborhood and thought I'd stop by for one last beer." A pause. "And who knows—maybe a kiss. I heard that you weren't too particular about who got your kisses these days."

He stretched an arm forward and lurched toward her. Before his fingers reached her another set of footsteps pounded on the snow and gravel. Elaine swiveled her head and saw Donnie running toward them, a two by four in his hand from that neat pile of lumber he had stacked for her on Tuesday. Before Lloyd could react, Donnie planted his feet and swung the board like Joe D'Maggio reaching for the fence. He connected with the big man's ribs and knocked him to his knees. Lloyd's head was bent, hands clutching his side. Slowly he sank fully on the snow. Breathing hard, Donnie backed up and lifted the board again. He hefted it, his eyes locked on the back of Lloyd's head.

"No!" Elaine screamed. "Donnie, don't! Don't! He's not worth it. Put the board down!"

The boy kept his eyes on Lloyd's prone figure. "Elaine, are you all right? I'll kill that asshole if he hurt you!"

She shook her head and grabbed the board from Donnie. It was quiet. Breath from all three of them steamed on the night air. Lloyd grunted. He wasn't dead, but the noise didn't sound very energetic, either. She and Donnie looked at one another for a moment, both shaking, tears running down their faces. A louder groan turned their attention to Lloyd, now on one hand and knees, one hand still at his ribs, trying mightily to regain his footing. She didn't think he had much fight left but had to be sure. She turned to the boy and lowered her voice. "Go over there, Donnie. Over by the side of the porch where he can't see you. I need you to take this board and just wait, okay? Please. Do this for me."

The boy dipped his head in agreement and retreated to the shadows. Elaine wiped her arm across her face and took a deep breath. She raised her voice for Lloyd's benefit, as though she were addressing a retreating Donnie. "Okay. It's all over now. Go home now, Donnie. Stop at Perry's and tell him what's going on." She checked to see that Lloyd was still looking at the ground and motioned Donnie deeper into the shadows. Then she crossed her arms, hugged herself against the cold and waited for Lloyd to stand. His breath sounded ragged but gradually it steadied and he finally stood, his back to her. Straightening his shoulders, he faced her.

"Huh, you sent your little lover watchdog home, did ya? I shoulda known he was behind me. Shoulda smelled him. I must be slipping. That little asswipe mighta cracked a rib or two of mine."

"Then you get your sorry butt gone and have that checked out, Lloyd! You were down longer than you thought." This lying was getting easier. "My little watchdog must be almost to Perry's by now. I wouldn't doubt that he and Richard and probably Charlie will be here any minute. Hard telling who's at Perry's Saturday night poker game. Jeff Warner's off duty tonight so he's probably there, too."

"You think Jeff Warner scares me? That pussy constable? Takes more than a county badge to tackle me!"

"Maybe, but his secretary'll have a field day reading his report about you peeking in a little kid's bedroom windows. Telling her church group all about it. How long before that gets back to the bar crowd? Who knows? Maybe they'll figure they've got the Undie Thief Mystery solved, too." The mention of the underwear theft brought a muffled chuckle from the shadows. Donnie better be quiet.

Elaine turned to Lloyd. "Who knows what else that girl might add? She sure likes gossip. Not much of a stretch from swiping undies and spying in little boy's bedroom windows to all kinds of nasty stuff! The boys in the welding shop and at the tavern'll have a field day, won't they?" Perhaps she'd gone too far? She needed to control her temper.

"Awww, shit. You know I wasn't looking in at your brat. I wanted a rise out of you, you snooty bitch! Thinking you're so much better than the rest of us with your college learning and grant writing and all other shit you lord over us. Oooo and I forgot, married to a gen-u-wine he-ro, too. You snooty cock-teasing bitch!"

Elaine counted to ten. If she provoked him, even hurt he might get violent and bring Donnie back into the fray. Her resolve disappeared when he spit at her, a large gob of beery saliva landing on her shoe. Without thought, she took one determined step closer.

"You are such a coward! Are you proud to threaten teenagers or slap your wife around! You are such a poor excuse for a husband! Don't look at me that way! I know what you did to Fanny! I saw the burn mark when she rescued Punkie. I was with her on the dock and I saw her back! You proud of that, too?"

Pure fury replaced Lloyd's look of drunken confusion. "Whadda you mean? Who else was on that dock?"

Elaine's mind raced. She'd already involved Donnie. Might've put that boy in jeopardy. She didn't want this bully tormenting Olivia, too. She studied his face. If she could stall, maybe she'd make him anxious. "Don't worry. I'm the only one who saw her back. What we all saw was how quick and courageous she is. And we," she was nearly spitting now, "couldn't even acknowledge what a champion your wife was! Couldn't even properly thank her for being smart and brave. Oh, no! Because she didn't want anyone else to see what you did to her back! She was still protecting you! Don't you get it, you jerk? Protecting you and you don't even know what a gem she is. Now it would be wise for you to leave before Bud or one of those other guys gets here."

Elaine started back to the house. She barely advanced a few feet before a large and unyielding fist encased her arm. Lloyd pulled her close enough to smell the stale beer and cigarettes on his ragged breath. A tiny beginning of fear niggled at her.

"Watch it, missy! Watch your mouth. Your hero husband can't be around all the time. Or your smelly little protector, neither!" He jerked his head toward the road that led to Trout Lake and the pulpcutter's dwelling. A slight sound came from the far side of the porch. The big man turned his head and squinted into the shadows but Elaine knew he couldn't detect Donnie if the boy stayed put. It must be torturing Donnie to hide but so far Lloyd had not harmed her. She willed herself to keep her eyes on Lloyd's face.

Maybe the drink was wearing off. He pushed her from him and backed away. Elaine watched him gingerly pat his side. His step appeared steadier as he turned his head to the road. With another burst of bright moonlight Elaine made out his truck. He shook his head, spit profusely and started toward his vehicle. "Be sure and give ole Bud my best, okay, Elaine? And tell your little sweetheart I'll be looking for him."

She stood, hands on hips until she saw his taillights fade. Donnie appeared at her side.

"That guy's an asshole, Elaine. And meaner than a one-eared alley cat. I'm staying here until your husband gets back." Donnie took her elbow and guided her to the porch. "Come on. Don't you want to go inside?"

"Soon, Donnie. I want to stay out here just a few minutes."

Donnie disappeared and suddenly her winter coat was draped around her as he helped her sit. He sat beside her still clutching the board, silent and vigilant. And that was where they stayed until Bud drove into his yard minutes later.

CHAPTER THIRTY THREE

the next day

Bud waited until the Sunday afternoon basketball game on the radio was almost finished, then kissed Elaine and headed out the door. She was helping Jimmy with a puzzle and called to him as he left the house. "Don't be too long, Bud." Her voice sounded lyrical but he didn't kid himself; she wanted him home more for ease of mind than romance. Though she earlier proclaimed she was fine, Bud saw her fingers fidgeting while she folded laundry.

Bud reflected on last night. Hearing what the Clarkson boy said was difficult. Elaine sat mute in the porch swing while Donnie related what had transpired. When finished, the teenager glanced at Elaine, set the board down and began to leave.

"Donnie," Bud called to him. The boy turned and Bud extended his arm to shake the hand of the pulpcutter's son. "I appreciate what you did tonight, Donnie. You can be sure I'll never forget it." Donnie nodded and started down the road toward home.

"Do you want me to give you a lift?" Bud called after him. The boy threw up a hand in a sort of backward wave and never slowed his stride.

Initially Elaine's safety was Bud's only concern. Then guilt at not being there to defend his wife seeped in. Those feelings gave way to an intense anger, a rage he hadn't felt since his combat days. What good was he if scoundrels like Lloyd could invade his home, and scare his wife? What might have happened if that scruffy, good-hearted kid hadn't been walking by? Bud got Elaine in the house, checked the windows and doors and maneuvered her into bed. He peeked in on his son and tucked the covers snugly about him. After entering their bedroom, he quickly undressed and crawled under the covers. He lay on his side, arms encasing his wife, spooning. On guard duty now, he slept little while Elaine slumbered. Toward dawn, his anger began its slow smolder, but left him clear headed and sure of what he needed to do.

Now he was in the Beast, heading into town, knowing with 100% certainty that Lloyd would be at Charlie's listening to the basketball game. There would be a small crowd there tuned to the radio, shooting pool, maybe playing some cards and nibbling on peanuts and pretzels while exchanging gossipy tidbits. It was before this audience Bud planned a confrontation. Lloyd's hatred for Bud was publicly manifested here with a sucker punch and it would be here that this nonsense ended.

Judging by the cars parked in front of the tavern, it appeared Charlie had a good crowd. Bud parked around the back of the bar between Charlie's garage where the barkeep stored both the shiny, new Chevy he drove only to Wausau on weekends and his old, beaten Ford pickup. Fifteen years old, faded to a sad, tired black, the truck had evolved into Charlie's hobby, something to tinker with on slow afternoons. It was his first vehicle and he was sentimental. He would sell it eventually, he told his customers. Bud gave its fender a friendly slap as he headed through the back door of the bar.

A quick stride down the short narrow hall where Charlie stacked extra beer cases, and Bud was inside. A quick glance gave him the lay of the land. The barkeep leaned on the bar, cigarette in one hand, bar rag in the other, listening to the broadcast. He'd just served old Mr. Peterson and his even older brother-in-law, Mr. Nordstrom tap beers. Charlie welcomed these two old widowers most Sunday afternoons and helped the old codgers get situated on the barstools. Charlie also made sure they got home in one piece. They seldom had more than two glasses of cold brew so sobriety wasn't the issue. It was their fading vision. How either of them still held a valid driver's license at 80 or so was a wonder to most of Mashkiki's citizenry.

Bud's brother-in-law Tommy was seated at one of the small tables playing cribbage with Ed Gunderson. John Langholz sat there as well, probably preparing to challenge the winner. Toots and Einar were focused on the pool table where, from the looks of things, Lloyd seemed to be getting trounced by Perry in a game of eight ball. It was Perry who first noticed Bud.

"Hey, Bud. You up for a game when I finish off ole Lloyd here?" Perry's easy grin disappeared at the look on Bud's face and the set of his older brother's jaw. He saw Bud focus on Lloyd. Toots and Einar tried to get a read on what was transpiring. To their knowledge, it was the first time both Bud and Lloyd were together in Charlie's since last fall.

"Nah," Bud's voice sounded strangled, even to himself. "I just came to ask Lloyd what he was doing sneaking around, looking in our windows last night."

Charlie straightened up and moved down the bar where his small, wooden bat was concealed under the bar. He hadn't occasion to use it often but today might prove different. Only someone completely daft could miss the menace in Bud's voice. Toots and Einar backed up. Tommy and Ed moved their chairs back, as John, too, watched the drama unfold.

Lloyd, pool cue in hand, turned and looked at Bud over his shoulder. "Don't know what you're talking about, Tilden. You talking about last night? All I know is I was driving down your road and saw that smelly pulpcutter kid, the one your wife seems to be so fond of, skulking around your house. I stopped to run him off for you. Anything else you may have heard is just damn error on somebody's part." He bent over the green felt to take his shot.

Bud caught the question in his brother's eyes and shook his head. He didn't need help. As he crossed the floor in rapid steps, the only sounds heard were the smack of the cue ball and the radio announcer praising the Badgers.

Lloyd sank the fourteen ball in the corner pocket and set his cue against the table. He shook a cigarette from the rumpled pack, his eyes never leaving Bud's.

Bud's voice was low and calm. "I guess I'm pretty glad Donnie Clarkson was passing by when Elaine confronted you about peeping in the bedroom window. And I think Elaine's glad the boy was there to help persuade you to keep your hands off her. Sounds like you couldn't comprehend her saying no!"

Lloyd reached behind him for his pool cue but Perry jerked it from his hand. "I'll take that for you. Just want to keep things on the up and up here, Lloyd."

Lloyd narrowed his eyes at the younger Tilden and then concentrated on Bud who had stopped within an arm's reach. A snarl emanated from the big man. "I don't know what those two told you, Tilden. Didn't appear there was much conversation between the two of them." His insinuation was a gauntlet thrown between them. "And you can be sure I wasn't pawing your missus. Nothing'd be further from my mind." He punctuated his statement with a Hah! that fell somewhere between derision and distaste.

Bud shook his head and acted as though he'd not registered the insulting remarks made about his wife. "You know Lloyd, I was awake most of the night trying to figure out why you are so mean and rotten. I can take your cussedness, I guess, and your cheap shots and even your coward-ass sucker punches but I can't take you bothering my family, scaring my wife and threatening her."

"Aw shit!" Lloyd sputtered. "Is that what she told you? You got it all wrong! I tell you I saw that stinking son of a bitching pulper kid and thought you needed some help on the home front. Heard your wife might be sweet on him, maybe sampling some young stuff from that kid when you're out of–"

A fist cut Lloyd's protests short. Surprise sparked Lloyd's eyes and Bud knew his enemy would come back at him swinging when he got his wits back. Lloyd Defoe wiped his mouth with the back of his hand. He saw blood smeared on it, and with a bellow, roared and charged Bud. Bud ducked a roundhouse punch and came back with an uppercut that rolled Lloyd's eyes back as his head wobbled from side to side.

Lloyd lifted his big hands, advancing on Bud. Whatever he planned for Bud, whatever excitement the small crowd felt they'd witness, ended abruptly. Bud feinted right and when Lloyd swung, Bud bounced back in front of his opponent. Two quick right jabs and another uppercut from his left fist and the fight was over.

The next few seconds looked choreographed. Lloyd lurched, his knees beginning to buckle. With footwork worthy of Gene Kelly, John Langholz came from his chair and slid the seat behind Lloyd. Tommy, the only man near Lloyd's size, grabbed the loser's shoulders and lowered him to the chair.

Bud stood looking at the welder, ignoring the pain he felt spreading from fist to elbow. He'd be damned if he rubbed his knuckles or showed any sign of weakness now. He glanced at the bar and noticed with some degree of glee that Tryg Peterson and Will Nordstrom hadn't even managed to turn their old arthritic selves completely around on their barstools; the fight had commenced and was over so fast. All was quiet but for the radio broadcaster who let the fans know what the score was.

"Okay Lloyd, I'm leaving now. Perry and Tommy will put you in your truck and when your head clears, it'd be a good idea if you went home. Take a nap, go chop some wood, I don't care what you do but keep yourself out of my sight for a day or two. I mean it. In a day or two, I'll be done being furious and it'll be alright between us again. Far as I'm concerned, anyway. It's a small town and we have to get along, but I don't want to see your cussed face for a couple of days. And Lloyd?" Bud paused here wanting Lloyd to hear him plainly. Wanted Lloyd to hear this in front of witnesses. "Stay away from my wife."

Bud dug into his pocket and slapped a five dollar bill on the bar top. "Charlie, I'd appreciate it if you buy a round for the house. Make sure you get Mr. Peterson and Mr. Nordstrom first, would you? And Charlie?

Keep the change."

Bud threw Charlie a wink and nodded at the old men still struggling to swivel their barstools and catch up with the action. "Always nice to see you gents."

Chapter Thirty Four

April 1956

Elaine awaited the arrival of the Canada geese on their way back north. It seemed they always stayed near the lakes and rivers near Mashkiki Rapids for their last hurrah in Wisconsin before moving even further north.

These early April days were so temperate, the air so refreshing. People's spirits were uplifted. Winter was over and already activity had picked up at the lodge. This morning, with Jimmy at Madlyn's acting as a guinea pig for the girls and their child care merit badges, Elaine assisted Dorothy and Richard with inventory. Now she just picked up her two-year-old and planned on his company while she ran her other errands.

Elaine rounded the corner near the post office, Jimmy in tow. His latest endeavor was taking extra-long steps and though his short little legs were no match for hers, her new shoes slowed her and gave him a tiny advantage today. Both concentrated on their feet and didn't notice they shared the walkway. Jimmy's movements halted when he tripped on large feet that appeared from nowhere.

Elaine recognized the scuffed toes of black leather boots even before she raised her eyes. The automatic apology from her little boy did nothing to erase the scowl on Lloyd Defoe's face. Elaine allowed herself a few seconds of pride in her tiny son's good manners before that pleasure gave way to alarm. It was the first time she'd encountered Lloyd since Donnie struck him a few months back. That was the night before Bud found him at Charlie's and soundly punched him according to Perry. She opened her mouth but a low growl from Lloyd crowded her speech.

"Better watch where you're going, squirt." Lloyd's hand shot out and gave her son's shoulder a quick shake as he brushed by Elaine. Large envelope in hand, the brute looked in a hurry to get to the post office.

Elaine noted an apprehensive look on Jimmy's face and began to draw him to her. "You're alright, aren't you, Jimmy? Mr. Defoe is kind of rough sometimes but you don't need to be scared of him."

Elaine watched Lloyd's eyes narrow and heard the low cuss that escaped his lips. Lloyd snarled and turned back with a quickness that belied his size. He stepped between the Tildens and again reached toward Jimmy.

"Stop it!" Elaine screamed. She pushed herself in front of Jimmy and smacked Lloyd soundly with her purse. She hit the welder again and pushed at Lloyd. "Stop!"

"Yeow! Well, aren't you the feisty little hellcat, Missy! Bud always acts so high and mighty about his college educated wifey but you got some fight in you, doncha? Things might be more interesting at the Tildens than I thought. Maybe you got enough spunk in you for Buddy boy and that trashy pulper's kid. I was just going to give your brat a pat on the head. I don't go around scaring babies!"

"Let's just leave it there, Lloyd," Elaine warned him. "After our last encounter, I don't think you can blame me for being a little edgy around you!" Pulling Jimmy behind her, Elaine squared off against the big man.

"Aww don't get your fancy undies in a bundle, Lainie!" Lloyd's use of Bud's pet name for her sounded obscene. He spat on the sidewalk and carelessly walked away from her. "You ain't that special."

Elaine watched the forced swagger in his step and wondered again how much energy it took for Lloyd to hate all of them. She felt a tug on her sleeve. A solitary tear trickled down her son's cheek and his lip was quivering but otherwise he seemed unhurt. Such a brave and cheerful little guy.

"Are you okay, honey? Is your shoulder okay?" Elaine searched her son for injury, but already he was giggling at a dog across the street. He was fine.

Elaine's thoughts turned to Fanny and little Davey. I hope Fanny can stand up to that creep she's married to. I hope Lloyd is good to Davey.

She hated to think what Bud would do if he heard about this. But ... did he have to know? She couldn't bear another fight. Maybe she wouldn't bring it up. Jimmy wasn't hurt, and children forgot things quickly. Maybe Lloyd did this on purpose, just to provoke Bud and force another confrontation, keep the animosity smoldering. She glanced around and saw no one in the vicinity who could vouch for what occurred. She thought her scream was blood curdling, but apparently it was more benign, just a loud exclamation. No one came out of the shops to investigate. Maybe she was blowing the whole encounter out of proportion. Besides when she'd told Bud about Lloyd's treachery with Fanny, he'd ignored her. This was nothing compared to that. She looked at Jimmy and made her decision.

"Let's go home now, okay, Sweetie? Mommy will make you chocolate milk."

She recalled the set of her husband's jaw whenever Lloyd's name was mentioned in conversation. No matter what he said, Bud hadn't gotten over his confrontation with the big welder in Charlie's bar. She tried to broach the subject with him a few days after the fight but his eyes looked frostier than ever. With some finality, he made it clear to her that he wouldn't discuss Lloyd's behavior with her. "It's over Elaine, I just want to let things get back to normal."

Elaine wondered if there ever was a normal. Maybe he felt conflicted because fighting Lloyd contradicted everything he told himself he would never do again. Still, Bud was firm so she would try to go along with his wishes.

Today's exchange with Lloyd bothered her, but he didn't frighten her as he had when he accosted her at home. The thump from Donnie's plank, and the subsequent knuckle sandwich received courtesy of Bud should've convinced Lloyd to stop causing trouble. But what Elaine remembered from her college psych classes was that bullies essentially were cowards and when backed into a corner, cowards turned vicious.

She walked past the post office, and spied Lloyd inside. His gaze followed her as she passed. She shook her head; enough time had been wasted this fine day thinking about Lloyd. There were better things to do. Like share some chocolate milk at home with the youngest Tilden man.

CHAPTER THIRTY FIVE

May 1956

She knew the instant she heard the first syllable tumble from Olivia's lips that something was terribly wrong.

"Elaine?" Olivia's tone lost its hesitancy and became sharp. "Elaine, listen to me and try not to ask too many questions. The less people know the better. Is Jimmy in bed? Is Bud there with you? Okay, tell him you have to go out for an hour or so to be with me. I don't know, tell him Perry and I had a little squabble. Just get out of there now! Come down to the clinic, to the emergency entrance. It's Fanny and Davey."

Elaine did as her sister-in-law asked and was now pulling into the clinic. Soon the sun would completely fade and the first smattering of stars appear. She saw Olivia's slim form outlined from a backlit doorway but before she could speak, Olivia crossed the lot and took hold of Elaine's arm.

"Listen, we don't have much time to get moving! There's no time for us to convince Perry or Bud. We have to do this ourselves!" The urgency in Olivia's voice matched the inescapable, talon-like grip of her tiny hand.

"What, Livvy? What's happened? Where are Fanny and Davey? Is she hurt? Was it Lloyd?"

"That jerk is what's happened, alright! That miserable damn Lloyd! We need to get out of here quick." Olivia took a breath and moved closer to Elaine, her face fierce and commanding. "Fanny called me an hour ago. Lloyd came home and started slapping her around. After we saw the burn mark, she got enough gumption to tell him that she would leave if he ever roughed her up again. Apparently he listened and he's left her alone all these months. But then tonight he came in drunk and startled her. She dropped her casserole dish and it shattered. When she went to sweep it up, he grabbed the back of her head and said she was a lousy wife to waste food. He shook her and told her to eat it from the floor. She told him she was leaving."

Olivia gulped as big silent tears slid down her cheeks. "Now did that make him think? No! No sir! When Fanny wrenched away from him, that miserable excuse for a man turned around and pointed at little Davey in his chair. Shook his finger at Davey. Then he sneered at Fanny and said something like 'Oh yeah, you think you can do that, you trashy little slut? You think you can just leave me when you feel like it? You think I'm gonna stand for that?" And then he reached down and yanked Davey up out of his chair. Yanked him hard and twisted his little arm bad! So bad that it broke! He broke Davey's arm, Elaine! Don't know if he intended to do that but what kind of a man hurts a little kid?"

Olivia looked around the lot and lowered her voice. "Davey screamed so badly, Fanny knew it was serious. When Lloyd stormed out to the barn–maybe for another bottle-Fanny called me. When I got there, Fanny'd already carried Davey out to the road. Lloyd was still in the barn so we got Davey to the clinic without any interference. Oh, Elaine, Davey was so brave and was trying so hard not to cry. Doc says the arm'll be fine but that he'll have to fill out a report in the morning with the sheriff's office. Doc said someone would talk to Lloyd. This is what it took for somebody to step in? I told him I was taking Fanny and Davey home to my house."

Elaine was shocked but somehow found her voice. "But tomorrow–"

Olivia interrupted. "Fanny's not going home with me. No ma'am. I had about five minutes to come up with a plan and the beauty is that it can work, Elaine. It will work! There's only a handful of us who know some of it. None of us know all of it. But Fanny's leaving Rapids tonight and not coming back. She's going and Lloyd won't know where. God knows I'll miss her. Next to you, she's my closest friend. But the most important thing is to get her and Davey away from here!" Olivia's eyes gleamed and the strength emanating from her petite frame hit Elaine in a wave.

"But I still don't get it, Livvy. What am I doing here? What do you want me to do?" Elaine was distraught. What Olivia was saying made some sense but this wasn't something done lightly. Did Olivia know what she was doing? Maybe she needed more time to think. Maybe the minister could assist them. She stopped. Now she was thinking like the men. She and Livvy had been unsuccessful in convincing their husbands to help. Maybe it would be the same with the sheriff.

Olivia was still speaking. "I also called—hold on! I think part B of my plan has just arrived." Olivia looked at the headlights of a dark vehicle as it turned, carefully dodged a few potholes and parked at the shadowed side of the building where it couldn't be seen from the street. Two familiar figures stepped out and waited for Olivia's approach. One held a burning cigarette, and as he turned, Elaine knew him. What was Charlie doing here? And what was Donnie Clarkson doing, driving Charlie's precious restored truck? What was going on?

"I called Charlie because I needed a man with sense. Someone I didn't have to argue with. A man with sense and a vehicle. When I told him what was going on, and what I wanted, he volunteered his truck. He told me he'd bring Donnie, too."

Charlie took a drag from his cigarette. "I've known what's been going on in the Defoe house for quite while." He looked at Elaine. "From Bud. For what it's worth, he talked to me about it and was sick about not helping you gals with Fanny before. But he figured it wasn't his business. Plus all the junk between Lloyd and him made him feel he shouldn't get involved. He thought if he did, things might get worse for you and Olivia. Or Fanny." He cleared his throat.

"Well, water over the dam now. We're here. That truck runs well, no one will notice it's gone, and no one will connect it to Fanny." Charlie nodded at Donnie who was looking at Elaine with some degree of intensity and continued. "Donnie was doing some work for me in the back room when Olivia called. Since Richard recommended him, Donnie's spent lots of time at my place helping me and working on the truck." Charlie smiled and used his elbow to nudge the boy. "He's a pretty fair mechanic and he's got some real talent with carpentry. I've been working on gun cabinets in my shop. Need a delivery man. Guess who just got himself a valid driver's license last week?"

Elaine glanced over at a grinning Donnie who was proudly fingering a new driver's license.

"So Donnie's going to be the driver. Since Donnie's never met Fanny before no one, especially Lloyd, will put two and two together. After everyone gets going later, I'll drive out to the Clarksons and tell Donnie's folks he's running some long distance deliveries for me and that he'll be gone for a couple of days, maybe longer."

"I was gone overnight back a week or two when I went to Wausau for Charlie so Ma won't fret. Mr. Clarkson will probably be glad there's one less mouth to feed." Donnie shared an easy smile with Charlie. Elaine recognized a bond there between the crusty bachelor and the lonely teenager. As Richard would say, Who'da thunk it?

Olivia chimed in. "Charlie and I have cash for Fanny and money for Donnie, too. Donnie'll drive her where she wants and he'll be the only one who knows where that is. And that might be a bus stop in Chicago or Sioux Falls or Minneapolis. Then she'll go wherever she wants.

"I'll drive Charlie home and then I'm using the Ladies Auxiliary key to the church basement and get them some clothes and blankets. Then home. If Lloyd shows up there, Perry and I will tell him he has to wait until tomorrow to talk to Fanny. Fanny says when she stayed at Aunt Lovey's–yeah, Aunt Lovey's! I guess we're not the only ones to know what a slimeball Lloyd is and have helped Fanny. Lloyd never went looking for them when they were at Lovey's. He just stayed at home and slept it off until Fanny called him to come pick them up. Chances are it'll be the same tonight."

Elaine looked at the small group assembled around her. Slowly she began to nod her head. "This just might work. Yes, it will! What do I need to do?"

"This might be a little tricky. If he's still in the barn, we can't call him. I need you to go out to Lloyd's and tell him Fanny's at my house. That should keep him home since he won't want to mess with all the Tilden men. If he has a mind to come in to town, then he'll come straight to my place and won't be anywhere near the church or County D where Donnie will head out. Just trying to cover all our bases. With any luck you won't have to get out of your car. You okay with that, Elaine? We think you should take Morag with you so it won't be as scary. Charlie was going to do it but we don't want Lloyd to even get a hint that Charlie might know about this. We don't want Lloyd to make any connection to Charlie's truck being gone."

Elaine thought about Lloyd and the twist he gave to Jimmy's shoulder. She fought the trickle of fear that ran down her spine at the notion of being alone with Lloyd in the dark. But Olivia was right. The fewer people involved the better and she had confronted Lloyd before with his abuse of Fanny so this would sound plausible to Lloyd. "Yes," she said to the trio of conspirators before her, "I can do that."

Charlie noticed activity at the clinic door and went inside. Shortly he was back, a drowsy Davey in his arms. Fanny trailed behind. Olivia clutched Fanny's hands and spoke in a low voice while Charlie gently deposited Davey in the wide front seat of his truck and tucked a blanket around him. Then he turned to Donnie and extended his hand. Donnie ignored him and enfolded the bartender in an awkward hug. Charlie clapped the boy's back and murmured in his ear.

Olivia herded Fanny to the open truck door and helped settle her beside her sleeping boy. "Just like we talked about, okay, Fanny?" Olivia said to her. Numb, Fanny merely nodded. There was another quick embrace and Olivia closed the door.

Elaine leaned through the open window and gave Fanny a kiss on her cheek. "You and Davey are going to be alright, Fanny. Everything is going to be alright!"

Before climbing into the driver's seat, Donnie turned and walked to Elaine. He hugged her, too and leaned close to her ear. "Don't worry about her," he whispered. "My Aunt Royanne will purely love meeting Fanny and Davey." And they were gone.

CHAPTER THIRTY SIX

later that night

"You can go a wee bit faster, Elaine. I can handle myself around the corners quite well, you know."

Elaine turned her eyes momentarily from the road as she turned to consider her friend. Then she pushed on the accelerator.

"And," Morag continued with portent, "We need to make some haste if we want to keep that bloody bawheid from searching for Fanny."

Elaine wasn't sure what a bawheid was but from the steely disdain in Morag's voice, it couldn't be good. In truth, Elaine was apprehensive squaring off with Lloyd on her own, even verbally. Morag was short but had a steel backbone when it came to backing her friends. Elaine tuned back to what her Scottish pal was saying.

"And if it's a fight he wants, well, then I might manage a solid kick right in his goolies. It's no more than he deserves hurting Fanny's wee bairn the way he did."

Morag behaving like a street brawler was an amusing thought and relieved some tension. Elaine stifled a nervous giggle and directed Morag's attention to the task at hand. "Remember Morag, we aren't to let on that we know that Fanny is really gone. We just want to keep him out of town tonight." Elaine filled Morag in on only part of the details of the evening, in keeping with Olivia's instructions.

"Right you are; I ken the plan."

Turning into Lloyd's gravel driveway, the women could see the Defoe house dark and silent. Muted light spilled from the milk house fifty yards away. The smell of rain and manure saturated the air.

"Lead the way, Elaine. I'm right here with ya." Morag zipped her jacket and hopped out of the car. They could hear the muffled sounds of a radio coming from the interior of the milk house as they approached. Their progress was halted by Lloyd's appearance at the door. His bulky silhouette blocked most of the light.

"Bastard!" Morag uttered under her breath. Elaine reached for her friend's hand, hoping to shush her friend and fortify herself.

"What're you do-gooders doing here? Yer hubbies know you're out and about? Don't know that I'm man enough to service both of you." Lloyd sneered at his visitors. Leaves swirled around the entrance as Lloyd ducked back into the milkhouse and the women, seeking shelter from the cold wind, followed suit.

Bile rose in Elaine's throat. Morag was right, he was a bastard. Just deliver the message she told herself. Engage him in a few minutes conversation. Anything to give the fugitives a little more time on the road.

"Evening, Lloyd. Olivia wanted us to tell you that Fanny and Davey are staying in town tonight. She said no one answered your phone and Morag and I were out running errands so we said we'd deliver the message."

Elaine maintained eye contact with him as she skirted puddles on the slick concrete floor. Talk to him for a few minutes and then go.

"Oh yeah? Is that a fact now? Maybe I should just go into town and see about that! Just where is Fanny? At that fat Tilden aunt's house again or with your nosey sister-in-law and that pussy Perry? Maybe I should pound that silly grin right off that asshole's mug! Just like all the Tildens, thinks he's so much better than me!"

Electricity fairly sparked off Morag. She stamped her foot at the welder and shook an admonishing finger at him. "Ya bloody eejit! I'd be careful as to what I'm spouting if I was you! You're pure dead brilliant with your big talk! But I dinna know about tackling one of the Tilden men. Breaking the wee lad's arm is not the same as facing Perry or Bud or even my own sweet Ed!" So much for holding her tongue.

Too late, Elaine realized that Lloyd was drunker than she first believed. His cheeks were purple with rage; his eyes menacing and evil. Before she could quiet Morag, the little Scotswoman flung another insult at the hulking man before her.

"Oh, you're a right scunner, Lloyd Defoe. We know all about poor wee Davey! May you be ashamed of yourself and rot in hell!"

More quickly that Elaine thought possible, Lloyd snatched a section of milking apparatus from near the cooling tanks and swung his arm in Morag's direction. The heavy hose and clip caught her left eyebrow and the woman sagged to the damp floor.

Elaine screamed and reached for Morag. Morag raised her hand and made a brushing motion with her hand, "It's alright, I'm na hurt so bad." Her pallor and the blood running down the side of her face belied that message. Elaine moved closer but her passage was halted by Lloyd's big, rough hands on her shoulders. Hands that now shook her as they shook Jimmy a few weeks ago. She pushed against his chest, but a brutal jerk made her head snap like a large, heavy peony on a slim supple stem.

Was that the crunch of tires on the gravel? Some one else was here? She willed herself not to glance toward the door. Perhaps she was mistaken. Lloyd would have heard tires, too and prepared for another visitor. His eyes were still fixed on hers with not even an eyelid flicker. Quiet now. It was all wishful thinking on her part.

"Well Missy, whadda you think should happen now? You think you can stop me better'n your dopey little bitch pal here? I think not! Maybe what you both need is a real man to show you how to behave!" He released her briefly and slapped her cheek as she twisted away from him. There was a roar in her ear and then a sting as her incisor cut into her lip. His blow had landed solidly.

Poor Fanny! How often had she experienced this? She and Morag needed to get away from this maniac. Lloyd grasped her arm once more. There was no doubt in her mind that he would strike her again if he could stop swaying. She maneuvered herself to kick at him, stomp on his instep, something! All this flashed through her mind as his coarse laughter assaulted her ears.

Suddenly Elaine saw the big man's eyes shift to the doorway. He wrapped his arms around her. Before he spoke or she turned her head, a flutter in her chest told her who she would see there. What she didn't expect to see was the crowbar Bud clutched as he stood, ten feet away.

"You okay, Lainie?" he asked quietly. Bud's focus moved to the floor beyond Lloyd. "Morag? How bad are you hurt?"

Morag mumbled coherently enough to let Bud know her injuries weren't crucial. "I can walk if I can just claim a second to get my wits about me."

" Well, now Buddy-boy! Finally come to fight your own battle, huh? Not gonna let the women do it for you? Didn't think you had the balls! Imagine that!" Spit flew from Lloyd and his eyes glittered with challenge and anticipation as he released Elaine. A sturdy logging pickaxe leaned against the wall. Lloyd reached for it and stared at Bud.

"Put it down, Lloyd! Morag and Elaine and I will get off your property and leave you be. You've done enough harm for one night, don't you think?" Bud's voice sounded reasonable but Elaine heard a deadly tone underlying his words .

Lloyd heard it, too. A low, guttural groan came from his throat as he pushed Elaine away and brandished the pickaxe. His eyes were crazed.

"You're not stupid, Lloyd. Let the women out of the milk house and then you and I can talk." Bud's voice continued to be soft as he wrapped both hands around the crowbar. Elaine recognized the famed Tilden grip as her husband set his feet into a solid softball stance and readied for the charge.

"Talk! Bullshit, Tilden! We're way past talking!" Lloyd's grip tightened on the pickaxe and he flung his body toward Bud.

He covered no more than a foot or two when Morag attempted to rise. As she did, her leg was thrust into Lloyd's path. Too much drink and wet concrete thwarted good balance. The rubber soles of Lloyd's boots skidded across the slick, slimy floor and his arms began to windmill even as his feet lost purchase.

Bud reached for him as Lloyd released the pickax to brace himself, but Elaine knew it was too late. Too late to break his fall. The thwack of Lloyd's head crashing against the galvanized steel of the cooling tank made her sick. It was an eerily familiar sound, one that played in her memory. It didn't immediately register. And then in a rush, it did. It was the sound of her mother's head hitting a lead pipe in the basement. The thwack of flesh forcefully meeting metal and extinguishing life: tragic, deathly, and accidental.

From the corner of her eye Elaine saw the pulpy mass of Lloyd's head, saw the blood already pooling under it, saw the vibrancy flee from Lloyd's eyes. She felt bile rising in her gorge and tears pushing from the backs of her eyes. She choked back her urge to vomit.

Bud strode purposely to the fallen man. He knelt at Lloyd's side and placed his fingers at the welder's neck, feeling for an elusive pulse. At length, he let his hand linger on Lloyd's head.

A sharp, whooshing sound punctured the air. Bud had been holding his breath. His shoulders quaked from the exhalation and his lips quivered as he attempted speech. Elaine stood with arms wrapped tightly about herself, blubbering like a baby, throwing her head back in one loud wail. One shriek, an acknowledgement of twin accidents, and her sensibilities returned.

Bud looked up to answer the questions in his wife's eyes. "Charlie called me. He thought I should know what was happening and where you were. Jimmy's with Madlyn and the girls." Elaine nodded numbly, her eyes on Lloyd.

"Poor old Lloyd," Bud intoned softly. "The poor sonofabitch was never content. Seems like bitterness corroded everything that could give him some joy. Oh God Lainie, did it have to end like this?" He patted Lloyd's forehead before he rose and turned to his wife who was helping Morag to stand.

His words jolted Elaine back to the world of feeling. Lloyd had just tried to kill one of them, maybe all of them, and Bud sounded like he felt pity for him!

"You feel sorry for him?" Elaine stood there, one arm around Morag, her other hand wiping blood from her mouth. The air vibrated with the emotional ferocity. "Good God, Bud! What is wrong with you? You feel sorry for him? He could have killed us! What about Davey? What about Morag? What about me? How can you say that?" She guided Morag to a wooden stool propped against the wall.

Before her tears started again and while shudders wracked her shoulders, Bud was beside her. His steely arms held her like cables securing the logs on his truck. There was no way she was moving anywhere and after a few seconds she stopped struggling and realized the confines of his embrace for what it was. Strength. Protection. Unconditional love.

She looked into his eyes and saw those familiar, intimate ice blue pools. Sorrow was there but concern as well. Concern for her. Like a powerful cleansing agent, that concern revealed with crystalline precision what had occurred. Bud entered the milk house with a crowbar in his hand and an inferno blazing in his eyes. It was a look she'd never seen in him before. It wasn't hate. Not deadly malice, but determined resolve and resignation. Resignation that, if necessary, he would again take another's life.

He'd been willing to kill for her. This man who dismissed all hero worship, who'd sworn off killing for all time, was willing to put himself in harm's way and commit to do what he promised never to do again. With no hesitation, he would have killed for her.

They stood there, both weeping, looking at one another, understanding one another's thoughts. How could ardor be so revived and heightened when another man's blood congealed on this chilled and murky floor? But this man, her man, brought mashkiki to her marriage, to her life. Who with her was the mashkiki.

Morag was crying as well, the three of them motionless, their breathing a background counterpoint to the drip of water sounding from the sink in the corner. Morag sniffed and tried to speak as she stood. "Oh my, Elaine! Bud, how can I ever-" Her voice broke and her words were swallowed by more tears. Both Tildens moved to steady her and include her in their embrace. A few moments passed and Morag cleared her throat. "Shouldna one of us be calling the sheriff? I think it's time we ended this night and got back to our homes and our kidlets."

"Yes," Elaine reached for Bud's hand, her eyes never leaving his. "We need to go."

Epilogue

late June 1956

Dear Elaine,

I suppose by now Charlie has talked with you so you know I am not coming back to Mashkiki Rapids. I have also sent my ma a letter and so she knows where I am. She and Mr. Clarkson and the kids will move on but she can keep track of me since she knows Aunt Royanne's address. I hope I get a letter back from her or my sister soon.

It's been a couple of weeks since we left but Fanny and Davey and I drove to where we were headed. I am now in O'Neill, Nebraska where my Aunt Royanne lives with her husband. He told me I should call him Uncle Stanley and so I do. He is a decent man who is good to Aunt Royanne and he has been very friendly to me also. I like him fine. He told me that he's been putting off hiring a hand to help on their place so that if I want to stay on and work for them he will pay me. He tells me I am a fine strapping lad and calls me Don but Aunt Royanne still calls me Donnie. Ha ha.

The very next day after we got here, Aunt Royanne and Uncle Stanley told me to clean out the little room off the kitchen that they were using for storage. Underneath all the boxes and stuff was a bed and they said that this room could be mine if I wanted to stay. The day after we got here, Fanny called a cousin further out west and the cousin wired her some money so I took her and Davey to the bus station. She didn't let me see where she bought the ticket to. Olivia told her to do it that way so she'd be harder to find if that sonofabitch comes looking for her. Aunt Royanne says I shouldn't cuss, so sorry.

Aunt Royanne has been telling me a little about when I was a baby. My real last name is Redbird. My father's name was John Redbird and he was a Lakota from South Dakota but he was raised in an orphanage so I probably don't have any cousins there or anything. She wasn't sure how my Ma came to know him but Aunt Royanne met him once and thought he was a nice man and good to my ma. He was a soldier, a heavy equipment mechanic and was killed when his unit was in Hawaii. She kept a letter sent to my ma from one of his soldier friends who told her that his nickname was Akicita. That means warrior or something in Lakota. I think that is neat. She also told me she will help me get my name all straightened out if I want since she has my birth certificate that my mother left with her. Also I have a middle name. It is Richard, like Mr. Tilden. And it's my middle name, just like Jimmy's. How about that?

When I start working for Uncle Stanley I can send some money to Charlie and pay him for the truck. I can also send a few extra bucks to Martha since I won't be there to get her new under duds. Ha ha. Uncle Stanley says I could also see about taking a night school course in the fall and finish up my high school diploma. I don't know about that but Aunt Royanne thinks I should keep an open mind, so I will.

Tell Mr. Richard Tilden about my middle name and that I am grateful for all the stuff he taught me and the stories he told me. I told some to Fanny and Davey on the drive and that kept the little guy from thinking about his arm. We also sang a little. Has Jimmy learned any songs yet? I bet he is getting bigger every day. I think he is a lucky little boy to have a mother like you. Maybe if you wanted to you could write me a letter to the address on this envelope and tell me what is happening in Mashkiki Rapids. I bet it is still real exciting there. Ha ha. If Jimmy wants, he could stick in a coloring book picture and I'd put it on the wall of my own bedroom next to my own chest of drawers with my own radio on the top.

Well, better go now. Uncle Stan needs some help with moving machinery.

Sincerely, your friend,

Donald Richard Redbird

P.S. I think Bud is lucky, too. Tell him hello from me.

QUESTIONS AND TOPICS FOR DISCUSSION

Mashkiki Rapids

1. To what degree is the title a metaphor for this novel?

2. The era of the Fifties had definite expectations on choices made by unwed mothers. Do you think today's younger readers can empathize with the pressures placed on Elaine to give her baby up for adoption?

3. In what ways does Elaine's memory of her mother influence her decisions?

4. Why is the town of Mashkiki Rapids so insistent on having a specific hero to claim?

5. Why does Elaine allow herself to be enticed by Perry?

6. Who is the most selfless character?

7. To what extent do the history and traditions of Mashkiki Rapids affect the actions and beliefs of the characters?

8. How do you feel about Perry and his relationship to others in Mashkiki Rapids? To Bud? To Olivia? To Elaine? Is he a sympathetic character?

9. Though perhaps not overtly discriminated against, any people of color or different heritage were ignored by a more dominant white culture. What led Elaine to breach this societal gap with the Ojibwe sisters?

10. Sociologists say that small town festivals and parades reveal much about the community's personality. What does the parade reveal about Mashkiki Rapids?

11. A character flaw may be defined as "a limitation, imperfection, phobia, problem, or deficiency present in a character who may be otherwise very functional." A character flaw may be visible in all characters, from hero to villain. What are some of the character flaws exhibited in the characters of Mashkiki Rapids?

12. Who is your favorite minor character? Why?

13. What role does Donnie play in the novel's plot?

14. How has Elaine changed by the end of the book? Bud? Perry? Olivia?

15. As far as theme is concerned, is this book more about loyalty or love, or growth of the human spirit?

About the Author

Anne Rud Miller worked as a public high school English teacher for thirty four years before beginning her writing career.

She was awarded first place in the fiction category of *WritersRead 2013* for a reading from Mashkiki Rapids and is published in WritersRead 2013, Volume I – an anthology.

Anne was selected to read her short story (fiction) in *Penokees Read 2013* which was performed at StageNorth in Washburn, Wisconsin and broadcast live on Wisconsin Public Radio.

She is also a recipient of a Chequamegon Bay Arts Council grant.

Anne Miller lives in Ashland, Wisconsin near her three daughters and is presently an adjunct instructor at Lac Courte Oreilles Ojibwe Community College.

CPSIA information can be obtained at www.ICGtesting.com
Printed in the USA
LVOW10s0438071013

355682LV00001B/5/P